TOR BOOKS
BY ISOBELLE CARMODY

Obernewtyn
The Farseekers

Isobelle Carmody

The Farseekers

Book Two of The Obernewtyn Chronicles

TOR®
fantasy

A TOM DOHERTY ASSOCIATES BOOK
NEW YORK

THE FARSEEKERS

Copyright © 1990 by Isobelle Carmody

First published in Australia by Viking
Penguin Books Australian, 1990.

A Tor Book
Published by Tom Doherty Associates, LLC
175 Fifth Avenue
New York, NY 10010

www.tor.com

Tor® is a registered trademark of Tom Doherty Associates, LLC.

Map by Ellisa Mitchell

ISBN: 0-812-58423-6
Library of Congress Catalog Card Number: 00-027940

First edition: August 2000
First mass market edition: July 2001

Printed in the United States of America

0 9 8 7 6 5 4 3 2 1

For Shane

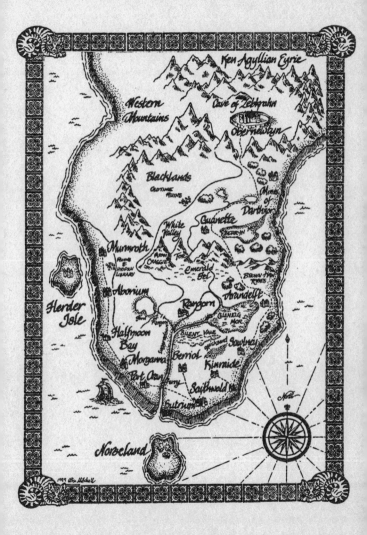

Part I

I

Roland shook his head decisively. "I can do nothing to hasten the healing, Elspeth. If you rested them more often..."

I sighed and rubbed the tender soles of my feet. "Kella said a warmer climate might help."

Roland nodded absently, returning satchels of herbs to his carry-all. "It's true cold doesn't help the healing process, but whatever miracles healers can do, changing the weather to suit their patient is not among them."

I was startled at the unexpected touch of humor from the dour Healer guildmaster. Hefting the weighty bag onto his arm, Roland gave me a piercing look. He added significantly, "If you would stay in your room in wintertime with banked fires instead of wandering around the draughty halls and beyond..."

"I *am* mistress of a guild," I said.

Roland was unsympathetic. "Garth finds no difficulty in remaining in his caves and the Teknoguild works do not crumble because of his inactivity," he said with faint asperity.

The Teknoguild was concerned with studying the Beforetime and researching the effects, past, present and future, of the Great White. I had little interest in such things, but I had met secretly with Garth only that morning. I wondered if Roland knew.

"Garth ... is Garth," I said with a smile. Roland's lip twitched.

There was a knock at the door, and Kella entered carrying a jug.

Roland waved his ward in impatiently. "Soak in that, then rub some of the salve into the soles. And stay off your feet!" he growled, slamming the door behind him.

Kella poured the liquid in a flat pan, smiling ruefully. "He's angry with himself because your feet aren't healing properly."

I lowered my feet gingerly into the shallow panniken. A sweet scent rose from the water. "Herb lore?" I guessed.

Kella nodded. "A recipe given us by the Master of Obernewtyn himself."

I smiled, never quite able to accept the grandiose title for Rushton. When I had first known him, it was as an enigmatic farm overseer. No one had been more astonished than I to discover he was the legal owner of Obernewtyn.

Kella was staring into the fire, its orange glow playing over her cheeks. "Rushton has not come back yet from the highlands," she said, a faint line of worry between her brows. I wondered idly if the healer were attracted to Rushton. It would be a pity for her. His brooding singleness of purpose made him blind to anything but his complicated plans for the future.

"It's good to see you smile," Kella said. The old fear of revealing myself caused me a moment of sharp fear, then I consciously relaxed. The need for hiding my expression was past, at least at Obernewtyn.

"Yet there is not much to smile at, even here," I said somberly.

Kella's expression sharpened. "You spoke to the newcomers?"

I nodded. "When I was in the orphan home, torture was nothing more than a rumor."

Kella's face was pale. The deliberate infliction of pain was

anathema to any healer, but torture was doubly dre...
both mental and physical pain forged into one. She dislike...
mind-bending activities of the Coercer guild, but this was far
worse.

As if reading my thoughts, she said, "Miryum claims there
are times when the end justifies the means, but even a coercer
could not condone torture."

Tactless Miryum was guilden of the aggressive Coercer
guild, whose function was to defend Obernewtyn and prepare
for battle with the Council, if it should come to that. There
was a growing rift between Healer and Coercer guilds. Where
a farseeker could read conscious thoughts, near and far away,
healers, like coercers and futuretellers, could descend into the
unconscious mind, deep probing. All three guilds shaped the
ability to deep probe differently. The mind of a coercer was a
weapon to suborn the will of other minds. The healer also
entered other minds, but with a probe honed tendril-thin for
healing. It was little wonder the two guilds were at logger-
heads—using the same ability to opposing ends.

"Anyone would think you were a futureteller," Kella said
resignedly, referring to the habit futuretellers had of drifting into
a dream in the middle of conversations.

I laughed. "It might be pleasant. You would never be surprised by anything."

"Not for me," Kella said. "I prefer to live in the present.
I don't want to know the future."

Without warning, the outer door to the Healer hall was
flung open to admit a wild-eyed Matthew. His anxious expression dissolved. "Here ye are! I've been searchin' all over for ye!"
he said accusingly.

I blinked at him innocently. "Oh? I must have forgotten
to say where I was going."

Kella snorted, knowing I disliked the lack of privacy that
went with being a guildmistress, and often evaded such formal-
ities as making my whereabouts known.

Forgetting his frustration, Matthew hurried over. "Rushton has just come back! An' he's called a guildmerge."

My heart jumped. Rushton often traveled outside the mountains, for there was no danger to the legal Master of Obernewtyn, but something serious must have happened for him to call a guildmerge so abruptly.

"When?" I asked.

"Now!" Matthew said. "He sent me to find ye. The meetin's to begin as soon as ye come."

"Did he say why?" I asked, astonished by the haste. I dried my feet quickly and slipped on my boots. Rushton usually gave plenty of warning of a guildmerge, to give the guilds time to prepare reports and requests.

"Nowt a word," Matthew answered, handing me my walking stick. "He was investigatin' a rumor that th' Council meant to establish a soldierguard camp in th' highlands. Do ye suppose...?" he began, aghast at the thought of a camp so close to Obernewtyn. It had been bad enough when a soldierguard training camp was set up just below the lower ranges. If the Council meant to put a camp in the highlands, it could only be because they intended to tighten their control of the high country.

"It might be no more than gossip," I said.

Most highlanders were simple, superstitious folk only too ready to gossip. Obernewtyn's unusual history made it an obvious subject for speculation. But this time, there might be substance to the rumors.

Ceirwan would know what had happened, since he had gone with Rushton. As guilden of the Farseekers, he would normally have reported at once to me, but Rushton's call for an immediate guildmerge made that impossible.

I wondered if any of the guilds would use the unexpected meeting to make requests. I had had no time to prepare a submission since meeting with the Teknoguild, but Pavo would be at the meeting and might fill in the gaps. If Matthew were right, it was important to act quickly in case Rushton suspend all expeditions.

I shivered. As ever in the mountains, there was a chilly underbite to the air and the old burn scars on my feet and lower legs ached. Roland had promised they would heal in time, but two years had passed and they still hurt at the first sign of cold weather.

My eyes went beyond the gray stone walls which surrounded Obernewtyn and its fields and farms, to the horizon and the jagged line of the western mountains separating us from the highlands. Those mountains were our best protection, especially if soldierguards did come to the highlands. In winter, snows cut us off entirely and, even in the mildest season, the road to Obernewtyn was difficult. The mountains kept us safe, yet the sight of them never failed to disturb me in some deep, incomprehensible way.

Long ago, in one of his queer fits, Maruman had told me my destiny lay in the mountains. Battered and half-mad, the old cat had been my first friend and had followed me to Obernewtyn. Expecting a grim existence there, perhaps a horrible death, I had found Matthew, and Rushton, and learnt I was not alone in my mutant abilities. When Rushton had been given control of Obernewtyn over his defective stepbrother, who had been manipulated by Alexi and Madam Vega, I had taken his offer of refuge and stayed on. Madam Vega and Alexi had been killed in their battle to keep control of Obernewtyn, and Ariel had fled to his death in the bitter mountain winter. I could hardly recall Madam Vega's face or even Alexi's, but Ariel remained a vivid nightmare image. Of them all, his angelic beauty and the manipulative lust for power that hid behind his fairness were, for me, the epitome of all that was evil in the world. Fortunately, the muddle-headed and malleable Stephen Seraphim was the sole reminder of the usurpers. To my surprise, I had been happy at Obernewtyn. Apart from his periodic wandering, Maruman also made Obernewtyn his home.

Yet I had the sudden chill premonition that the long healing time of peace was drawing to an end.

"What is it?" Matthew asked.

"I was thinking of the past," I said. "Everything that happened in the caves with Alexi and Madam Vega, the Zebkrahn machine exploding, these..." I touched my scarred legs. "It all seems like a dream now."

Matthew nodded grimly. "'Tis easy to forget," he said softly. "But sometimes I dream of Ariel an' I..." He shook his head. "I wish I had killed him. If he had nowt died in th' storm..."

I looked up, surprised at his vehemence.

When I had first met him, Matthew had been thin and frail looking with a limp and hungry, intelligent eyes. The limp had been long since healed with a reset bone, and Matthew now stood a head taller than I, with strong, wiry limbs. Ceirwan was convinced he was developing deep probe ability, saying he often seemed to know our thoughts before we sent them. I had dismissed that, thinking it no more than the natural result of our closeness. But it might be so. There was so much about our abilities we did not yet understand.

Farseekers converse mind to mind over varying distances. I had thought myself the only farseeker able to deep probe. Multitalents were not uncommon among us, and choice of a guild was based on the dominant ability. In rare cases, two abilities were of equal strength, and then choosing came down to simple preference.

As if to confirm his ability to know my private thoughts, Matthew said, "Maybe we should use this guildmerge to raise th' matter of Zarak changin' guilds."

Zarak was that rarity, a Misfit with two equal abilities— that of communicating with animals, beastspeaking; and farseeking. He had chosen the Beasting guild.

I shook my head decisively. "Now is not the time. Besides, I think the matter can be better resolved on a personal level.

But something will have to be done soon, I agree. Zarak is proving to be a disturbing influence in the wrong guild."

Matthew nodded fervently. "Not that Lina isn't capable of gannin' up to mischief on her own, but Zarak . . ." He trailed off as we approached the front steps to Obernewtyn.

The new doors were less imposing than the old, being too plain to complement the ornate stone scrolling of the entrance. I had a fleeting memory of watching the original doors burn, and with them the concealed maps showing a route to the Old-timer weapon machines. To the others, the burning had been simply the easiest way to get at the inlaid gold we had used to make armbands for the guildmasters. That had been my suggestion, and Rushton had agreed. Perhaps my wounds had made him humor me. He had been very kind then, I thought pensively. These days he seemed distant and preoccupied.

As if conjured up by my thoughts, Rushton was waiting for us in the circular entrance hall.

He looked tired, and it was clear from his clothes that he had not bothered to change. I felt a rush of gladness at the sight of him, for though Obernewtyn ran smoothly even in his absence, I never felt as safe as when he was there.

He met my look with an ambivalent stare. It was almost a challenge. Before I could speak, he sent Matthew to find someone from the Futuretell guild, then he ushered me toward the guildmerge, matching his steps to my own limping progress.

"What has happened?" I asked.

Rushton turned to look at me. "The Council is showing a renewed interest in us. Two men were up in the highlands asking questions about Obernewtyn."

"You think they were from the Council?"

He shrugged angrily. "I know nothing, except that I am tired of my ignorance. Do you remember when I went to claim Obernewtyn in Sutrium?" he asked unexpectedly.

I remembered. Sutrium was the center of Council activities. It had not been easy for him to convince us to wait for his return. Many had wanted to leave, fearing his trip would lead to their capture and burning. That we had chosen to wait had been an act of faith in Rushton. We had never regretted it.

"I remember," I murmured.

"I thought the Council trusted me. Maybe I was wrong. With farseeker or coercer help, I could have made sure. Now it would be different."

"Now?" I echoed.

Rushton looked at me, his green eyes glowing with sudden excitement, as if he had resolved some inner doubt. "It's time we found out what the Council is up to. Time we made a move into their territory."

"Sutrium?" I whispered.

"Sutrium," Rushton said.

II

As usual, guildmerge was held in the circular room which had once served as Alexi's experiment chamber. The bookshelves concealing the alcoves adjoining the central chamber and the enormous fireplace were all that remained of the old laboratory where he and Madam Vega had pursued their research.

The steep passage hidden behind the pivoting fireplace was now used only for easy transport of knots of firewood into the meeting hall in winter. Like other such passages at Obernewtyn, it was no longer a secret, although Lina was convinced the old buildings must be riddled with passages and was forever to be found tapping the walls and listening for telltale hollowness.

Obernewtyn's first master, the reclusive Lukas Seraphim, had been a morose and secretive man, and the great gray buildings reflected his personality.

Louis, who could still remember the man who had carved Obernewtyn out of the wilderness on what was then the very fringe of the Blacklands, said he had possessed a mind that was as much a labyrinth as the greenthorn maze separating the main house from the farms.

Since Rushton had taken over, much of the buildings had been altered to provide better access to all parts of the rambling wings, and each guild had been allocated a certain section of

Obernewtyn as its base. The chamber where guildmerge sat had once been accessible only through a concealed panel in Madam Vega's chamber. The walls had since been knocked down and two broad doors installed.

Though cavernous, the domed meeting room was kept warm by the padded shelves of books on all sides and an enormous fire. There was nothing in the room but a long trestle table and a number of chairs. I seated myself near the fire, surreptitiously toasting my sore feet.

The buzz of talk was louder than usual, partly because of the abrupt way Rushton had called the meeting, and partly because it was a full guildmerge—almost all wards and guildens as well as guildmasters were present. Even the irascible Garth was there, looking impatient and bored.

On the other side of the table sat Ceirwan, still clad in riding clothes. I felt momentarily irritated by the guildmerge rule restricting communication during meetings to the spoken word, but I did not try to reach him. Matthew returned and seated himself next to Dameon, opposite me. The blind Empath guildmaster smiled at me unerringly, sensing my attention. Empaths could read emotions the way farseekers read thoughts, though few were actually able to converse mentally. Some empaths, like Dameon, could also transmit emotion. The twin Empath guilden, Miky and Angina, sat beside him, deep in animated discussion.

Rushton had walked to the head of the table and was now talking to Domick, a fierce frown of concentration on his face. The Coercer ward responded quickly, stabbing his finger in the air for emphasis.

Next to them, Maryon sat staring into the distance, a slight smile on her lips. No one could mistake her for anything but a futureteller. She had come back with Matthew, but the seat beside her was empty. I wondered what was important enough to keep the Futuretell guilden, Christa, away. Roland was alone in representing his guild. This was not unusual. The healers put their patients before anything else. Next, and completing the table, were the Beasting guild——Alad looking unusually grim.

I was conscious of an expectant atmosphere among us as Rushton began to speak, reminding us of the day we had taken over Obernewtyn, of the first guildmerge which had ended with our pledge to abolish the name of Misfit in the Land. He invited those with business to raise their hands. Traditionally, Rushton spoke last at guildmerge. This meant that whatever had prompted the sudden guildmerge must wait until all other matters had been dealt with. His eyes widened speculatively at my hand among those few to rise.

Alad rose to speak, again raising the need for animals to be represented on guildmerge by one of their own. As before, no one could decide which animal should represent all animals, and whether the animals should propose their own candidate. The increasing dominance of the volatile younger horses' attitude was raised. With a hint of impatience, Rushton suggested the matter be passed on to the next guildmerge.

The Beasting guildmaster frowned. "This is the third time it's been put off. It's time we dealt with this once and for all."

"It will be dealt with. Next time," Rushton said tersely.

"The animals themselves requested a decision one way or the other. There will be trouble if it is left any longer," Alad said coldly.

Rushton lifted his brows questioningly, "Threats, Alad?"

The guildmaster shook his head. "Just a warning, Rushton. They have the right."

Rushton said nothing and Alad sat looking disgruntled and preoccupied. I was surprised at his persistence. Everyone knew it was only a matter of time until animals had a representative. That and rumors of trouble from the horses made me decide it was time I visited the farms again.

The Coercer guild then proposed a competition, a contest of coercer skills, pitting one against another until a champion be announced. Master, guilden, and ward would be excluded.

This resulted in a heated discussion about the value of competitiveness. The Futuretell ward argued persuasively against it, saying it would produce antisocial and aggressive tendencies in an already aggressive guild.

"The aim of Obernewtyn is to have all minds working together for a common goal, not to isolate winners from losers and devalue those whose skills are less violent," she said.

The Healer guild was even more seriously opposed. Rushton interrupted what looked like an erupting argument to suggest the coercers draw up a complete plan for their proposed tournament. This would then be voted on by a full guildmerge.

He nodded to me and I stood. "I request that the ban on Teknoguild expeditions be lifted."

Rushton frowned. He did not like anyone to step outside the procedures which governed guildmerge and made it work smoothly. "This is a strange request for the Farseeker guildmistress to make, Elspeth," he said. "Surely it's up to Garth, especially since he graces us with his presence today."

There was a titter of humor, since everyone knew of the Teknoguild master's reluctance to leave his laboratory. Garth scowled.

"This request concerns my guild," I said quietly.

Rushton's eyes bored into mine. "What interest could you have in the Teknoguild expeditions? If I recall, you were among those to vote for the ban."

I took a deep breath. "If the ban were lifted, I would propose a joint expedition."

Rushton shook his head emphatically. "If I refuse to let teknoguilders kill themselves roaming on poisoned Blackland fringes, I would hardly let farseekers replace them!" he said with impatient sarcasm.

The death toll among teknoguilders had always been high. The ban had been enforced after a disastrous Teknoguild expedition in which Henry Druid's people and the teknoguilders clashed over a newly discovered ruin on the Blackland fringes.

The argument had ended in a mysterious explosion which killed most of both parties. Either the Druids, as Henry Druid's men named themselves, had deliberately set off a forbidden weapon, or some ancient device hidden in the ruins had been accidentally triggered. Either way there had been no further Teknoguild expeditions, and no more had been seen of Henry Druid or his followers.

Henry Druid had been among the first to oppose the Council's book-burning laws. A Herder novice, he had been cast out by the Herder Faction and had fled to exile in the high country. Rushton had been befriended by the old ex-Herder, and for a time their paths had matched. But the old man's fierce hatred of the Council was exceeded only by his hatred of mutations, and in the end it had become too dangerous to continue the connection.

Apart from the one incident with the Teknoguild expedition, the Druid and his followers seemed to have disappeared. Sometimes that absence made me uneasy. Like Alexi and Madam Vega, Henry Druid had wanted power in the form of Beforetime weapons. What if he were to discover the machines that could set off the Great White again?

I choked off that train of thought. "The expedition we propose will not be to Blackland fringes."

Rushton looked puzzled. "Then I don't see any difficulty. Teknoguild expeditions were banned because they never want to go anywhere but the fringes. But that still doesn't explain your interest. I would be surprised to find you had any aim in common with the Teknoguild."

It was true I had often opposed their interests. Of all guilds their abilities were hardest to define, being little more than a vague empathy for inanimate things, a slight power to move things by will alone, and a passionate interest in the past. Unlike the other guilds, the Teknoguild was based outside Obernewtyn's walls in the network of caves discovered and used by Alexi and Ariel, who had assisted him in his experiments.

They were believed to be the remains of a Beforetime establishment and had contained a number of machines. I had not been there since Alexi had tortured me using the Zebkrahn machine to force me to use my powers to locate an Oldtime weapon cache.

Pavo's request to come to the cave network that morning had been unexpected and unnerving. In the end I had gone, as much to lay my old fears to rest as out of respect for Pavo, who was more concerned with understanding Oldtimers than unearthing their mechanical secrets.

Also, I had been curious.

Walking back into the cave had been a disturbing experience. The past had seemed to lie tangibly beneath the present. The entrance to the cave network had been littered with boxes and sacks of Beforetime papers, books, and other relics unearthed in previous expeditions. The passage had been well lit by candles set in sconces at regular intervals. There was no sign of the hissing green candles Alexi had favored, yet I had seemed to smell their sickly sweet odor.

Coming from the sloping passage with its smooth walls into the main cave, I had been forced to stifle a gasp, having forgotten how big it all was, and how bright the Beforetime sphere of light which lit the area. High up in the shadows, stalactites hung poised like spears. Yet it was also very different than I remembered. Woven rugs and thick mats softened cold floors, and the walls were almost covered with paper, scrawled with lists and notes and diagrams. Tables and chairs were occupied by busy teknoguilders who barely registered my entrance.

Only the Zebkrahn machine had looked the same, though I knew it could no longer be used to coerce and torture, having long since been modified. Now it served as nothing more than an enhancer, enabling farseekers to double their normal range limit. Even so, my skin had risen to gooseflesh at the sight of it.

"Pavo asked me to come to the Teknoguild cave network,"

I began bluntly in answer to Rushton's questions.

Pavo gave a dry cough and rose. "It might be better if I explain, guildmistress," he offered diffidently. As in the cave that morning, I was struck anew by his pallor.

"I did not know Elspeth would raise this matter today, and so I have not brought my notes, therefore you will have to take my word on some matters. A while back we uncovered evidence of an enormous book storage, which we believe is untouched since the Beforetime. However, because of the ban, we set this matter reluctantly aside. Last week, we succeeded in getting the Zebkrahn machine to penetrate the blocking static over tainted ground." He paused to remind everyone that, previously, the machine, like farseekers, had been unable to project across or through tainted ground or Blackland wastes.

"The machine is now able to monitor areas previously out of reach to us, even to farseekers as strong as Elspeth, whose range is normally better than that of the machine," Pavo said. "It was necessary for Elspeth to see the machine, not to admire the new modification, but so that she could see what it revealed." Pavo looked at me, and all eyes swung expectantly my way.

I said obligingly, "The Zebkrahn was registering a Talent at its outermost limit."

"But . . . that's impossible. Th' machine has to be focused through a farseeker," Matthew objected.

Pavo shook his head eagerly. "Only in the case of ordinary or weak Talents. That is to say in most cases. But the Zebkrahn would need no farseeker focusing to register Elspeth."

"But . . . that means this Talent mun be as strong as Elspeth. . . ." Matthew said.

"Perhaps stronger," Pavo corrected gently.

"Such a Talent would be worth rescuing," Gevan of the coercers interjected.

"The two, the new Talent and the book storage Pavo told you about, are in the same region, and since it is so far away, we thought of a joint expedition," I said.

There was a buzz of excited talk, but Rushton ignored it. "So far . . . ?" he enquired coldly. "Exactly how far?"

My mouth felt suddenly dry. "Somewhere between Aborium and Murmroth."

There was silence, then someone sighed heavily. Aborium was on the other side of the Land, a coastal town. The only way to get there was to travel the main coast road, bypassing soldierguard camps and all the main towns, including Sutrium.

Rushton's face was pale with anger, realizing his brief words to me before the guildmerge had prompted me to propose the expedition. He saw, as I had, that he could not dismiss my proposal since he meant to propose his own equally dangerous expedition.

"That would mean traveling through Sutrium," Roland said brusquely. "A crazy dangerous idea. Our false certificates would not deceive the soldierguards for a moment."

Pavo coughed again. "It is not necessary to journey through Sutrium, or to travel on the main road. We have devised a route which will avoid both." He pulled one of the maps on the table toward him and spread it out. "I have a better map, but . . ." He pointed to the red circle denoting Obernewtyn. "The expedition would travel out of Obernewtyn and down the main road, but would turn off to cut directly across the White Valley and through an Olden pass between Tor and Aran Craggie in the lower mountain ranges, and down to the lowlands. From there, it would be an easy trip across the Ford of Rangorn and down to the coast."

Rushton examined the route. "You are sure this pass exists? I have never heard of it."

The teknoguilder stood self-consciously, nodded, then sat down. Someone laughed, easing the tension in the chamber.

"T'would mean winterin' outside maybe, if an expedition were to leave at once," Matthew said tentatively.

"It would be best to act at once. Surely the gain is worthy of some risk," Pavo said anxiously. "Think of what we might learn from an untouched collection of Beforetime books, and who knows what talent this Misfit will bring to us."

Rushton nodded for us to resume our seats, his expression inscrutable. His eyes swept the assembled faces.

"Well," he said at last, "I called this guildmerge for a particular reason, but guildmistress Elspeth has preempted me. I, too, meant to propose an expedition.

"While in the high country these last few days, I heard rumors of men asking questions about Obernewtyn. Strangers, perhaps Councilmen, perhaps not. They were asking questions about the damage caused by the firestorm, wanting to speak to anyone who had actually seen Obernewtyn. This means the Council may know I lied about the storm. If so, we will be investigated, probably after the next thaw."

There was a muffled howl of dismay.

"Or," Rushton went on, "it may mean nothing. The problem is that we have no idea what the Council knows.

"Up until now we have striven to avoid any contact with the Council, to hide and grow in strength, until we were powerful enough to confront them. We are not yet strong enough for the final battle, or any sort of open confrontation, but it is time we moved on to the next stage of our plans.

"I called this meeting to propose an expedition to Sutrium, with the aim of finding out if we are in danger and if the Council has any real knowledge of our existence. We can no longer hide in the dark, shivering. We must look, in the next year, to establish a safe house in the lowlands, preferably right in Sutrium."

"What is a safe house?" Miryum asked.

"The safe house will form the nexus of our inner defence. It means we can move with more confidence among the lowlanders. Most important, it means we will be in a better position to know what the Council is up to."

"What if someone is caught and . . . tortured into giving up the safe house location or, worse, to tell the truth about us and Obernewtyn?" Matthew asked. A few nodded fearfully at this.

"Don't you understand that we are no safer hiding up here?" Rushton said urgently. "Even if the rumors are just gossip, the soldierguards will come to hear of it, especially if they set a camp in the high country. The question is, do we wait until the Council descends on us before we act, or do we act now, while we can still move with relative freedom?"

A thoughtful silence greeted his words.

"Then, do you propose two expeditions to the lowlands?" Roland asked.

Rushton smiled slightly. "I vote that we accept the expedition proposed by Elspeth, with the addition of another person, whom I will choose, who will leave the main party after Rangorn and move into Sutrium. An expedition that can have two purposes can as easily have three. Now we will vote on the expedition with its three-fold purpose, and on the establishment of a safe house in Sutrium. Yes, first." He lifted his own hand.

I raised mine, hiding a reluctant smile. Rushton was never truly defeated. He knew Garth would never have agreed to the move on Sutrium without the lure of the coveted library. In the end, the vote was unanimous. Perhaps all felt that the time had come, whether we were ready or not, for a less passive strategy. At any rate, no one liked the idea of waiting like a lamb to be slaughtered.

Rushton rose to close the meeting formally, but was interrupted by a commotion outside the doors.

Christa entered, her smooth face worried.

Seeing me, she beckoned urgently. "Elspeth, it's Maruman. He's having some sort of fit. You had better come quickly."

III

Maruman had been taken to the Healer hall. As usual after days of wandering, often on tainted ground, his fur was filthy and singed in places, and dried blood matted the fur on one paw. But he looked no worse than he had on any other return. The wan afternoon light slanted obliquely from one of the high, slit-like windows to lay across his body, making it seem insubstantial, while candles burning all round the hall gave the room a ghostly orange tinge.

In the bed alongside the old cat's was a girl, heavily bandaged. She had been literally wrested from the Herders' purifying flame and had been unconscious since her arrival. One of the futuretellers sat beside her sunk in deep concentration.

I let my eyes rove around the room.

Two of the Guanna lay on a treatment bed near one wall. For a moment I had a vivid recollection of the night the dog Sharna had been torn to pieces by the savage wolves while trying to help me. I knew the healers were trying to treat the minds of the wolves who had been trapped and driven insane by Ariel. He had used them to guard the grounds and help him hunt down and kill runaways. But his sadistic treatment had made healing almost impossible.

I looked up to see Alad come through the door.

"He looks like he's asleep," I said.

Christa shook her head, nodding at the meditating futureteller. "She can hardly think for Maruman's emanations. I don't understand how you can't feel them," she added.

"I have my shield up," I explained. I dissolved the protective mental barrier and almost staggered beneath the force of gibberish flowing from Maruman's mind. I had seen him during other fits, but none so severe. "I see what you mean."

I saw from Alad's expression that he had lowered his own shield. "Usually I find the flow of beast thought soothing," he said ruefully.

Looking at the sleeping cat, it was hard to believe the insane babble rose from his mind.

"He was lying outside the Futuretell wing when we found him. It looked as if he had dragged himself there," Christa said.

"It seems worse than usual. Is it a fit?" I asked.

She looked down at the old cat. "The truth is that generally his mind is such a mess it is a wonder he can think straight even some of the time. I can't imagine what caused the damage in the first place, perhaps a traumatic birth. The amazing thing is that his mind seems to have adapted itself. There are the most extraordinary links and bypasses—yet somehow it all functions. The fits he usually has are the result of some sort of upward leak in his mind, where material from the deepest unconscious levels rises to distort his everyday thinking, hence the wild futuretelling, but this . . ."

"What do you make of it?" I asked Alad.

He sighed. "I'm a simple beastspeaker. This is beyond me. I've sent for Gather. He has a small Talent for deep probing as well as being a strong beastspeaker. No one else has that combination. Christa suggested it since she has no Talent as a beastspeaker and Maruman will not allow her to enter him. Perhaps he will permit a beastspeaker to deep probe."

"I can deep probe," I said.

Alad raised his brows, then looked at the cat pensively.

"You could try. He's less likely to oppose you. I'm afraid if it goes on much longer he'll die of exhaustion. He looks calm enough, but this is pulling him apart."

I stared down at the battle-scarred old cat, tears pricking my eyes. He looked so vulnerable. He would have hated that. I stroked him, fighting for control.

"Is there no healer free to ease him?" I asked gruffly.

Tactfully Alad examined the window. "They have done all they can. He's in no pain."

"What can I do?" I asked.

"Go into his mind," Alad said. "See what you can find out. Make him wake, if you can."

"I've never tried to deep probe him before. What if he resists? I might hurt him."

Alad shook his head impatiently. "He'll die if you can't help him. He is more wild than tame, and you know as well as I, the wild ones are hardest to reach, even in a normal communication."

With a feeling of dread, I sat on the stool beside the bed. I stroked Maruman's coarse fur gently, willing him to wake. I was repelled by the idea of entering my old friend's most private mind. I could not have borne such an intrusion myself. I was uncertain I could overcome my own mental block, let alone any Maruman might throw up.

Alad patted my shoulder. "It might be that you are the only one he will permit to enter him. You might not have to force your way."

I bit my lip then closed my eyes. Loosing a deep probe tendril gently into the first level, I forced myself to ignore the screaming gibberish that assaulted me the instant my screen was down. For a moment I was swept along like a leaf in the dizzy maelstrom of Maruman's unconscious mind. I had a fleeting temptation to let myself go, but concentrated on Alad's hand on my shoulder, forcing myself to the next level.

I slipped through effortlessly.

Alad was right. Maruman was letting me in.

I drifted deeper, concentrating to avoid the forgetfulness which was one of the greatest dangers inherent in entering an unconscious mind.

Deeper still and suddenly the susurration of the upper levels ceased. It was very quiet and still.

"Maruman," I whispered. "Maruman?"

I sensed a ripple in the fabric of the cat's unconscious mind. In a sense, I knew, I was inside his dreams. I went deeper still. Again I whispered his name.

This time he responded. "Elspeth Innle ..."

"Come with me," I invited trying to draw him to the upper levels and wakefulness. I was buffeted gently by his refusal.

"Can not. Mustwait," he responded.

I was puzzled. "Wait for what?"

There was no answer. I asked again. "Mustwait until Seeker comes."

This was a name Maruman sometimes called me. More confused than ever, I said, "I am the Seeker."

"Deeper. Must come deeper," Maruman responded instantly.

"Whymust?" I asked.

"The oldone wishes it."

I shivered violently, becoming suddenly conscious of my physical presence in the Healer hall. I forced myself to concentrate, but I was unnerved. It struck me that Maruman had let me in easily because he had wanted me to enter his deepest mind. Why? I could only know that by slipping deeper but I was almost at my limit. The desire to rise was powerful and my energy was running away quickly. Before long I would have no choice. I would not have the strength to remain. If I were to go deeper, I had to do it immediately.

Yet I hesitated.

At the depths of the mind is a great unconscious mind-stream. It was into this that the futuretellers dipped for their predictions. Without training it was possible for a mind to literally dissolve. I was already deeper than I had ever gone before.

I braced myself. Fighting an irresistible urge to rise, I pushed my mind fraction by fraction into the depths. All at once the void seemed to brighten and, below, I was aware of the shining silver rush of the mindstream.

Now I felt an opposite tug from the stream itself, a siren call to merge. My innate fear of losing myself gave me the strength to resist.

"I have come," I grated.

"Deeper," Maruman urged. "Must come deeper."

I was frightened now, for it was possible Maruman did not realize the danger. I hesitated and felt myself begin to rise. I clamped on my probe and forced it deeper. Now I could feel the wind of the stream and its incredible cyclonic energy below. It seemed to sing my name in an indescribably lovely voice, willing me to join. Again, fear of losing my identity helped me to resist. Then, suddenly, the pull to join the stream and the pull to rise equalized and I floated motionless.

Then I was on a high mountain in the highest ranges, the air around me filled with cold gusts of wind. I was inside the body of Maruman. I felt the wind ruffle his/my fur. I/We waited.

An illusion, but as real as life.

I/We licked a paw and passed it over one ear.

Then I felt the calling. It was not a voice so much as an inner compulsion. Maruman/I rose at once and began to walk, balancing with easy grace on the jagged spines of rock leading to a higher peak. It was there, I sensed, that the calling originated.

Then I heard my own name, but the voice was not Maruman's.

I was so astonished that the mountain illusion wavered and for a moment I saw, overlaid, the Healer hall. I was in

Maruman's deepest mind, and yet heard a calling that used my name!

"Do you know me?" I ventured.

"I have always known you," came the response.

"Who are you? What are you?"

"I/We are Agyllian," it answered, in a tone a mother might use in speaking to a small child. "I have used the yellow-eyes to communicate with you, Elspeth Innle, knowing you would come to his deepest mind. He is weary to death and it would be kind to let him join the stream, but he is not ready to go yet and neither, I think, are you ready to let him go. His pain and his strange mind make him receptive to us and allow us to use him."

"Then it's you making him sick," I said indignantly.

"Be at ease. He permitted it. He will suffer no harm, but he can sustain us little longer lest he pass into the stream of his own accord. I come only to warn you that your tasks have not ended, and to remind you of your promise. The deathmachines slumber, waiting to be wakened. While they survive, the world is in danger. When the time is right for you to seek out the machines, you must be ready to act swiftly and without doubt. You must not allow the concerns of your friends or your own needs to sway you. When the time for the dark journey is near, you must come to us and we will provide you with help."

"Journey? What journey?" I cried, but I was alone.

The mountains dissolved and I used the last of my strength to rise to where the upward drift would carry me to the surface of Maruman's mind. I was vaguely conscious that the upper levels were now quiet.

"Are you all right?" Alad asked tensely as I opened my eyes. I was slumped in the chair, soaked with perspiration and vaguely amazed to find it was dark outside.

He reached out and touched Maruman gently. "He'll recover. He's sleeping normally now. What did you do?"

I was too tired to answer. Seeing I was nearly asleep in

the chair, Alad and one of the healers helped me to my room.

Yet lying in bed, I found myself unable to sleep, and even the following day I was preoccupied with the memory of the voice inside Maruman's mind.

Had it been a deep probe illusion? They were common among Futuretell novices unused to the strict mental discipline required to deep probe successfully. But I had not been in my own mind. Such an illusion ought to have been a distortion of Maruman's thoughts, but apart from imagining that I was using Maruman's senses as I occasionally used Matthew's, there had been no sense of invading the cat's dream.

It was possible the illusion had risen from my own conscience, and from my fleeting worry about what Henry Druid, if he still lived, might find in his meddling with the past. Perhaps that and my visit to the Teknoguild caves had stirred up too many old ghosts, and the vision in Maruman's subconscious was the result.

Perhaps not.

It was hard to separate reality from illusion in the deeper levels of a mind but, if I had imagined it, why had Maruman been released from his torment the moment I had left his mind? If it had not been an illusion, what had spoken through Maruman to me?

And what of its words? The voice had warned me about the weaponmachines, reminding me of my vow to destroy them before they could be used. It had warned me to be ready to act when the time was right. But how would I know?

I shivered. I wanted to ask someone's advice, but suspected everyone, even Dameon, would tell me I had imagined the whole thing.

Yet they did not know that the weaponmachines had survived. Ironically Alexi's tortures had enabled me to see this, but I had kept the secret, believing the knowledge too dangerous even for Rushton.

Both Maruman and poor Sharna had believed me to be a

mysterious being in beast mythology named the Seeker, who they claimed was destined to fight a dark battle to save what remained of the world. It was too fantastic to believe.

Or was it? I was certain the voice in Maruman's mind had not been human—perhaps it had been some kind of animal. Was it possible those of the beast world knew something the humans, or funaga, did not? I wondered if I should speak to Maryon or one of the other futuretellers to ask for a future reading.

Fortunately, a busy guildmerge meeting to sort out details of the coming expedition drove all these thoughts to the back of my mind. After the meeting I went to see Maruman. He had not wakened, but the sleep was natural. The best kind of medicine, Roland had said reassuringly.

Coming across the lawns from the Healer hall, I found myself thinking of the guildmerge and Rushton's plans and feeling more certain than ever that things were about to change at Obernewtyn. Glancing up, I half expected to see dark clouds gathering overhead, but the sky was a clear and cloudless blue.

Inside, I noticed Dameon making his way down the hall toward the kitchens with Matthew.

I watched them approach, wondering what kept Dameon from running into things. His empath ability would not help him see, yet he was never clumsy.

"Elspeth?" he said unexpectedly in his soft beautifully spoken voice. His father had been a member of the Council before his death, and Dameon had been a product of that privileged class before a cousin had arranged to have him judged Misfit and claim the estate. It was one of the beauties of the Misfit charge that it could not be absolutely proven or disproven.

"Are ye sure ye canna see?" Matthew asked the empath, walking behind because of the narrowness of the hall at that point.

Dameon smiled sweetly. "I possess neither sight nor the

wondrous magic of your precious Oldtimers," he teased. "I knew Elspeth was there because of your reaction to her."

"You empaths!" Matthew exploded. "I thought I had th' shield in place then. Ye'd think emotions at least ought to be private."

"You need to perfect that shield," Dameon admonished. "Do you think I want to be privy to your emotional turmoils, entertaining though they are?"

Matthew blushed to the roots of his hair. "One canna always be screenin' every thought," he muttered.

Dameon laughed aloud. I bit my lip to conceal my own amusement. Dameon smiled accurately in my direction. There was a touch of sadness in his face that had not always been there. I looked up to see Matthew give me a speculative look. Annoyed that he seemed to know something I did not, I was tempted to probe him.

"Come, or we will arrive for midmeal at firstmeal," Dameon said pointedly.

Rushton called the empath his conscience and suddenly I understood why.

Dameon held out his arm and I took it with a wry smile. "I hear young Lina has been up to her tricks again?" he asked over his shoulder.

Matthew scowled blackly. "It was nowt so much the prank as her gettin' me so flustered I sat next to Miryum at nightmeal. That girl has as much grace an' wit as a lump of stone."

"Yet she is guilden," Dameon said with faint reproach.

Matthew looked put out. "She has Talent, I grant ye. But all she ever thinks about is the latest way to make people do things they dinna want to do. I dinna see how ye can bide her," he added, belatedly remembering Dameon spent a lot of time with the coercers in his work with Rushton.

The sound of cutlery clinking and laughter flowed down the hall from the kitchen to meet us. There had long been vague plans to open up another room as a proper dining area, but somehow the alcoves adjoining the kitchen remained the main eating area.

Guilds had got into the habit of sitting together for meals, but most of the masters sat at the head table with Rushton. He seemed to think of meals as another kind of strategy meeting.

Dameon saw me seated, then went to join his guild members. The empath spent most of his time working with Rushton, and he had long ago offered to forgo his place as master of the Empath guild, to make way for Miky and Angina, who managed it in his name. The twins had refused emphatically. No other guild had quite the same love for their master as empaths. They made little official demand on his time, but at social occasions they were possessive.

I was seated beside Rushton. Domick was on the other side of him, and they were both absorbed in something being said by Gevan, master of the Coercer guild. Rushton's soup was untouched.

I sighed and wondered if he ever noticed anything he ate, or enjoyed a conversation just because it was fun.

I noticed Louis Larkin standing just inside the kitchen courtyard door peering about short-sightedly. He hated coming to the house, preferring to eat in the farm kitchen. I wondered what had been important enough to bring him to the main house.

I sent a probe to Matthew, telling him to find out what Louis wanted. "He says he must talk with you," Matthew sent after a moment. "Will not tell me. Can't crack grouchybugger's shield."

I sighed. Louis was just as hard to get along with as he had always been. His hair stuck out like coils of wire on each side of his head but was sparse on top. His cheeks and nose were red with cold, but he insisted I come outside before he would talk. Matthew came too, closing the door behind him. It was growing colder and my breath came out in little puffs of cloud.

"Hmph," Louis grumped. "I'm surprised ye've th' time to spare for a beastspeaker." Louis regarded my decision to lead the Farseekers rather than the Beasting guild as the worst sort of traitorous defection.

"What is it, Louis?" I asked resignedly. There were times when he reminded me of Maruman at his most difficult.

"No need to snap my head off," Louis said smugly. "T'were a bit of gossip I heard, I thought might interest ye."

Louis was a remarkable source of odd bits of information. He hardly ever left Obernewtyn, but he always seemed to know what was going on in the highlands. And he knew everything that went on at Obernewtyn.

"I heard ye were wonderin' if th' Druid had left th' high country," Louis said, looking over his shoulder as if he thought someone might be listening. I was never sure how much of his eccentric behavior was affected and how much genuine.

"Have you heard anything?" I asked.

He nodded smugly. "Th' word is that th' Druid has nowt left th' high country. No one has seen a sign of his people in many a long day, but now an' then, there are disappearances."

"That could be our fault," Matthew said. "Them missin' could be Misfits we rescue, despite th' trouble we gan to make them seem natural."

"Ye'd be right of course! It could nowt be that th' Druid is doin' his own recruitin'. 'Tis nowt possible the disappearances are the reason th' Council takes an interest in th' high country!" Louis huffed sarcastically.

"But, if the Druid is taking people, where is he? And why haven't we been able to locate his camp in farseeking searches?" I asked.

Outrage in the old man's face melted into genuine puzzlement. " 'Tis strange enow. I would have said th' Druid had gone. But if he's nowt away from th' White Valley, yer expedition route mun be more dangerous than goin' th' main way."

"Have you mentioned this to Rushton?" I asked.

Louis gave me a look of sly entreaty. "Fact is, I only just heard it. Ought to tell th' Master but I've a yen to go on this expedition. I'd like to see th' lowlands once, afore I die," he added pitifully. "Ye could put in a word for me."

"Rediculous," Matthew said. "Ye'll live forever, ye old fake!"

"I will speak to Rushton," I said. Louis's eyes were fixed on my face, and whatever he saw there made him smile sourly.

"Ye do that," he said.

After he had gone, Matthew looked at me incredulously. "Why did ye let him bluff ye? Rushton'll nivver agree!"

"Because if Rushton heard this, he would be bound to cancel the expedition, or at least delay it. And Louis knows it. Besides, he might . . ."

"What th' devil?" Matthew muttered, hearing a wild yell from the courtyard behind us.

Zarak and Lina of the Beasting guild ran up to us. Both were white faced.

"Guildmistress, we have to talk to you!" Lina gasped. She elbowed Zarak hard.

"Well?" I snapped, in no mood for her antics. Zarak looked up, his eyes miserable and frightened, and suddenly I was filled with apprehension. "What is it?"

Lina answered. "We were sitting in the courtyard next to the maze and Zarak was . . ." She glared at Zarak, who was now staring at his feet. I restrained an urge to shake him.

He burst out, "I know I'm not supposed to farseek, but you don't know what it's like—being able to make your mind fly, and not being allowed to do it. I only meant to go a little way, but it felt so wonderful. Then I bumped into someone else. A stranger!"

I stared at him coldly. "You know even Farseeker novices

do not farseek beyond the mountains." He nodded. "Do you know why we have this rule?" He nodded again. "Tell me," I snapped.

"Because they might bump into a wild Talent ... and not be able to shield well enough to stop them ... tracing back to Obernewtyn," he mumbled. "But I swear it was someone untrained as I am. He couldn't have traced me. He thought I was an evil spirit."

I felt a sneaking sympathy for Zarak, who was in the wrong guild because his father was a beastspeaker. But I showed none of these thoughts on my face. Zarak had to learn to curb his curiosity, for all our sakes.

"Then since you know the rules it is not a matter of ignorance, but of deliberate disobedience." Zarak hung his head, flushing. "Therefore you will go at once to Javo and tell him you will be available for heavy kitchen work until I say otherwise. You will be suspended from the Beasting guild for the same period. I will speak to Alad and your father. Or do you want to lodge an appeal at the next guildmerge?"

Zarak shook his head.

Matthew nodded approvingly. "A fool who knows he is a fool is near to becomin' wise."

Lina fidgeted and looked at Zarak. "You'd better tell them everything," she advised.

Zarak bit his lip. "I might be wrong. It was so quick," he said, then floundered to a halt.

"What did ye do?" Matthew shouted.

Zarak said nothing.

"The person Zarak bumped into," Lina said with a sigh. "Zarak thinks it was a Herder."

IV

"Do ye think it were a Herder?" Matthew asked dubiously when the Farseeker guild met the following day.

"I don't know," I said. "Misfits have come to us from almost every walk of life. Why not from the Herder cloisters?"

Matthew frowned. "But would nowt they just burn any Misfit they found among themselves? They have th' right, over their own people."

I shook my head. "The Council might, but the Herders are subtle enough to think of using a Misfit for their own purposes. Especially if it were our sort."

"You think this accidental meeting was no accident?" asked an older farseeker.

I shrugged. "It may have been accidental on Zarak's part. But if the Herders have discovered about Talented Misfits . . ."

"Maybe he was wrong about not being traced," Ceirwan said.

I shook my head. "I think he was telling the truth, but we'll have to make sure. Have you traced the old path from Zarak's memory?"

Ceirwan nodded. "It's a cloister all right—in Darthnor, of all places."

"Darthnor. A town full of pro-Herder bigots an' fanatics. Wonderful," Matthew said darkly.

∽

Later that day I went down to the farms. Ostensibly I wanted to organize wagons for the expedition to the lowlands. But I was also curious to talk to Alad about his outburst in guildmerge. The Beasting guildmaster was nowhere to be seen, but I noticed a dark horse grazing nearby. That reminded me of the rumors of friction between humans and the younger horses.

It looked up warily at my approach. "Greetings, funaga."

I was surprised at its guarded tone. "Greetings, equine," I sent. "Do you know where Alad Beasting guildmaster is?"

The horse looked at me measuringly. "Who knows where the funaga go?" it sent coolly.

All at once I realized whom I was talking to.

Alad had encountered the black horse in Guanette. He had belonged to a gypsy troop. Half starved, he had been trying to pull a cart loaded with furniture, five plump children, and a fat, dirty gypsy man cursing and lashing out with a whip. Alad had told me the horse's imaginative mental curses had attracted his attention—that and his strength of mental projection.

He had ended up buying the horse and bringing him to Obernewtyn. Despite a deep hatred of humans, the horse had chosen to remain, becoming almost at once the spokesman for his kind. He had arrived, a dusty, bedraggled bag of bones, wild-eyed and filled with hatred of the funaga. Now he was lean and muscled, his coat gleaming and sleek. Only the eyes were unchanged, still filled with anger and suspicion. Suddenly I was sure this equine was behind Alad's difficulties with the horses.

"I remember when you came to Obernewtyn," I said gently.

The horse tossed its head, nostrils flared wide. "I was brought here a slave. I did not choose to come," it snarled.

Taken aback I said, "We had to do it that way. It would have looked odd to buy a horse and set it free. You chose to stay."

"That is so, funaga. There is no place in the world not infected by the funaga. Here is the same as anywhere else."

From the corner of my eye, I saw Alad approaching.

"We are not like the people who owned you before. Here, all work together. We are equals."

The horse snorted savagely. "You talk like a fool. We have no place in the funaga conclaves."

"It's only a matter of time..." I began, but the horse cut me off with its own thought.

"Alad-Gahltha asked that we be treated as true equals. Again this was set aside. Wait, they say. We have waited long enough. Now we are tired of waiting. From now on, we work only for our food and shelter. We will carry no funaga, and we will pull no cart beyond these mountains. We will not risk our lives to help the funaga. We will not fight the funaga's battles unless they are also ours."

There was no doubt in my mind that the proud, bitter horse meant it.

"That won't make anyone like you or take..."

The horse spat violently at my feet. "Like! I care nothing for the likes and hates of the funaga. Allies we will be, or nothing. I have heard the funaga plan a journey to the lowlands. We will see how they fare with no equine to draw their carts or carry them in the dark lands."

I blinked. "But we're not going to the Blacklands."

"The places where the funaga dwell are dark," the horse sent bleakly.

"I tried to warn Rushton. And it's not just the horses," Alad said from behind.

I ignored this and addressed the horse again. I knew as well as he that no expedition could be undertaken on foot, especially one so far and through such terrain. We needed the horses. "What if the journey were a test—to see if your kind and mine could really be allies, working together, trusting one another?"

The black horse stood very still, but he did not respond. "A way to find out if your kind and mine can work in accord," I went on softly. "A test in which funaga must pretend to have no special abilities and equines must pull carts, be ridden by funaga, and reined."

The horse reared violently and Alad started back swearing. I had expected the reaction, knowing the younger horses would not even tolerate a modified rein and would only work with beastspeakers.

The black horse bucked and reared, driving bladelike hooves deep into the ground. At last he calmed and turned to face me, his coat dark with sweat. "What if all who journeyed were slain? What if this journey failed?"

"If the equines did their part faithfully, the test would be judged a success—regardless of the outcome. And one of your kind would sit at guildmerge."

I knew I was offering what I had no right to offer, but I had no doubt Rushton would concur. He knew we needed the horses.

Alad should have brought the black horse before Council and let it make out a case. Its obvious hatred of humans would have been balanced by its intelligence and strength of mind. The horses were worthy allies, though I doubted animals like the black horse would ever be friends to their former masters.

"It shall be as you have stated, funaga," the horse said finally. "I will find those to draw your cart for this testing. But I will join your expedition also. Not to draw a cart, but to bear you. Then we will see whose kind is best fitted to lead."

"Elspeth you can't!" Alad cried aloud. "Rushton will have a fit!"

The black horse did not take its eyes from mine and there

was challenge and cold amusement in his look. He was daring me to agree, certain I would refuse.

I took a deep breath, ignoring the horrified Beasting guild-master. "It will be as you say, equine. Together we will deceive the lowlanders into thinking I am your master."

The horse neighed its laughter.

V

"Who are you?"

"Young," I assured Ceirwan.

"Where are you? I know you're there. I feel you."

The probe was clumsy and its movements graceless and badly focused, but I was surprised to find he had sensed my presence since I was tightly shielded. I let my probe brush against his fleetingly, testing.

His mind stabbed out in fright. "Are you a demon?"

Even while he grappled with my shielded probe, I entered him at a deeper level, deep probing to find trace memories of the encounter with Zarak. The meeting had had a huge impact on his mind. I was amused to find he thought Zarak a minor demon come to test his faith.

I decided to risk contact. If he reacted by calling out to his masters, I would stun him and Domick would manufacture a coercive block.

Rushton had insisted Domick monitor the attempt after being reluctantly convinced we had to establish how much damage had been done and whether Zarak's probe had been traced back to Obernewtyn. I suspected Domick had orders to cripple the boy's mind if there were any risk of the Herders using him.

"Do your elders know of us?" I sent.

The boy's mind recoiled from my mental blast. I had deliberately made it harsh and even slightly painful. While the boy believed he was dealing with demons, we were in no real danger.

"It is the way of a priest to undergo his tests in silence, Demon. My master has warned me your kind would try to shake my faith," the young Herder sent proudly.

I had read from his thoughts that he was a novice or apprentice priest. Born and bred on Herder Isle to servants of the priests, he had been chosen to join the priesthood. After initial training, he had been sent to Darthnor cloister to serve out his apprenticeship in the highlands. Ironically, he had become aware of his powers under the rigorous mental training of the priesthood.

He was speaking the truth about having said nothing of his encounter with the demon. He believed, at least superficially, that this was because the private agonies of a priest must remain locked in his own mind. Herder teaching said anything outside normal abilities was a mutation, but he had refused to admit his secret fear that he might be a Misfit.

He was no hardened fanatic for all his reactions. We rescued few older folk since most were unable to accept that their mutant abilities might not be evil. Those we encountered whom we judged a bad risk we simply blocked, making it impossible for them to use their powers.

This horrified the healers, but in truth the Misfits were happier to seem normal. Many believed Lud had cured them. The Herder boy's youth was a mark in his favor, since most of our rescues were of children. It was his youth that stopped me simply having Domick expunge the memory and block his mutant powers. Instinct told me he was worth rescuing, but because he was a Herder, I had to be sure he would respond the right way. I had promised Rushton I would do nothing until I was certain he could be trusted.

"How do you know I am a demon?" I asked, curious to know how much dogma he had swallowed.

The response was immediate. "You are a greater demon. The other was a lesser novice. Only demons can talk inside a man's head. My master says many are driven mad by such things, but you will not find me easy to break."

I sensed Ceirwan's amusement. "A puppy," he sent in ardent relief.

"If we can bring him in we would have an insight into the Herders' world. It's always possible those men asking questions about Obernewtyn were from the Herder Faction."

Ceirwan looked unconvinced. "He is a novice. Unlikely to know their inner secrets."

"He is one of us," I insisted stubbornly. "If we leave him, the Herders might end up finding out what he is anyway, sooner or later. Then he might betray us at their behest. He is not fully committed to their way and, deep down, I think he knows it. He's suppressing it because he is frightened."

"A rescue would have to be completely foolproof," Ceirwan warned.

"Are you still there, Demon?" the boy sent.

The wistful inquiry in his voice decided me. I remembered my own long mental loneliness, thinking myself a freak, living in fear of disclosure.

"Do others of your kind speak to demons?" I asked.

There was a significant hesitation in his mind before he answered. "Demons test many priests."

"I have not encountered any other human who could communicate with me," I sent, trying to sound like a demon.

Still probing his lower mind, I sensed him shy away from the half-formed thought that followed my comment. I was reminded of my own childhood in the orphan home system. I had not known at once that I was a Misfit, but some instinct of self-protection had kept me silent about my abilities. My brother, Jes, had been even more frightened. His hatred of my mutant abilities had warred with his love for me. He had spent a lifetime suppressing, even from himself, the fact that he, too,

was a Misfit. In the end, he had been killed trying to escape
from an orphan home after I was sent to Obernewtyn. For all
his apparent devoutness, the Herder boy was afraid, loath to
speak of his abilities because of a gut feeling of danger.

"I want to bring him out," I told Ceirwan aloud.

The memory of Jes made me determined to rescue the boy
before leaving for the lowlands. With this in mind, I contacted
him every night, working on his buried fears. At last he broke
down, confessing his knowledge that he was a Misfit, his belief
that his masters had begun to suspect him.

"Surely such a small mutation would not matter," I said,
at the same time evoking an old nightmare in the boy's mind
based on a burning he had once witnessed.

I was startled at the strength of his reaction. He screamed.

The noise brought an older Herder. Fearing the worst,
Domick struck. I deflected his blow with an ease that made him
glare suspiciously.

"I said I'll handle this," I hissed aloud.

I was relieved to hear the Herder boy tell his master he
had been dreaming and injected my own calm control over his
outward expressions. The priest departed with a final hard stare.
My own heart was thudding, reacting to the boy's fear.

"He knows," he sent forlornly. I had not meant to make
an approach so soon, but the desperate loneliness I sensed in
his thought decided me.

"You could run away," I suggested.

"Where could I go that they wouldn't find me?" the boy
asked miserably. "If they suspect, they won't let me get away.
They are interested in Misfits. They don't send them to the
Council." I saw a fleeting thought that confirmed rumors of the
Herder interrogation methods and shuddered. What would happen when they discovered our kind of Misfit? What would happen to the boy if they did guess the truth? Suddenly I was very
curious about the mysterious Herders.

"You know I am no demon," I sent gently, after a moment.

"Yes," the boy sent simply.

"Once, I was an orphan. Like you, I was different. I didn't fit in and I was afraid of being found out and burnt, or sent to the farms. Now I live free, with others like me."

"Misfits," he sent, using the hated word.

"Like you," I sent. "You could join us," I added lightly.

Hope flared, swamped by a sudden regressive fear that I might, after all, be a demon tempting him of the loss of his soul. "The other one. The first one I met. Is he there?"

I called Zarak and shielded his beam while they talked. In the end, the young Herder agreed to join us.

"He wants to know if he can bring his dog," Zarak asked with a grin.

∽

Zarak, Matthew, and Ceirwan brought him out. Officially Zarak was still in coventry, but the Herder boy trusted him, and had insisted he be present.

Gradually over a matter of days, the boy gave his Herder masters the impression he was becoming increasingly homesick. He talked constantly about his family and refused to eat. He let his masters think he was having trouble with the mental disciplines of the priesthood. When he escaped, it was made to appear as if he had run away with his dog and had drowned trying to cross the Suggredoon.

It was a good scenario, one of the best we had designed. It had to be or Rushton would never have passed it. It was artistically managed, even to the point of having clothes washed up on the bank, and beastspeaking scavenger birds to hover ominously about the spot when the Herder search party arrived. It was one of the few rescues that had gone without a single hitch.

The boy proved not only to be a powerful farseeker, which we had known already, but also an equally strong empath, which explained how he had sensed my presence when I was shielded. The joint ability was unusual. There were only two other farseekers among us with weak empath Talent. To my regret, the boy chose the Empath guild, little wonder since Dameon had taken him gently in hand from the start. Within days he had developed the empaths' traditional adoration for their gentle leader.

His name was Jik.

The expedition was due to depart in only a week when I met with Rushton to discuss the final plan. Discovering my name on the list of those to go, Rushton had exploded. He was furious to hear of my agreement with the black horse and even angrier that I had not spoken of it to him sooner.

"I won't be threatened," he shouted.

"It is an agreement," I said calmly. "We really don't have any choice. We need the horses. And I am the strongest farseeker and a perfectly good candidate for this expedition."

Rushton shook his head. "I will agree to this test in principle, but you won't be the one riding the black horse. I won't risk a guildmaster on an expedition."

Using Alad as translator, Rushton argued with the black horse, but it was useless. "He says why should the equines risk one of their leaders if the funaga will not? He says a test should involve leaders," Alad said.

"Then offer me as his rider," Rushton said grimly.

The horse agreed this would be a fair exchange, but guildmerge outvoted Rushton, saying he was more valuable than any other at Obernewtyn, being the legal Master. He must not be allowed to risk himself. Incensed, Rushton found his own rule, permitting a unanimous guildmerge to outweigh his lone vote, used against him.

I was taken aback at his reaction. I understood his reluctance to risk a guildmaster, but to offer himself as a replacement was senseless. Even he must see he was more important to Obernewtyn than I.

Ceirwan was to run the Farseeker guild in my absence, along with two other farseekers, since Matthew had also been appointed to the expedition. Unspoken was the knowledge that Ceirwan would become master if I failed to return.

On the final list were myself, Pavo, Kella, and Louis Larkin, with the Coercer ward, Domick, as Rushton's choice for our spy. The expedition was to be disguised as a gypsy troop. The carts had been built by the Teknoguild.

The black horse snorted its loathing at the sight of the gypsy rig. It had appointed two older horses to draw the carts. "Gypsies are not well loved by the funaga. Too fine horses will encourage robbers," he sent in terse explanation.

"What about you?" I asked.

The horse perked its ears forward complacently. "They will not find me desirable," he sent cryptically.

The night before we were to leave, Rushton came to the turret chamber. He had collected our false Normalcy Certificates. Written on old discolored parchment they were good forgeries, but I hoped we would not need them. The names had yet to be filled in.

"It's done then," Rushton said. He stared into the fire. There was a drawn-out silence and the fire crackled as if the lack of sound made it uneasy.

"Is something wrong?" I asked.

"Are you afraid?" he asked unexpectedly. I had a sudden vivid memory of him asking the same question in that room when it had been his.

This time, I nodded soberly. "It will be dangerous, despite bypassing Sutrium and the main ways."

Rushton turned to face me, his green eyes troubled. "Don't . . . risk too much for this Misfit," he said. "Whoever it is might not want to join us. You . . . are perceptive, but you don't always see what is in front of your eyes."

I had the notion he had meant to say something else and shifted uncomfortably. I had never felt really at ease with him since being forced into a mind link. I began to wish someone else would come in.

Rushton stood abruptly, shook his head and walked across to open the window shutters, breathing deeply as if the air in the turret room were too thin. He turned, leaning back against the open window, his face in shadow. "You ... are important to Obernewtyn. We can't afford to lose a guildmistress. Even now it is not too late to change your mind..."

I shook my head, relieved at the change of subject. "I want to go. Besides, I promised."

"You belong here," Rushton said sternly.

I wished he would come back into the room so I could see his face. There was a note in his voice that puzzled me.

"Have you been so unhappy here?" he asked.

I laughed. "I've never been more content in my life. But I am glad to go away for a while. It's as if I'm too safe and comfortable—like an old house cat. As Maruman would put it: I'm being tamed by comfort."

"And look at him," Rushton said darkly. "Someday you will have to come out of your ivory tower."

I shrugged, not understanding the reference. "Alad said he is recovering, though he still sleeps. He remembers nothing of coming back here."

Rushton nodded. "He will miss you."

Before I could answer there was a knock at the door.

I was surprised to find Dameon and Maryon outside. Their eyes went beyond me to Rushton.

"What is it?" he asked brusquely.

"I have futuretold th' expedition," the Futuretell guildmistress announced in her soft highland accents.

"What have you seen?" Rushton asked eagerly. "Will it be a success? Will those who travel return?"

I held my breath.

Maryon looked grave and serene. "I have seen that th' boy Jik mun travel with th' expedition. If he does nowt go, many, perhaps all th' rest, will nowt return."

I gasped aloud. None were permitted on expeditions except full-fledged guild members.

"Surely another empath?" Rushton said.

Maryon shook her head. "The prediction deals specifically wi' th' boy, but it is unclear. I dinna see any direct action on his part. It is my belief that he matters in some obscure manner—perhaps something he will do, or say, will offer a turning point for the journey. Whatever it means, he mun gan on this expedition, or Obernewtyn will fall to its enemies."

"That settles it, the expedition will have to be put off until Maryon can clarify the prediction," Rushton said.

Again the Futuretell guildmistress shook her head. "The boy was only part of the foreseeing. Th' fate of Obernewtyn hangs in balance of this journey an' it mun proceed as planned. The expedition mun return to th' mountains wi' their prizes before winter freezes th' pass, else we fall."

Rushton shook his head. "I don't know what to make of this."

"You need not fear Jik would betray us," Dameon said.

Rushton looked taken aback. "I don't doubt his loyalty if you vouch for him, but he's a boy! It's bad enough ..." His eyes darted momentarily in my direction. I felt irritated knowing he was thinking how it would damage Obernewtyn to lose a Talented guildmistress.

"I don't think we have any choice," Dameon said. "For some reason or other, Jik has to go on the expedition. There is no time to wait for clarification."

"Which might never come," Maryon added.

Rushton ran one hand through his hair and sighed. "I sensed it was time to end our isolation, but I little thought what that would cost." He turned and nodded at the pile of Normalcy papers. "Jik will have to use the extra one I had made for the Talent you hope to find. It's too late to make another."

When they were gone, I went to the window and breathed in the cool night air thinking how strangely things came about. A fortnight before, Jik had been a Herder novice. Now, suddenly, he was vital to Obernewtyn's future. If Zarak had not disobeyed me . . .

I shook my head. One could go mad thinking of alternate possibilities. Kella was right. The present was enough to deal with.

VI

The day of the departure dawned grim and unseasonably cold.

Gray clouds scudded across a metallic autumn sky. Wind blustered and rain fell in short violent flurries.

I shivered, staring out over the gardens from my balcony. I could imagine vividly in that moment the mountain valley blanketed in ice and snow, the mournful sound of wolves echoing across the frozen wastes. The lowlands would be much warmer than the mountains, even in wintertime. Perhaps, at last, the scars on my feet would have the chance to heal completely. I had avoided speaking to Roland about my feet for fear Rushton would hear of it and use them as reason to ban me from the expedition. He seemed savagely opposed to my going. Fortunately, Kella understood and had been treating me without telling Roland.

The healer made me think of Maruman. I had gone to see him before firstmeal but, though conscious, he was still dazed and barely coherent. I had wanted desperately to talk to him about the vision I had seen in his unconscious mind.

As with all expeditions, no amount of forethought could avoid the last-minute rush as remembered necessities were hunted up. Feeling harassed, I looked up with relief to see Ceirwan and Matthew approach.

"See, I've been practicin'," Matthew sent on a tightly shielded probe. The momentary mischief in his eyes faded as he looked around.

"Until today it hardly seemed such a great thing to be doin'," he said pensively.

I had said nothing of Maryon's prophecy. Rushton believed it was better not to let it be known the expedition carried the fate of Obernewtyn on its back. I would tell the others when and if I needed to. Dameon had suggested I tell no one of the part of the prophecy concerning Jik. "It would not be fair on the boy. Maryon said it may be that his part is something quite obscure, something not apparent until much later, though his presence means the difference between survival and failure."

Jik was excited, but it was a subdued excitement. He was younger than Lina and Zarak, but more serious and quieter of nature. He seemed bemused by the news that he was to be part of the expedition.

We were delighted to discover he had been to Sutrium before coming to the highlands, and had seen enough to give Domick some idea of the present shape and disposition of the town. He had also been to Aborium, where we might need to renew supplies for the return journey. All the Herder vessels berthed there. I had the impression Jik had not liked the sprawling seaport and resolved to ask him why.

Jik's dog, Darga, was to accompany us as well. A nondescript short-haired dog with a ferociously ugly face, he was one of a breed used by the Herders to guard the Herder Isle. Darga had been a miscolored runt in his litter, expected to die when Jik had volunteered to nurse him.

Zarak and Lina stood beside Jik, their faces openly envious.

The three horses to travel with us had been supplemented by another. I would ride the black horse, who sent terse instructions that he would answer to the title Gahltha, which meant leader. Domick would ride the newcomer, a small, wheat-colored mountain pony with doelike eyes. Named Avra, she had been brought wild to Obernewtyn the previous wintertime, having injured herself in a fall. Alad told me she was the black stallion's chosen mate. The two mares to pull the carts were Mira and Lo.

The horses stood together as Alad harnessed them and installed the hated bit and bridles. Privately Alad had warned me Gahltha had chosen horses that were completely loyal to him. It was clear where their allegience would lie if it came to a choice between equine and funaga aims. They would follow me as leader of the expedition only under instructions from the black horse.

None of the equines seemed inclined to closer acquaintance, and I hoped I had not made a mistake in choosing Louis over a full Beasting guilder. I could beastspeak, of course, but the animals had more time for those of the Beasting guild. Naming his selection, Gahltha had said he had trained the horses to fight funaga. He sounded as if the thought of fighting pleased him. I hoped fervently that he would remember which funaga were his allies if it ever came to battle.

With Kella, Jik, and Darga in one caravan, and Pavo and Louis in the other, the caravans were authentically crowded. Gypsies traveled traditionally in extended family groups, begging, singing, and dancing for money and providing amusing and impromptu plays. The descendants of those who had originally refused Council affiliation, they were little liked or trusted for all their variety of skills. In some ways it was a dangerous disguise, but it was one of the few ways a number of people could travel about without drawing attention. Travel was not undertaken lightly, for people everywhere were suspicious of strangers in their midst.

To complete our disguise, we were unnaturally tanned and wore the layers of the colored clothing favored by gypsies. The dark skin was the result of a powerful berry-based dye. I doubted anyone would have the slightest suspicion we were anything but a motley gypsy troop.

The last guildmerge proved a disorganized affair. Along with a feeling of genuine need to get the expedition underway, and the flurry of last-minute preparations, there was the underlying feeling that time was getting away from us.

"We have been lucky up to now that our secrets have not been penetrated, that we have not been reported or caught out somehow," Rushton told us. "But luck and caution will not keep us safe forever. Sometimes, only an aggressive move will do. Now is the time to begin to fight the Council more openly." He went on to say that by "more openly" he did not mean revealing ourselves. He stressed the need to maintain our disguise at all costs. We had all set up coercive blocks that would erase our memories in an emergency. These were Obernewtyn's safeguard in case one of us was caught and tortured. Only Jik had not been able to be blocked, being too untrained; Domick or I would wipe his memory if the need arose.

Rushton adjured us to work together and not forget that the three aims in the expedition were equally important.

At the last, he wished us good fortune. "This journey is the beginning of a new stage for us. I wish you success, for your sake and ours." If anyone noticed the slightly ominous note in his final words, it was not apparent.

All Obernewtyn turned out to see us go, but the festival air did not last long. We had barely stepped outside when it began to rain heavily.

I climbed awkwardly into Gahltha's saddle, ignoring his derisive whinny. He might not want to be ridden, but he knew an incompetent rider when he had one.

Wrapping an oiled cape about my head and shoulders, I nodded to Domick. We had decided he would ride in front of the carts, and I at the rear, at least until we left the main road.

The rain had sent everyone running inside but, looking back, I had a final glimpse of Rushton standing alone on the top step, apparently oblivious to the downpour.

Even at that distance, I could see the same odd tension in

his stance that had puzzled me in the tower room.

I wondered what he was thinking and impulsively lifted a hand to wave.

Instantly he responded, raising his own hand. I stared over my shoulder until the gray curtain of rain came between us.

I felt an unexpected regret at the thought that I would not see him again for a long time, perhaps many months, if we failed to make it back before the pass froze.

Part II

The Lowlands

VII

I had been nervous about riding, but was relieved to find it less traumatic than I had expected. Under the terse instructions of the black horse, I had tied the reins to the saddle. There was no need to direct the horses until we reached the lowlands. I had not wanted to ride at all. Gahltha said coldly that I would have to learn to ride properly before we reached the lowlands. No gypsy would be as inept in the saddle.

I noticed Domick casually slouched in the saddle as if it were an armchair and envied him his skill and confidence.

Gahltha began instructing me the moment we left Obernewtyn. When I did not know what to do with my hands, I clutched at the saddle, hanging on for dear life. He forbade this, saying I must learn to ride by balance. A gypsy did not rely on his hands or stirrups. This seemed impossible enough until he warned me that I would have to be able to ride without a saddle, since gypsies rarely used them.

The steady rain kept me from talking aloud to those in the caravans, so I contented myself with the occasional farseeking observation to Matthew, and concentrated on trying to coordinate all the contortions Gahltha seemed to feel riding required.

"Heels out so you do not jab me in the ribs, or I may forget and buck you off," he sent.

"Knees tight or you will be off the first time I stumble."

The first hours were punctuated by Gahltha's staccato instructions. He made no comment to me except to give me orders. I had the feeling he was enjoying every minute of my discomfort.

The rain continued throughout the remainder of the day, drumming steadily on my oiled coat and on the roofs of the caravans.

The weather was so bleak that we passed into the realm of Blackland storms almost without noticing. The last time I had passed the stretch of tainted ground, I had been coming to Obernewtyn for the first time, filled with apprehension for the future. Now I was leaving, still full of apprehension.

We passed the area without mishap, and soon after left the main road for the White Valley. Fortunately vegetation and undergrowth were sparse, or the carts would have been useless.

I felt Jik clumsily seeking entrance into my thoughts. "Will the caravans be able to go through the Olden way?" he asked.

"Pavo thinks so. It was once an important Beforetime thoroughfare," I sent.

"Why doesn't anyone else know about it?" Jik wondered. "I never heard any of the priests up here mention it, and I never saw it on any of the maps."

The question had also occurred to me. "Pavo says it is probably because there has been no need of it. People prefer to travel the main coast road through the towns. And no one much uses the White Valley. The highlanders believe it to be haunted."

When night fell, it was still raining. After a hasty conferral, we decided to go on as long as we could, since it would be impossible to make a proper camp or cook in the sodden valley.

To my surprise, Gahltha was the one to call a halt, saying the horses pulling the cart needed to rest. I was surprised at his consideration, then reminded myself this was for horses, not humans. But I was glad to stop just the same. Climbing down from his back stiffly, I was convinced every bone in my body was fractured and wondered if it could possibly be any worse to ride bareback.

Relieved of the hated trappings, the horses wandered off to graze, untroubled by the rain. Domick and I hung our soaking oil cloaks under an Eben tree in the hope that they would dry by morning.

We all climbed in one carriage to talk. Darga had jumped out the moment the cart stopped; even so it was too cramped to change my damp clothes, so I wrapped a blanket around my shoulders.

"We might as well close th' flaps an' keep out th' night air," Matthew said, untying the strings.

Kella had lit two candles in shielded sconces and the interior of the van glowed dimly in the flickering light. It warmed up quickly with the flaps closed, and I felt myself drifting off to sleep while watching Jik and Kella prepare a simple nightmeal. I felt so tired it was an effort to eat, but Kella insisted.

I tried to shift my position, but my legs seemed to have set in their riding position. Laughing, Kella produced a strongly scented green paste which she promised would ease the muscle strain.

I sighed regretfully at the thought of my favorite chair in front of the turret-room fire. Jik interrupted my weary daydream to ask why he had been included on the expedition.

I had imagined Dameon had provided some plausible reason, but it appeared he had left it to me. Trying to give myself time to think, I asked Jik why he had not asked Dameon himself.

He shrugged diffidently. "Lina and the others kept saying how lucky I was. I thought somebody would tell me why sometime."

I nodded, knowing I could not burden him with the true

reason. "Your knowledge of Herder lore was the deciding factor.
We know so little about the priesthood. They seem to be growing stronger and more powerful. You might well be able to keep
us from making some obvious mistake. And, of course, there is
your knowledge of Sutrium."

Jik frowned. "I was only there two days. And novices are
the lowest of the low. I don't know any more than you would
know," he added in a troubled voice.

I patted his arm reassuringly. "Don't worry about why
you're here. Just concentrate on remembering everything you can
about Sutrium and the Herder Faction."

I heard squelching noises outside just as Gahltha's cold
probe slid into my mind.

I pulled aside the flap and looked into his dark, wet face,
almost invisible in the night. Directly behind him, Avra was a
pale blur.

"What is it?" I sent, matching his brevity.

"There are fresh equine tracks nearby, less than a day old.
Funaga rode the equines. Avra found the tracks." Gahltha sent.
"They traveled the opposite way to us, making for the main
road."

"Maybe someone else uses the Olden way," Jik said when
I told the others.

I sent a questing thought on an unshielded beam to Avra.
"Do you know how many funaga there were?"

"More than here, two times more than here," Avra sent,
as shy as Gahltha was arrogant. I bit my lip. That meant double
our number—as many as twenty. I felt suddenly cold remembering Louis's words about the Druid. Louis, too, looked
thoughtful.

We had been incredibly lucky to miss the riders, but that
did not solve the question of where they had come from. There
were no mapped villages in the White Valley. Louis said the
highlands were full of small settlements unknown to Council

mapmakers, made up of people who wanted to be free of Council domination without openly opposing them.

"Perhaps this is such a settlement," he offered without conviction.

"Riders do not have to indicate a settlement. Perhaps they were hunting," Gahltha sent.

I shook my head slowly. I did not think anyone would hunt in the White Valley. "We'll stay the night here and go at dawn."

I asked Gahltha to warn Darga and the other horses to keep an eye out for any sign of funaga that might give us a clue about why they had been in the White Valley. Then I dropped the flap, shutting out the bleak night.

"He doesn't like you," Jik said in puzzled wonder.

I nodded wryly. "Gahltha was badly abused by his old masters. I don't think he likes any human."

"But it's different at Obernewtyn. No one would hurt him there." Jik said indignantly. "It's not fair for him to blame us."

I smiled gently. "Not much in life is fair."

I realized Jik had not been able to hear Gahltha, but had sensed the dislike as an emotion. That seemed to be a new use of empathizing, or perhaps a new Talent. I made a mental note to tell Dameon when we returned.

"What do you think they were doing here?" Kella asked.

"I don't know," I said. "But if they are in hiding, they won't want to see us any more than we want to stumble into their midst. I'm going to farsense our route. If there is any sign of a settlement, we'll change course and bypass it." I closed my eyes.

For a moment I was half mesmerized by my own exhaustion and the monotonous sound of rain on the canvas roof of the caravan. I forced myself to concentrate, and then my probe was flying swift and low along the path we planned to take. I touched briefly on the minds of various nocturnal creatures, but found no human mind. At one point I was startled when a cloud of shadowy birds rose, flittering and shrieking indignantly, disturbed by my questing. Finding nothing, I came back along the same path, swinging out on both sides.

My probe brushed briefly along the static barrier on the fringe of the Blacklands, then I went back further toward the road, along the banks of the Suggredoon. I was surprised to realize we were less than an hour's ride from the river. We planned to follow the Suggredoon down to where it disappeared underground at the foot of the lower ranges. Not far from there we would find the Olden way.

Making a last sweep of the area, I encountered a numb area. I tried to penetrate it, but it was like trying to see in a blinding snow storm.

Defeated, I withdrew and opened my eyes.

"Are you all right?" Matthew asked.

"Did you find anything?" Domick asked.

I told them the result of my farsensing. "It sounds like Blackland static," Matthew said.

"It was like that, but denser and cloudier, and in the wrong spot," I said. "Maybe it was tainted water—that feels different but still gives off static."

"But no settlement," Domick persisted.

"I couldn't sense even a single person, let alone a settlement," I said, feeling relieved. "I think Gahltha must be right. Maybe it was a hunting party."

Matthew looked doubtful. "I dinna think anyone would come here to hunt. 'T'would be like takin' midmeal in a grave-yard. Maybe it were soldierguards lookin' for escapees?"

I chewed my lip. "It wouldn't be possible to have a machine that would create that kind of blocking static, would it?" I asked.

Pavo looked thoughtful. "That would mean someone had found a way to modify a Beforetime machine. The Zebkrahn took years to modify—first Marisa then Alexi and then the

Teknoguild worked to change what seems to have been no more than a thing originally devised to measure brain waves. I doubt it could happen again. Besides, I think you would know if it were a machine."

"It must be some sort of poisoning then," Domick said dismissively.

It was a cold night. I slept restlessly, dreamed of running through dark tunnels and woke with the feeling that I had forgotten something important. After racking my brain, I pushed the nagging feeling to the back of my thoughts.

Pulling the flap aside, I was delighted to find sun streaming through the treetops. The others stirred in the blaze of light, blinking and groaning. The ground was soaking wet, and there was no question of lighting a fire, but it was lovely to stretch our legs and walk around. I was very stiff but suspected I would have been worse without Kella's healer wizardry.

Gahltha and the other horses emerged from the trees as we were finishing a scratch firstmeal. Darga accepted a bowl of milk with a polite flap of his tail. We tied the oilskins which were still wet on top of the caravans and washed our faces in a streamlet. Domick worried that the water might be tainted, but Darga pronounced it safe. He had an acute sense of smell and could tell when water was bad.

We set off far more cheerfully than the previous day. I felt happier, despite Gahltha's insistence at my riding bareback. Mounting him was an awkward debacle because my legs were too stiff to flex easily. But once up, I felt more comfortable than I had on the saddle, though less secure.

The sun shone in a golden autumn way, and Jik played a jaunty harvest song on his gita, accompanying himself in a surprisingly sweet singing voice. Even grim Domick appeared to enjoy the impromptu concert, and the horses perked their ears as if they liked the sound.

Later, I listened to a communication between Darga and Avra about funaga. I was amused to hear their interpretation of human parenting, but Gahltha snorted loudly at Avra's observation that children seemed less dangerous than grown funaga.

"You do not know anything about the funaga and their ways," he told her icily. "They are all the same. I have been beaten savagely by a funaga child who laughed at my pain and jeered when I bled. Like poisoned ground, funaga bear poisoned fruit."

I shivered at the venom in his voice.

Gahltha's pace quickened after that. On a flat stretch he broke without warning into a trot and I promptly fell off. My only consolation was that the wet ground was soft. My anger made no impression on Gahltha, who insisted that I would not have fallen if I had been gripping with my knees the way I was supposed to. Louis laughed uproariously, and though the others restrained their amusement, my next fall sent them all into gales of laughter.

I kept my temper with difficulty, realising Gahltha wanted to goad me. And, also, I knew he was right, however sarcastic he was. I had been sitting lazily.

By the time we stopped for midmeal I was covered in mud. It was not worth changing, so I merely washed my hands and face to eat. The afternoon was worse than the morning despite my forlorn hope for an easy walking pace. Gahltha decided I must progress to riding at a gallop. Again pride kept me from protesting that he was progressing too quickly.

So we cantered and galloped, and when the wagons moved too slowly for Gahltha, he would run ahead, then turn and run back. By late afternoon I was beginning to feel the rhythm of his movements, and to understand that knowing and feeling the rhythm was the main part of riding, apart from balance. Once or twice I even found myself enjoying the speed.

We had been traveling parallel to the Suggredoon most of the day, but after midmeal, the river broadened suddenly, swollen from the night's rain. The undergrowth thickened too, slowing the caravans to a walking pace. Avra went slightly ahead with Domick, seeking the easiest path for the caravans. Later Gahltha and I took over, leaving Domick free to range farther ahead.

We hoped to reach the foot of the mountains before nightfall, but Domick returned just as the sun fell behind the mountains. One look at his grim expression told us his news was bad.

"I found the place where the Suggredoon goes under the mountains, but I couldn't find any pass. We went a fair way up from the river, but there was nothing. It looks like the Land has changed, blocking off the pass," he reported glumly.

"The opening could be aslant so that you would have to be coming from the other way to see it," Pavo said.

"I hope you're right," Domick said. "But that's not all the bad news. Just ahead there are great patches of swamp and wetlands. The wagons won't have a hope of going through, and it will take days to go round."

There seemed no point in pushing on in the darkness. We decided to make camp on a high, grassy knoll beside the Suggredoon.

Louis, Jik, and Matthew went to forage for dry wood while Kella organized nightmeal. Domick unharnessed the horses and checked the wooden wheels for stress cracks. Pavo was sitting near the wagons poring over his maps.

I went to bathe in the river, but just as I reached the edge of the clearing, I heard Kella and Domick begin a heated argument. Sighing, I turned back. The last thing we needed was guild rivalry.

Before I could intervene, Pavo broke into a violent fit of coughing. Kella stared at him for a moment, then went over commanding him to open his mouth.

"Don't be stupid, I swallowed a fly." He laughed and waved her away. But Kella's face was deadly serious.

"What is it?" Domick asked her.

The healer ignored him and laid a hand over Pavo's thin

chest. The smile faded from his face and, suddenly, I felt frightened.

"Why didn't you tell anyone?" Kella asked in a subdued voice.

Pavo smiled sadly. "What good would it have done, eh? I don't need a healer to tell me what the matter is."

"Rushton would never have let you come, if he had known," Kella said.

Pavo turned away abruptly. "Don't you think I know that?"

"What is it?" I asked, coming back into the clearing.

Kella looked at me bleakly. "The rotting sickness. It's in his breathing."

"Are you sure?" Domick asked.

"It's not hard to feel, once you know. And the coughing is always a sign. There's nothing I can do for him. Nothing," she added flatly.

Pavo still had his back to us, rigidly unmoving.

"You'll have to . . ." I began.

"No!" The mild teknoguilder whirled, eyes ablaze. "I won't go back. You said yourself there's nothing to be done. I accept that, but I'll go the way I want. I won't be a problem. Tell them," he demanded of Kella.

She nodded. "He'll cough and there will be bouts of pain. He won't be affected badly until near the end—three or four months . . ."

I gaped. Pavo stared into my eyes, his own pleading and determined at the same time. "You will need me to get to the library."

I wished Rushton were there to decide, instead of me. After a long moment, I nodded and Pavo's shoulders slumped visibly as if he had been holding his breath.

"Thank you," he said.

I felt tears in my eyes and was relieved to see Matthew and Jik arrive, laden with dry wood. Jik froze and stared about him, sensing the tangle of emotions. I sent a quick shielded instruction to Matthew, and he began to make a fire, diverting Jik's attention.

We slept inside the caravans again because of the sodden ground, but left the flaps open for fresh air. Obernewtyn seemed very far away.

Near dawn, I was jolted awake by Domick poking his head into the wagon.

"Quick, there are people coming, men," he hissed urgently.

I farsensed the area and almost fainted with horror. There were at least a dozen men approaching the clearing. "It's too late to escape. You get away. I'll send the horses away and contact you once I find out what this is all about. I'll farsense Gahltha to find you. Quickly," I whispered.

He nodded, melting silently into the gray, predawn shadows.

My heart thundering, I farsensed Matthew and Jik, warning them to let me do any talking. I wondered what sixth sense had woken the coercer even as I farsensed the horses, urging them away.

Our only hope, I knew, was to be taken for the gypsies we appeared to be. I cursed my stupidity in not taking better precautions after Avra had found the tracks.

"Ho. What have we here?" called a gruff voice. I leaned out of the caravan. Three men stood in the open, illuminated by the dying embers of the fire. Behind them, the dark sky showed pink and gray traces of the dawn. I sensed the other men waiting in the bushes.

"Who are you? What do you want?" I shouted.

"Gypsies," sneered one, a fat, bristle-bearded man with a great pouting stomach and pale glistening eyes.

"Perhaps," said the voice which had first hailed us. It belonged to a muscular young giant with ginger hair. The third man was frail and unlike the other two, clad in a long, fine woollen gown much like the garb worn by Herder priests. I was terrified that we might have fallen into Herder hands. I prayed the priest would not recognize Jik, and hurriedly warned him not to draw attention to himself. With his dark skin, dyed hair, and gypsy clothing, he did not look much like the Herder boy we had rescued.

"Who are you to be waking us in the middle of the night?" I demanded. Gypsies were not known for their manners.

"Get out of those wagons, all of you!" snarled the black-bearded man.

"This is a funny time to want your palm read," I grumbled. "If you mean to rob us, you'll be disappointed." I climbed out and put my hands on my hips as the others followed. I watched the man in the robe closely, but he did not seem to recognize Jik. "Well, you have us all out. Now what?" I asked.

The ginger-haired woodsman quirked his brow speculatively. "Is this all of you?"

"Enough for you," I said cheekily. Gypsies were never subservient.

"Are you the leader of these people?" asked the man in the robe. He had a curiously colorless voice and very cold eyes.

"For now," I answered after swift thought. "My father is the leader of our troop. We are to meet with him in Arendelft." I nodded at Pavo. "My cousin there fell sick and our party split in two. Though I don't know what business it is of yours," I added rudely.

"What are you doing here if you are headed for Arendelft?" asked the robed man.

My heart jumped. "We heard there was an Olden way through the mountains," I said, weaving truth with lies. The best lies are the ones that are mostly true, Louis always told us. He was glaring belligerently at the men and I hoped Matthew had told him to keep his mouth shut.

"There is no such pass." The robed man stepped forward and I resisted the urge to step away. "Enough of this. We will bring them back to camp." More men stepped out of the trees.

I pretended to look surprised. "Find the horses and bring these vans."

"Where are you taking us?" I demanded.

The robed man did not answer, but the ginger-bearded woodsman grinned over one shoulder. "You are to meet the great man himself. The Druid."

VIII

Through the trees I could see a settlement. I realized we were headed for the blank area I had been unable to penetrate the night before. This and the knowledge that we had been captured by Henry Druid filled me with apprehension. We could hardly have got into a worse mess deliberately.

But more disturbing was the fact that, as soon as we entered the area of blankness, my powers were useless. I could not even reach Matthew who was directly behind me. And I could not reach Domick, outside the area.

Mindbound for the first time in my life, I was overcome with panic and the feeling of being trapped. Glancing over one shoulder, the look of rigid terror on Jik's face acted like a bucket of cold water on my own fear. I made myself smile reassuringly and the stark tension in his movements subsided. I concentrated on calming myself. I had to find a way to free us, and that would only be possible with a cool head. Methodically, I tried reaching all the others, including Darga, who padded along quietly beside Jik. I could not sense a single thought. Again I tried Domick, then Gahltha.

Nothing.

I tried examining the block itself. No wonder the Druids had seemed to disappear so completely. The block had to be a machine, modified like the Zebkrahn. There was something mindless about the static.

Behind, Louis grunted in astonishment at the size of the walled encampment visible through the trees. The wall itself was no more than a barrier of thin, dark-stained striplings set upright in the ground, reaching high enough to obscure all but the tops of thatch-roofed buildings and a number of gently smoking chimneys.

I was less concerned by the size than by what such a block must mean. The Druid must know about Misfit abilities. He had been a Herder and there had always been rumors that the Herders knew more than they told. Perhaps they had always known about Misfits and simply kept it from the Council for some reason of their own.

Somehow Rushton had to be warned that the Druid had mind weapons. What would happen if the Druid discovered we were Misfits?

Or did he already know that?

Rounding the outer wall we came to a wide gateway, firmly bolted. A ruddy face appeared at an opening in answer to the red-haired woodsman's call, "Who is that wi' ye, Gilbert? I diven't know them faces."

Gilbert gestured impatiently at the door. "Open up, Relward."

"Bain't he a gypsy?" Relward inquired staring doltishly into my face. He chewed his lip ponderously, then, unlatching the gate, planted himself firmly in the gap.

"Step aside, dolt! You try my patience," Gilbert snapped.

Relward shook his head. "I canna let strangers in. Take him," he nodded at me, "an' them others to th' compound. Her can come in," he added, nodding at Kella. Despite the seriousness of our situation, I felt indignant at being taken for a boy.

"I'll decide where they will be taken, Relward," Gilbert said through gritted teeth. "But I'm not sure we should have a gatekeeper too blind to know the difference between man and maid."

The bumpkin's eyes widened. He stared at me accusingly as if I had deliberately transformed myself to confound him. Then he gaped, seeing the robed man. "Master," he bleated. "I dinna know ye was there." He tripped over his feet in the effort to get out of the way. The robed man ignored him and swept into the camp.

Gilbert grinned covertly over his shoulder at me. "Do not think we are all such fools as that—or so blind," he murmured in a low voice. I stared at his back in astonishment.

There was nothing makeshift about what lay within the walls. It was a complete and settled village with graveled streets and stores. There was even a blacksmith and extensive holding yards and stables for horses within the wall.

People came out into the street to watch us pass, their eyes curious. Almost everyone seemed to wear arms, including the women and older children. The prospect of escape seemed dim. I wondered what Domick would make of our disappearance. He might decide to return to Obernewtyn but, were I in his place, I would wait and try to find out what had happened.

At the very center of the settlement was a wide green expanse and garden beds. I was oddly reassured to see children playing on a swing, though they stopped their game to watch us pass.

Only one building edged on the square, a big stone house that reminded me vaguely of the main Councilcourt in Sutrium. Broad stone steps led up to the entrance and double wooden doors like those at Obernewtyn stood open, revealing a long hall with a shining timber floor and a high, sloped ceiling. Two young men emerged from one of the many doors leading into the hall. They smiled at Gilbert, but their good humor faded when they saw the rest of us.

"Gypsies," one spat. Gilbert frowned, but made no comment, shepherding us through a door into a room.

Left alone except for Gilbert, I did not try to talk to the others. Taking my lead, they stood silent too. I tried again to breach the block, but with no success. It was incredible to think such mental blindness was considered normal.

"Gypsies, eh?" Gilbert said, leaning against the door. "Where were you really headed? The main road is much quicker than any so-called Olden way."

I stepped up to him boldly. "I told you already, or are you as deaf as that gate warden was blind? We are to meet my father in Arendelft."

Instead of becoming angry, Gilbert threw back his head and laughed with real amusement. "I wondered why a scrap of a girl was the leader over grown men, but now I see you carry the sharpest weapon in your wicked tongue."

"Why have you brought us here?" I demanded.

Gilbert smiled. "I am the one asking the questions. Tell me, where have you come from, if you insist you are going to Arendelft?"

I hesitated. "We have been in the high mountain country."

I heard a smothered gasp from Kella, but fortunately Gilbert was too intent on my answer to register it.

"Then . . . you must have seen Obernewtyn?" he said.

I shrugged carelessly. "Of course." From the corner of my eye I could see Matthew looking at me as if I had gone mad.

"Why did you go up there?" Gilbert asked guardedly.

"Why does a gypsy travel anywhere? For silver. My father said there would be winter lodgings there, and work to trade for it. He wanted to try trapping a snow bear. One sold in Sutrium last moon fair for a Councilman's ransom." I smiled as if the thought of such wealth excited me, then I let my face fall.

"But everything went wrong. There was a curse on that place and we laid another in leaving. A firestorm had all but laid it to waste. There was nothing left but a few rough huts made of the ruins. The people left had no room or food to spare. Then my cousin fell sick, and I had to wait for him while the rest went on without us. And now this." I snorted petulantly.

"So, there was a firestorm," Gilbert murmured.

"We were supposed to meet the troop at Arendelft in time for the harvest of Eben berries," Matthew said.

Gilbert looked at him and grinned. "So, you can speak. I thought you were all mute, having this grubby wench speak for you."

I held my breath hoping Matthew would have the sense to see he was being deliberately needled. He only shrugged sullenly and fell silent.

The robed man returned, and Gilbert spoke to him in a low voice. His pale eyes rested thoughtfully on me.

"Take the men to the compound, the boy to the other children for the time being, and the girl to Rilla. You will come with me," the robed man instructed me coldly. He led me down the hall to another door.

"... but how can we have missed it..." A deep voice floated out as we entered the room. I blinked, dazzled by sunlight streaming from a huge window overlooking an enclosed fern garden. There was a long table in the room covered in books and papers and surrounded by chairs. A number of robed men, and several dressed like Gilbert, clustered around the head of the table.

"Forgive me, Lord," said the man who had brought me there.

Those bending over the table drew back, revealing a whitebearded man seated in their midst. He wore the same plain cream-colored robe. He had the thin face and body of an ascetic, but his features were curiously mismatched—beaky nose, a jutting chin, and beetling silver brows. His eyes were his sole visible beauty, dark and strangely compelling. Such eyes might easily see into a person's mind. I met his penetrating gaze uneasily.

"What is it, Douglass?" he asked in a low, sweet voice.

"This is the gypsy girl I mentioned a moment ago. But I had not realized then, she and her family have been in the high mountains," he added pointedly.

The old man's eyes glittered. "You have been to Obernewtyn?"

I nodded, wondering again if I had made a mistake in mentioning Obernewtyn. I had thought only to give credence to Rushton's lie, but it was clear the Druid's people had not believed the firestorm story. I told them what I had told Gilbert. "Why have you brought us here?" I asked at last. I wanted to impress on them that I was a gypsy interested in nothing but my own skin.

"Tell me what you saw at Obernewtyn," the old man invited.

"I've told you everything. They wouldn't let us stay because there was no room. Some of them were sick." I let distaste show in my eyes.

"Douglass told me you were looking for a Beforetime pass."

I nodded.

"There is no pass," the old man said. "Now, what is the truth of this avoiding the main road? I suspect you were trying to leave the highlands without being seen. Gypsies are known for being light fingered." I hung my head to hide my relief. He thought we were thieves trying to reach the lowlands without being arrested!

"What are you going to do with us?" I asked, more boldly.

"What was the name of the Master of Obernewtyn?" the old man asked.

A chill ran down my spine. "There was a youth in charge, if you would call him master. He seemed half out of his wits if you ask me. Kept raving about Obernewtyn belonging to him and wanting to restore it. Who would want to bother with such a ruin?" I chewed my lip as if trying to recall. "Rafe ... Rushton, I think his name was."

An unreadable look flickered over the old man's face.

For a long moment there was silence in the room, and I heard the muted sounds of children at play. The old man rose slowly and came round to stand in front of me.

"Do you know who I am?" he asked.

My heart sank. If he would tell that openly, he had no intention of letting us go. "Are you... the Druid from the old stories?" I asked shyly.

The old man gave me a quick, rather beautiful smile. "I am," he said. "It pleases me to know my name has not been forgotten. And what do gypsies know of Henry Druid?"

"My father told me the Council and the Herder Faction forced you into exile. He said you were not dead no matter what was said, and that you would one day return."

A fanatic gleam flashed in the old man's eyes. "Your father is wise, for I do mean to return."

The door opened suddenly and a pretty, blond girl entered. She scanned the room lazily, her eyes stopping on the Druid. "Father, you promised to come to midmeal. We are all waiting." She pouted.

The Druid smiled indulgently. "I will be there very soon, Erin. In the meantime take this girl to Rilla for me."

"Another gypsy?" she inquired disparagingly. Without waiting for an answer, she gestured languidly for me to follow.

The Druid's voice followed us into the hall. "And Erin, tell Rilla the two girls will attend nightmeal with us tonight. See that they have some suitable clothes."

Erin nodded and closed the door behind us. She led me wordlessly out of the building, across the green and down a number of streets to a square building near the edge of the settlement. A delicious smell of cooking food flowed out the door. My mouth began to water, but we bypassed the door, going round a narrow path to another building at the rear. The less appetizing smell of soap suds met my nostrils. I cast a regretful look over my shoulder.

Erin glanced at me with as much interest as if I were a piece of cheese. Her eyes were hard and bright like pieces of blue glass.

Another girl came out to meet us. Plump and pretty, she introduced herself as Rilla.

Erin looked bored at this exchange. "This one needs a good scrubbing. I don't wonder Relward mistook it for a boy. Still, do what you can. Both these gypsies are to come to night-meal at the Druid's table tonight."

"Your friend is already bathing," Rilla said, when Erin had gone. My stomach growled loudly as if defining its own priorities and Rilla laughed. "Ye'd nowt be let into th' kitchen lookin' like that. But bathe quick and ye can have yer fill before yer tum gives up growlin' an' takes to bitin'."

The bath house was filled with billowing steam. I squinted, making out a number of tin barrels all round the walls with fires burning beneath. In the center of the room were two vats. Kella's head popped above the rim of one and Rilla pointed me to the other.

"There now," she said kindly, handing me a drying towel.

I turned to set the towels down and caught sight of myself in the mirror. I gaped. No wonder I had been mistaken for a boy. I scarcely looked human. My face was barely visible for filth. I had not bathed since Gahltha's riding lessons. My clothes were stiff with dirt and my long hair one lank rattail. With a grimace, I stripped off my clothes and slid into the boiling water. I scrubbed thoroughly, massaging gritty dirt from my hair and ears. Kella handed me a thick calico robe like the one she wore as I clambered out.

"Was it the Druid?" she asked worriedly.

I nodded. "Do you notice anything else since we came here?"

Kella sighed. "You too? I hoped your powers would be strong enough not to be affected. What do you think it is?"

"Some sort of machine, but no one mentioned it. Maybe

this is how they test people to find out if they are Misfits. Yet I'm almost certain they believe we're real gypsies."

"Rilla won't be long. I think she's been told not to leave us alone. What are we going to do?" Kella asked urgently.

"I'm going to try breaking through the barrier tonight. If that doesn't work, I'll have to get to the machine and break it or switch it off somehow. If only Pavo were here. I wonder why we've been separated?"

"Did they say anything about this nightmeal?" Kella asked.

Puzzled at her tone I said, "We're to eat with the Druid. What else should I be told?"

"We are to eat with the Druid and all unbonded men," Kella said pointedly. "Have you noticed how few women there are around here? Rilla let it slip. Tonight we are going to be looked over like batches of scones. For bonding."

I stared into the clouds of steam. "We have to get away, and soon," I said.

Rilla returned carrying a green dress in one arm and a blue one in the other. "These will match your eyes," she said. Her eyes widened. "Well, ye do clean up nice an' proper."

I had never seen such fine clothes before, let alone dreamed of wearing them. But where had such finery come from, if not Sutrium? And how would an exiled Herder priest obtain such luxuries?

"These will make ye pretty fer tonight," Rilla said, holding out the dresses.

"Lambs to the slaughter," I murmured ironically. I held mine up as if it were a shroud cloth. And well it might be, for I had no intention of being bonded to anyone!

IX

It *was an odd, strained occasion.*

The Druid and his guests ate long and late into the night. They were formally attired and the courses of food were lavishly presented. It was hard to believe we were in the middle of the White Valley.

The Druid's armsmen, as those of Gilbert's type called themselves, drank heavily, both red and white fements as well as a spicy warmed cordial. The latter could be made anywhere, but the highlands were no place to grow the delicate fement grapes. Like the dresses Kella and I wore, the fements could only have come from the lowlands, probably Arendelft.

The Druid's daughter, Erin, sat by his side, clad in a dazzling blood-red dress. Her long hair was elaborately plaited and beaded around her head.

Beside her, Gilbert smiled welcome. "So, gypsy girl, how are you finding our rough and ready camp?"

Laughter met his words. All the Druid's captives were probably as astounded at the lavish way the Druids lived. Gilbert himself was hardly recognizable in a fine white shirt and black velvet jacket, though he was less extravagantly clad than many of the other armsmen. None of the white-robed Druid acolytes were present.

"What? No words for us, gypsy girl? Have we disarmed you at last? Perhaps the fire was quenched when the dirt was washed off," Gilbert teased.

Erin laid a dainty hand on his arm. "Dirt will wash away, Gilbert, but that particular hue of skin will remain the same grubby gypsy color, no matter how hard she scrubs."

The table fell silent, but before I could draw breath to respond, Gilbert laughed, smoothly drawing his arm from beneath hers. "I find that dusky tone more pleasing than the fashionable pallor of a fish underbelly," he said, smiling into my eyes.

I found myself seated some way down the table. On either side, the men spoke only a few polite words to me. Their eyes said they shared Erin's attitude. It was funny in a way. If they had known I was a Misfit, I would have been far more despised.

A while later, Erin's voice rose above the buzz of talk. "Father, I am only saying that this desire to bond the armsmen is going too far. Surely you want to maintain some sort of standard. Yet you permit grubby gypsies to dine with us." I had no doubt she had raised her voice deliberately.

I stood abruptly. "Lord, my father told me enough to make me admire Henry Druid, but I will not be insulted by a painted doll!" There was a gasp from some of the men, and Erin's pouting mouth fell open in astonishment.

There was a long silence. I did not take my eyes from the Druid's, but I was not to hear his reply since someone had begun to clap.

"Well done, Lady Erin. I salute you for your wit," Gilbert said. He raised his mug to Erin. "I feared our gypsy girl had lost her tongue." He drank deeply, and a few hardy souls around him laughed.

Erin's face filled with rage, but the Druid laid a restraining hand on her arm. I wondered at Gilbert's recklessness. Why had the Druid let him make sport of Erin? It was clear Gilbert had some rank in the camp, but now I wondered exactly what his position was.

He grinned at me down the length of the table, but I did not smile back. Beside him, Erin's eyes glittered with malice. Perhaps Gahltha's cynical comment that poisoned trees bore poisoned fruit was right, for I was certain the Druid shared his daughter's prejudice.

I finished my meal, ignored by my companions. I had a fierce longing to be back at Obernewtyn, where people were judged by their actions rather than their ancestry. Rushton would laugh to know how much I hungered to be home. He had seemed honestly disturbed by my desire to leave. With a painful lurch of my heart, I realized I missed him.

A young boy and an old man played a merry dance tune on a drum and a small flute. I was not surprised to see people rise to dance. I had never learnt how. Orphan homes did not organize such frivolous pursuits. On both sides of me the seats were empty, my dinner companions having deserted me for less controversial partners. My outburst had made me an outcast despite my finery.

I looked up to find Gilbert standing beside my seat. "Come, let me see if you dance as well as you talk."

I lifted my chin. "I wonder you dare ask a gypsy to dance."

Gilbert frowned. "Hatred of gypsies is a foolish, unfounded prejudice which I do not share."

"It seems you are alone in that. Who are you, that you can safely voice such unpopular opinions?"

"I lead the armsmen. The Druid values my expertise. But I am known for my outspoken nature. It has not got me killed so far."

I smiled a little despite myself. At another place and time, I would have liked the smiling armsman as a friend. But the knowledge that he was the leader of the Druid's fighting force made me nervous. His friendship might be no more than a strategy to put me off guard.

As if reading my thoughts, Gilbert slid into the seat beside me. "I am my own fellow," he said softly. "I am no whisperer of other's secrets. If you will not talk, then dance with me," he invited.

I found I did not want to hurt his feelings with a plain refusal. I lifted the hem of my skirt and showed him my scarred legs and feet. His face tightened at the sight of the scars. "And I made you walk back to camp. Why didn't you say something?"

I smiled and shrugged wryly. "You didn't seem the sort to worry about a prisoner's feet."

"Then we will talk," he said firmly. "You may direct the course of our words."

The opportunity was too good to miss. "Tell me how you came to be here."

Gilbert smiled and obliged. It proved an unexpected tale.

He had been born to a seafaring family in Aborium, but his father had been taken by slavers and his boat sunk. As a child, Gilbert had worked as a harbor laborer to support his mother and sister, until they died of a mysterious plague that swept the coast one year. Weary of the sea and lonely, he had gone inland to seek his fortune as a hunter. He had been searching in the White Valley when the Druid recruited him. He smiled wryly at the euphemism.

"At first I was determined to escape but what was there to escape to? I had no home to go back to and I loathe the Council. And, as you see, this is a pleasant enough life for one so skilled and useful as I."

"The Druid has a good supply of luxuries," I said.

He grinned. "He has a friend in Sutrium." He stopped abruptly and I babbled on, pretending not to have noticed his slip.

"Are there really such things as slavers?" I asked.

He nodded. "There are at that, black-hearted souls. They prey on small fishing vessels like those belonging to my father, shanghai the crew and sell them. Those taken are never heard

of again. I have heard it said the Council sells Seditioners they
do not want brought to open trial. Who knows where they end
up? It is a wide, strange world."

"But... what do you mean? There is only this Land and
the two islands," I stammered. "The rest is Blacklands."

Gilbert shook his head. "A myth spawned by the Council
who have a vested interest in ignorance. There are other places
on the earth where the white death never reached, or where the
poisons have faded. I remember once my father told me the
Land was but the tiniest portion of a huge island. It is possible
there are parts of it untainted."

I stared. "But how is it no one knows this?"

Gilbert smiled, and it was not a pleasant smile. "Any sea-
farer stupid enough to talk of such things disappears, no doubt
himself sold to the slavers. It's a convenient way for the Council
to rid itself of troublesome babblemouths."

"But why?"

"The Council do not want their subjects sailing off in
search of greener pastures and freer lands," he answered simply.

I was fascinated. I had never dreamed of questioning
Council teachings claiming the Land and two islands were all
that remained of the world after the holocaust.

"Why not take to the sea yourself and go where there is
no Council?" I wondered.

Gilbert sighed. "I could have done that, but a harsh law
is better than none. What lies beyond our horizons are, by all
accounts, wild loreless places where there has been no attempt
to establish normal growth, a world where incredible mutations
of plant and beast run riot. No, better to work here with the
Druid to overcome the Council. Besides, I get seasick," he added.

I laughed then sobered quickly. "You think the Druid and
his acolytes are any better than the Council?" I hardly expected
an answer to such a question, but he was as outspoken as he
had promised.

"I don't know. I hope so. He is hard, but there is always

hope of change. At least he has standards and rules to live by."

I looked at him sharply. "The world is full of mutations. Who has the right to decide what is normal?"

Gilbert looked taken aback at the change in my tone. "I do not believe gypsies are inferior," he said, mistaking my words. "In fact, I don't mind mutants. But don't tell the Druid. He is fanatical on the subject. Most of the others think as he does. Perhaps I'm not fine enough to distinguish between the smells of people as if they were so much spoiled meat."

I frowned, deciding whether the Druid knew or guessed about Misfits, Gilbert knew nothing. Perhaps only the Druid's acolytes knew about the machine blocking my abilities.

"And what about freedom? He would not let you leave here."

The armsman smiled. "No one keeps me where I do not want to be. But freedom is not a matter of that. You are a gypsy, so you think freedom is only to move from place to place. Real freedom is a thing no one can take from you, because it is of the spirit. I keep it here." He tapped his head, then rose. "I have promised a dance, but we will talk again."

I watched him go, surprised to find myself wishing we could have gone on talking. I had meant only to extract information, but he was astonishingly open with his words and opinions, and he had allowed me to question him without asking me questions in return. With a sudden depression, I wondered if he was as open simply because he believed himself invulnerable in the camp.

I shook my head. He was an enemy, yet I had liked him. And I was as certain he had liked me. It had never occurred to me that I might be found desirable. Yet clothed in the fine dress, I had only been able to gape at my reflection. The girl who looked out of the mirror at me with her cloud of dark silky hair and mysterious green eyes had been a dazzling stranger. Passing through a room into the Druid's dining hall, I had caught sight of myself in a long mirror and, in that moment, had the curious wish that Rushton might see me so transformed.

To my relief, the meal ended without talk of bonding. Like all farseekers, I knew bonding for me would be more than a physical communion. A mind meld would be far more intimate than any bodily merging. It would be an ultimate kind of nakedness with one of my own kind; to bond with an unTalent would be like bonding to a statue.

I found myself thinking of Gilbert as I prepared for bed. If one had to bond with an unTalent, he would at least be kind and funny. Rushton's dark, brooding face came into my mind like a dash of cold water.

Dismissing all thoughts of the nightmeal from my mind, I concentrated my senses for an attempt on the static barrier preventing me from reaching the others. Kella had been housed in a separate room, so there was no chance for us to make plans.

The block lay like a wet blanket over my senses. I felt suffocated as I tried to farseek. I used more strength, but the blocking seemed to respond, strengthening in direct proportion to the force I used.

Finally I lay back with a defeated sigh. It was no use. I would have to find the machine and somehow damage it.

X

"What are ye up to, Emmon?" Rilla demanded suspiciously of a slight boy with a lop-sided grin who had entered the kitchen.

He looked exaggeratedly hurt. "Th' Druid sent me to bring the gypsy called Elspeth," he said in a wounded voice.

I had spent the morning with Kella helping to do the encampment washing. I had tried questioning Rilla, but she appeared to know no more than Gilbert about the blocking static preventing me from using my abilities. But she had told me the Druid acolytes worked in a shed forbidden to all others. Kella told me Rilla's dead bondmate had been one of the Druids slain in the last Teknoguild expedition.

"I don't think she knows much about it," Kella had said. "It seems as if the Druid only tells people what he thinks they need to know. Rilla has no idea the people they ran into were from Obernewtyn. But she did say the Druid suspected the explosion had been caused deliberately using a Beforetime weapon. I think his reaction to Obernewtyn means he suspected Rushton, at least."

I wondered what the Druid wanted of me.

As we left, Emmon stole a slice of meat and got a hard smack for his troubles. Outside he rubbed his ear and grinned broadly. "T'was worth it. Come on."

We had not gone far when I realized we were going in the wrong direction.

"Well, that's true ..." Emmon admitted. "As a matter of fact, I were nowt told to bring ye at once, so we've time to spare. I'd rather walk about than wash clothes or work at spellin' an' th' like. Wouldn't you?"

"Won't we get into trouble?" I asked warily.

He shook his head. "You won't. If we gan caught, I'll say ye knew nowt of it."

"Will you show me around? I haven't had much chance to see the camp," I asked.

Emmon nodded enthusiastically. He marched off, at once beginning to describe the variety and uses of buildings we passed. I tried leading him to talk of the Druid, in the hope of getting a clue about the block over the camp, but he seemed to know as little about it as I did. I concentrated on memorizing the camp.

We passed a long windowless series of buildings which Emmon pronounced as storehouses.

"Where do all the Druid's supplies come from?" I asked.

Emmon grinned. "From th' Council's own stores. Th' Council dinna know their own trusted agent is a friend and oath kin to th' Druid."

Oath kin? That meant someone as close as blood without being related. The Druid had an oath kin on the Council. The Druid was as canny a strategist as ever. With a chill, I realized the rumors about Obernewtyn could have been generated by the Druid's friend.

"Is it true ye've been to Obernewtyn?" Emmon asked suddenly, as if reading my mind.

"True enough," I said.

He shook his head in wonder. "That's th' library." He pointed to another building. It seemed his dislike of spelling did not run to books. The Druid had obviously instilled his followers with his own love of books.

"I hear Erin dinna take to ye much," Emmon said.

"Who told you that?" I asked sharply.

Emmon smiled. "I'll take ye to visit a friend of mine."

Before I could answer he ran off, and I was forced to follow. I found him outside the door to a small cottage. As I reached his side, he knocked firmly on the door.

"Who lives there?" I asked. I heard footsteps inside. "Erin's twin sister lives here," he whispered, as the door swung open. I gave him a furious look, but it was too late. The door opened and a delicious odor wafted out.

"Gilaine, it's me. I've brought a visitor," Emmon announced. He sniffed and sighed. "Honeyballs."

I stared at the girl who had answered the door.

There was no question whose sister she was. But they were as much alike as the sun and the moon. Where Erin's hair was spun gold and elaborately dressed, Gilaine wore her long, ashen tresses loose about her shoulders. Erin's eyes were bright blue, but Gilaine's were gray as clouds with the sun behind them. The greatest difference though, lay in their expressions. Erin's face was haughty and querulous, but Gilaine's was gentle, the smile on her mouth only echoing the smile in her eyes. I was immediately drawn to her.

"This is Elspeth. She's one of them gypsy folk," Emmon said, slipping behind her into the house.

Gilaine smiled. I wondered why she did not speak. As if in answer to my thought, she raised a finger to her lips. At first I thought she was trying to tell me to be quiet, then I realized: she was mute.

"The honeyballs are burnin'!" Emmon wailed. Gilaine smiled, gesturing for me to follow her.

The cottage was tiny, consisting of three sections. A closet with a bed in it, a front hall, and a cozy and relatively large kitchen. The honeyballs turned out to be tiny crisp sweets. Mouth full, I asked Emmon why I had not seen Gilaine at the nightmeal. He managed to look wrathful over bulging cheeks. "She is nowt asked," he said.

The old Druid was a perfectionist. He hated anything flawed. Gilaine was mute. Poor Gilaine, I thought. Seeing my look she smiled sadly and shrugged.

We stayed with Gilaine until it was time to go. I was surprised to hear Emmon confess his deception, but she only shook her head helplessly and ruffled his hair with an expression of mingled concern and exasperation.

Crossing the green to the meeting house, I spotted Jik playing ball with some younger children and asked Emmon if I could talk to him.

"Well, yer nowt supposed to, an' ye know what a stickler I am for rules. But if I was to gan over an wash my hands at th' spring, I'd nowt see what ye were up to. I'm a gullible fellow," he said with an engaging smirk.

"Do you know where the others are being kept?" I asked Jik as soon as we could speak. There was no time for greetings.

He shook his head. "I think they're someplace outside the walls."

"What about the block, can you feel it?"

He nodded, saying he said he had heard no talk of machines, but that the Druid's helpers had a special place to work in where no one was allowed to go.

I nodded impatiently. "Keep an ear out, but don't ask any questions that will make anyone wonder about you. Remember you're a gypsy. Where's Darga?"

"He disappeared when they brought us inside," Jik said, miserably.

"Darga's a smart dog," I said, "He's probably gone to look for the others, or Domick."

Jik's face brightened. "Do you think so?"

"Come on," Emmon called.

I patted Jik on the shoulder and ran to join Emmon.

I was taken in to the Druid by one of the acolytes. I

wondered curiously if the Druid were trying to start up his own opposing order. I had the feeling the Druid's order would be as bad as the Herder Faction, whatever Gilbert believed. Entering the Druid's meeting chamber, I heard a tantalizing snatch of conversation.

A voice said, "If she is telling the truth, I don't see any need to waste more time on the mountains. I said all along it was your old friends that we bumped into. Herders."

"That may be, but I think it is too late to stop the soldierguards from investigating Obernewtyn." That was the Druid. I hesitated at the door, hoping to hear more, but the Druid looked up.

"Come in, Elspeth. I want you to tell me again all you saw at Obernewtyn . . ."

I was there for the rest of the afternoon. Fortunately my story was simple, and I resisted the temptation to embellish in case he asked me to repeat it again. I quickly realized what he really wanted to know was if Rushton were continuing Alexi's research.

I was unsure how much he knew of the truth. It was common knowledge Alexi and Madam Vega had been involved in illegal research into the Beforetime, and that Rushton had stopped them, at the same time rescuing two Councilmen. At one time, Henry Druid had befriended Rushton, knowing him to be the true heir to Obernewtyn. Rushton had told him that Alexi and Madam Vega were searching for weaponmachines from the past. Yet he could not have known Alexi based his search on the work of his stepmother, Marisa Seraphim, a brilliant scientist devoted to studying the technology of the past. She had discovered and resurrected the Zebkrahn machine. In his eagerness to possess his stepmother's secrets, Alexi had murdered Marisa, only to find her notes cryptic and secretive. Originally the research Alexi conducted into Misfit abilities had been a cover, but he had learnt that some Misfits possessed a remarkable sensitivity to the written word, which might be used to decipher Marisa's notes, if he were able to find a Misfit with a strong enough sensitivity. He quickly found that pain enhanced sensitivity.

Trapped into revealing my abilities, I managed to keep Alexi unaware that I was strong enough to decipher his stepmother's notes without help. Ironically, under torture by Alexi and Ariel, I had seen not only the map Marisa had secretly commissioned to be carved into two doors, showing the whereabouts of the weaponmachines, but somehow, I knew the machines were those which had caused the terrible holocaust known as the Great White. The Druid could not know that because I had told no one, not even Rushton.

As far as I knew, Henry Druid had learnt nothing about Alexi's Misfit research from Rushton, who had recognized the Druid's obsessive hatred of mutations was a danger to us and gradually severed communication. Ironically, this must have convinced the Druid that Rushton was continuing Alexi's search for Beforetime weapons. The snatch of conversation I had overheard told me the Druid no longer saw Rushton as an enemy. Just the same, while taking care to present myself as an ignorant, self-centered gypsy, I made sure Rushton sounded as if he were verging on mania, trying to rebuild the shattered Obernewtyn.

Dismissed at last, I went back to the wash house.

"What did he want?" Kella asked. "You've been ages."

I told her of Emmon's antics, then recounted what I had heard.

"Nothing that will help us escape?" Kella asked disconsolately. I had told her of my abortive attempt to breach the block that morning. We talked over what I had overheard, convinced the words referred to the Teknoguild expedition.

"But it sounds like they now believe the people they bumped into on the ruins were Herders. How odd that they should jump to that conclusion," Kella said.

I nodded. "I think there is much about the Herders' activities that is secret. The important thing, though, is that the

Druid now seems to believe Obernewtyn is a ruin. The problem is, it might be too late to stop the soldierguards coming to the mountains. I'm almost sure this friend on the Council organized the investigation. It wouldn't be hard. The Council is so suspicious anyway."

Kella wiped her hands slowly on her apron. "We have to warn Rushton."

I nodded. "But first I have to do something about this machine. Let Rilla think I'm still with the Druid. I'm going to try to find it. I think I can home in on it if I put my mind to it."

"Don't get caught," Kella said.

I climbed out the window at the back of the wash house. Walking slowly, I let my mind rub against the oddly pliant nature of the blocking static. Again I was reminded of a blanket, and brushed my mind against it instead of using force. I had the eerie feeling it liked that, rubbing up against my mind like a kitten. I thought I could sense a core and moved in that direction, hoping I was not imagining it.

Before long, I found myself in a part of the camp I had not seen before. I walked purposefully, trying to look as if I were running an errand, avoiding the eyes of the few people I passed.

Two men coming out of a doorway looked at me, but made no move to stop me. As soon as I rounded a corner I ran, keeping to the walls. I was determined nothing would keep me from at least locating the machine. A young girl looked out of a window curiously. I slowed abruptly to a walk, but her eyes followed me up the street.

I noticed a bank of ominous black clouds roiled on the horizon. An omen, though for good or ill I couldn't decide.

Suddenly I found myself on the very perimeter of the settlement. There was no one in sight. This part of the camp looked deserted. Uneasily I wondered if the whole thing were some sort of trap.

I was about to turn back when, suddenly, I sensed the source of the block was very near. I couldn't resist. It came, I was certain, from a long, low-slung building with a flat roof. There was only one door in the building and no guard. My trapped powers prevented me from knowing if there were guards inside.

Pressing one ear against the door, I heard faint voices.

Dry-mouthed I pushed the door. It swung open soundlessly.

I gaped at the complete unexpectedness of what lay inside. The building contained a single, long, almost bare room filled with babies and very young children. On the far side of the room, a thin, dark-haired girl wiped the face of a bawling tot.

In the middle of the room, helping a group of mesmerized children to build a tower, was Gilaine.

She looked up idly, and her face registered my own shock.

I could not think of a single thing to say. The room was obviously a kind of communal nursery, but I was convinced it was also the source of the block. The machine had to be concealed somewhere in the room.

The dark-haired girl came over. "Yes?" she said pleasantly.

Gilaine touched her arm and made a few intricate hand motions. "Gilaine says you're a friend. Come in."

Gilaine made another agitated hand movement and the girl nodded. "I'll do it. You talk to your friend," she said kindly.

"What is this place?" I asked Gilaine, when we were alone.

She frowned and pointed to the children. One of the toddlers waddled after her and lurched drunkenly at my knees. Reaching out to catch him, my hand brushed against Gilaine's.

The baby gurgled in delight, oblivious of our stunned looks. The moment our hands touched, I had immediate access to her mind—and she to mine! Gilaine was a Misfit. An empath and farseeker like Jik.

She had pulled away almost immediately. I leaned forward slowly, not wanting to alarm her, and touched her forearm.

Again contact was established. It seemed the block did not work if I was actually touching the person I wanted to communicate with.

"Gilaine?" I sent gently. She recoiled violently. I stood waiting, and she reached out, touching my shoulder with a tentative finger.

"Elspeth?" her mind responded. It was a weak signal, despite the strength I had found in her mind.

I nodded. Gilaine sat on a chair as if her legs would not hold her, and pulled the toddler onto her lap. I reached forward, pretending to look at the baby, and touched her. "We must not make ourselves obvious/dangerous," I sent, at the same time wondering if Gilaine were the trap.

"You . . . are not like us," Gilaine sent timidly.

"Us? There are more of you here?" I asked, astounded. She nodded imperceptibly. I sensed that she did not want to talk about them.

"Does He/Druid/father know?" I asked.

She shook her head vehemently. "Not know. Must not know." The baby began to struggle to be put down. Gilaine jiggled her knees up and down and he gurgled contentedly. "Fatherdruid thinks Misfits feebleminds or dreamers. He doesnot know about us/you. He thinks Misfit/mutant evil," she stressed.

"You? Do you think this is evil?" I asked.

She shook her head, but without much conviction.

"Dangerous foryou and friends here. Why stay?" I asked.

She shook her head and fleetingly, a face pressed from her thoughts into mine. I was amazed to recognize it. It was the face of the boy I had met in the Councilcourt in Sutrium, waiting to be sentenced to Obernewtyn. Startled, I remembered the youth had spoken to me of refuge in the mountains, and of running away. Was it possible he had meant me to run away to the Druid? He had even mentioned Henry Druid, saying the rumor of his death was a lie. I fumbled in my memory for the name. "Daffyd," I murmured aloud triumphantly. Gilaine almost dropped the baby in fright. The startled child hitched in a breath and began to scream. When it was quieted, Gilaine touched my hand. "How do you know that name? Did you read my behindthoughts?" she asked suspiciously.

I shook my head without bothering to explain that I could, but chose not to. People always thought you wanted to eavesdrop on their private thoughts, whereas the notion actually embarrassed me. "I saw his face in yourmind. Remembered the name. I met him once, in Sutrium." I gasped aloud. "You mean he is one of you? Us?"

She nodded, still warily.

I wondered what had possessed him to envisage the Druid as a refuge for a Misfit. "Where is he?" I asked.

"Druid sent him to Sutrium/lowlands. Druidbusiness."

I noticed the dark-haired girl watching us curiously. We had been silent too long. In another moment she would begin to wonder who I was and why she had not recognized me. I was putting Gilaine in danger and said as much to her in a low voice.

Rising, I sent a final vital question, "Where is the blocking machine?"

She frowned. "Machine?"

"The block on our minds. Surely you can feel it?"

"Feel what?" Gilaine sent.

Confused I sent a brief image of the block.

"Oh, that," her mind sent, amused. "No machine. Lidgebaby." She pointed to a cot near one of the walls. "Lidgebabymind."

My mouth fell open. The incredible numbing effect blanketing the camp which had resisted all my strength was the uncontrollable mental static of a Misfit baby!

XI

Something woke me.

It was a dark night and the moon showed full beyond the window glass. Rain was falling softly on the roof of the wash house and its adjoining sleeping chambers.

Then I heard a voice, calling softly. "Elspeth?"

I sat bolt upright in bed, afraid to answer in case it was a trap. Trying to think how I would react if I really was nothing more than a gypsy, I climbed out of bed and went across to the window.

"Who's out there?" My voice came out low and anxious, not quite a whisper.

"Shh!" the voice hissed urgently.

Apprehension prickled along my spine. "What do you want? Who are you?"

There was a pause, as if the caller was wary too.

"I come from a friend," the voice whispered at last, reluctantly.

I frowned. "I have no friends here."

Again there was a pause. "Gilaine," the voice grated, with a hint of irritation.

I bit my lip and peered into the rain-streaked night, wishing there were a moon. Whoever was out there had the perfect cover. I could see nothing. I wondered if Gilaine had really sent them.

"I have a key to unlock your door," the voice said.

I made up my mind. If it were a trap, I would blame gypsy curiosity.

"All right." A moment later, there was a faint click and the door opened to admit a man wearing a dark, hooded cloak pulled low across his face. With an imperious gesture, he slipped back outside. Pulling my own cape hastily over my nightdress, I padded out barefoot, closing the door behind me.

"Who are you?" I demanded.

"My name is Saul. And you don't need to know any more than that," he added brusquely.

We hurried along, keeping close to the walls, cloaks flapping in gusts of wind blowing along the dark, empty streets. Coming to a cobbled square, Saul stopped, scanning the square and the streets leading into it intently. Trees growing up through the cobbles flung bare branches about, sighing mournfully. After a long moment, he flicked his hand curtly and strode directly across the square.

On the other side I stopped. "Wait a minute. This isn't the way to Gilaine's house."

"It is the way to my house," Saul answered.

His house proved to be as small as Gilaine's, but looked dark and deserted. He opened the door and light spilled out onto the wet ground. Dark heavy curtains had hidden the light from prying eyes. Reassured, I followed him inside.

Removing his cloak, Saul shook it and hung it on a peg in the wall. Studying him covertly in the light, I decided he was handsome in a cold sort of way. He was tall, but too thin and his skin pale. His hands were as long and slender as a woman's, and his facial features sharply defined beneath a fringe of straight, light brown hair. He looked at me fleetingly with eyes the color of mud-stained ice. I smiled tentatively, but he did not respond. I pretended to stumble following him along the hallway leading to the other section of the cottage, clutching at his arm to steady myself.

I had a brief impression of an intelligence bordering on brilliance, resting on a frighteningly unstable personality. "Get out!" commanded an icy mental voice. He pushed me away with a look of revulsion.

I followed him wordlessly into the kitchen knowing I had seen such stress before in people unable to tolerate the realization that they were Misfits. I guessed Saul had been ruthlessly orthodox before his discovery that he was a Misfit. His personality was disintegrating under the stress of being what he loathed. I wondered if the others knew.

The kitchen was almost the exact replica of Gilaine's, but without cooking smells, flowers, or plants. It reminded me of an orphan home kitchen before Council inspection.

Seated at a scrubbed timber table were Gilaine, the two musicians I had seen at the Druid's nightmeal, and an older, heavy-set man I had not seen before.

For a moment they looked up at me with collective appraisal. Then Gilaine rose. Smiling welcome, she touched my arm. "I am glad you came. See? I am getting better at this strange way of communicating, but Lidgebaby does not like it. This is Saul, who brought you here. I think you have seen Peter and Michael." She gestured at the musicians. "And this is Jow, the brother of Daffyd."

"This is dangerous," I said aloud.

Gilaine nodded gravely. "You told me this afternoon you had to get away. We want to help, but you must answer questions first," she sent.

From the expressions on the faces of the others, I guessed they had been less eager to help than Gilaine. I wondered what she had said to convince them, especially Saul, who made no pretense of liking my presence and was prowling back and forth like a caged animal.

"The others with you—Misfit also?" Gilaine asked.

I nodded, aware we would not get out of the camp without help. I had to take the risk. And I did trust Gilaine. I guessed she was reporting my answers to the others, but could find no trace of their communication, though her hand rested on my arm. She seemed not to need physical contact to communicate with the others.

She looked back at me. "Have you really come from Obernewtyn?"

I nodded, and again told the story I had told the Druid, with one difference. I told her we had welcomed Pavo's illness as a way of splitting off from the rest of the troop. "It was getting too dangerous for us to stay. Gypsies live close together—they hate mutant/Misfits."

"Then you never meant to rejoin your father?" Saul asked accusingly, when Gilaine had relayed my answer. "You say Obernewtyn is a ruin. How can we believe you?"

I shrugged. "Believe what you want. Why would I bother to lie?"

It was odd how sure everyone seemed to be that the firestorm story was a lie. No one had been up to the mountains since Rushton had claimed Obernewtyn but our own people. No one could really know, but they seemed so certain. I decided to ask my own questions.

"How did you discover your powers?"

Gilaine smiled. "The night Lidgebaby was born," she sent.

The baby coercer had woken the entire group to operancy. Gilaine sent a graphic picture of the night the baby had been born. She had been in bed asleep, when the sound of a baby screaming woke her. She was in the street in her nightgown before she realized the cry she was hearing was inside her mind. She had dressed quickly, her mind reeling, unable to resist the summons. Only when she reached the street outside the birthing house did she begin to understand that had happened, for she was not alone. They had all answered the call: Saul, destined to become an acolyte; Jow, an animal handler; his younger brother Daffyd; and the two musicians.

Daffyd had woken first to the peril of such a gathering, and they had dispersed, planning to meet in less dangerous circumstances, the first of many such meetings. They all understood two things at once though. They would never again be alone in their own minds, for Lidgebaby was with them constantly, linking them irrevocably to one another, and they were in terrible danger.

In that dramatic birthbonding, Lidgebaby had forged an indelible emotional link between the group. None could ever consciously harm the baby. All were coerced to love and protect.

Little monster, I thought, keeping my mind shielded. No wonder I could not hear their communication. They talked through the baby, using their own powers only to maintain contact. It was the combined network of minds, and the child's mental overflow, that was blocking me.

It was an incredible situation and gave me a clear idea of Lidgebaby's mental prowess. A baby, his coercive demands were selfish but basically innocent. What would happen when he grew up and became conscious of the power he wielded? I shuddered, seeing them smile in the collective memory of that first enslavement/wakening of their Misfit minds.

Seeing my eyes on him, Saul frowned and turned away.

"Where will you go, if we help you?" Gilaine asked.

"We hadn't thought far ahead. We meant to use an Olden pass we heard about to get to the lowlands without going along the main roads."

Saul snorted. "No one could get through that pass alive."

I stared. "You mean there is a pass?"

Gilaine nodded. "But Saul is right. No way to go there. Dangerous."

Jow shifted in his seat and the others fell silent. For the first time I glimpsed Daffyd's features in his face. "Where then?" he said aloud.

I shrugged. "To the coast I suppose. We thought of getting a boat. I've heard there are places..." I hesitated.

"Over the sea," said the boy musician wistfully.

"I have heard there are places over the edge of the world, where there is no Council or Herder faction," Jow said pensively.

"Why do you stay here?" I asked. "It's terribly dangerous?"

Jow shook his head. "Better to wait until winter is over. And we must wait until Lidgebaby is weaned."

"Couldn't you get the mother to go with you?"

"The mother is bonded to an acolyte and has already had one babe burnt. She denounced it," Jow said.

I stared at him in horror. "Why are you offering to help us?"

Jow frowned. "You are a danger to us as long as you stay. You are a danger to the baby. We'll help you, but you must understand we can't let you talk if you are caught. The acolytes are very persuasive."

I nodded, understanding what he left unsaid. "How can you help us?"

"There are two things," Jow said. "First, we can absorb Lidgebaby's emanations so that you can communicate with your friends in the compound. Second, we will organize a diversion to give you all time to get away. The soldierguards from the training camps below the lower ranges will leave in a few days to witness the ordination of new Herders in Sutrium. That will mean the main road will be safe for a week or so, and you can cut right through the camp and make for the coast between the lower mountains and Glenelg Mor."

I bit my lip. It would take several days to go that way, but it seemed there was no choice.

At a word from Jow, Saul seated himself at the table and the group linked hands. "Be quick," Jow said. "I'm not sure how long we can hold it. Tell your friends the word firestorm will be used to identify us."

They closed their eyes. For a long moment, there was silence. A log cracked noisily in the fire, spitting out an orange flame. Beads of perspiration stood out on Jow's face.

Then the block was gone.

I gasped in delight, realizing how the restriction had oppressed me. I sent a specific probe tuned to Matthew's mind. There was too little time to locate him physically. He was asleep when I found him, and I woke him with an ungentle mental jab.

"Wha?" his mind inquired stupidly. "Elspeth!?" he sent, recognizing my probe.

"I don't have much time so listen carefully," I sent. "Some Misfits here are going to help us escape. They'll be using the word firestorm as a password. They'll create a joint diversion to give us the chance to get away."

"We canna use th' Olden way," Matthew warned.

I told Matthew Jow's alternate plan. "They know nothing about Domick. I'm going to try to reach him. He may have gone back to Obernewtyn."

Matthew interrupted eagerly. "I farsensed him." I was astonished. It was impossible to communicate over distance with anyone but another farseeker unless communicator and communicant possessed some deep probing ability. It seemed Ceirwan was right about Matthew developing deep probe powers. But there was no time to think about that now.

"Are the horses with Domick?"

"An' Darga," Matthew sent. "Wait a minute! If ye haven't escaped, how can ye be contactin' me?"

"The Misfits here helped me stop the block for a bit. It's not a machine. The block is caused by a baby with coercive powers."

"A baby!" Matthew echoed.

"Where is this compound? Show me," I demanded.

Matthew made his mind passive so that I could use his eyes. At once a ghostly vision unfolded in my mind. He was looking down a long narrow rift between two mountains. There was a fence dividing a bare foreground from a heavily vegetated background. I thought I could see patches of glowing gas in the moonlight beyond the barrier. It took a moment for me to realize what I was seeing.

"The Olden pass . . ."

Matthew confirmed it. "Poisonground/poison gas an' gigantic growling beasts."

"Why build a compound there?" I wondered.

In answer, Matthew turned again. Dirt, rocks and dispossessed trees lay in mounds on either side of a broad gape in the ground. On one side of the hole were a row of rough huts. "Th' ground here is safe. We're here to pander to th' Druid's favorite obsession. Oldtime ruins. He thinks th' machine what made th' Great White is here somewhere. Mad as a snake is our Druid, to think it would still be workin' after all this time."

Not so mad, I thought with a feeling of cold dread.

"How is Pavo?" I asked.

"He says he refuses to die in a dirty, damp Druid hole," Matthew sent. "He's convinced you'll be along any minute to rescue us. Elspeth is a survivor, he keeps sayin'."

"I wish I shared his faith. There's no hope now of getting to the lowlands and back before wintertime. And Maryon has predicted disaster for Obernewtyn if we don't make it."

"If only you could farseek Ceirwan at Obernewtyn," Matthew said.

I shrugged. He knew as well as I that our ability to farsense over long distances grew progressively weaker the closer we came to the coast. Pavo believed this had something to do with the density of air. As well, the tainted mountains threw up a violent static impossible to penetrate from below. Only the Zebkrahn could penetrate the static, but it did no more than register Talents. There was not even the hope the Teknoguild would see from the Zebkrahn that we had stopped moving, since we were veiled in Lidgebaby's mental static. The one slender chance was that Domick would register on the machine, and Rushton might wonder at the lone Talent and send someone to investigate. But we could not afford to wait.

"I want you and Louis to take Mira and Lo and go back to Obernewtyn as soon as you're free. Make sure you don't leave tracks or get caught. Someone has to warn Obernewtyn about the Druid," I told Matthew. I made him repeat my news until he was word-perfect, before bidding him good-bye.

Next I sought Domick. This was harder, and he responded by trying instantly to repel me.

"You!" I saw him assimilate my ease in demolishing his defences. "Have you escaped?"

I told him all I had told Matthew.

"Then we are still going?" Domick asked when I had finished. "You know we can't make Maryon's deadline if we go that way. We are already cutting it fine because of the delay here." Rushton had told him of the futureteller prediction.

"We dare not head back to Obernewtyn anyway, since the Druid would follow," I said flatly. "I'm sending Matthew and Louis to warn Rushton. The rest of us will continue, if only to draw the Druid's attention away from the high mountains. I'll contact you as soon as we get outside the baby's static. In the meantime, stay out of sight. A group of armsmen went out this morning to hunt. Now where are you?"

Domick was unable to let me use his eyes, but projected a picture with painful force into my mind. Cross guild farseeking had its drawbacks. The coercer was right at the foot of the mountains. Tor, he sent in explanation. "I've been hiding in the cave where the Suggredoon goes into the mountain. There's a good wide ledge. Pity it doesn't go right through. That would be a quick way down, but the ledge breaks off a short way in, and the walls are smooth as soap."

Severing the contact, I found myself back inside the room. The group was still hand linked. Gathering my exhausted senses, I reached out to Jik. He was overjoyed to hear Darga was safe and little else registered. I was in the middle of explaining the escape plans, when the contact was severed neatly as Lidgebaby's static filled the air.

I opened my eyes in time to see Gilaine pitch forward. Jow picked her up gently and laid her on the floor, using his coat as a pillow. She moaned and her eyes fluttered open. I went to her side, stricken with guilt.

"She was the focus. Lidge likes her best," Saul said petulantly.

"Did you get through?" Jow asked.

I nodded. Gilaine reached out for my arm, and projected a message to us all. "It will be difficult. Perhaps they should stay and leave when we go."

"They can't stay!" Saul broke in angrily. "They endanger the baby. They endanger us all. It was bad enough to reveal ourselves...."

The older musician shook his head reproachfully. "Saul. Saul. We have already gone over this. Once Gilaine was revealed, it was the same as if we were all exposed. If the Druid forced her name from Elspeth, she in turn would be forced to betray us. I'm sorry, Gilaine, but it would be better for them to go."

She hung her head.

A queer expression flitted across Saul's intense features, and I felt certain he was thinking Gilaine's death would have solved everything.

"We won't be staying," I said firmly.

Jow nodded. "You'll have to move quickly then. The best way for you to go is also the most dangerous. You'll climb above the place where the Suggredoon flows into the mountains and scale the river that way. It will give you a good start over the Druid's armsmen. We'll make sure it looks as if you've gone round the river."

I knelt down beside Gilaine. Dark pools lay under her eyes, a curious white dot in the centre of the shadows, as if someone had set a floury finger there. I looked at Jow. "You'll never have cause to regret this," I promised. "And some day, you might be glad."

Lying back in my bed later, too overwrought to sleep, I kept thinking how strange life was, moving people about like pawns on a gamesboard. I had met Daffyd as a complete stranger years before, and now he had come back into my life. And he, too, was a Misfit and one of our kind! I vowed I would bring Gilaine and her friends out when I got back to Obernewtyn. I fell asleep wondering what Daffyd would think when he heard the story. I dreamed of running again, and of someone calling my name.

I woke to Rilla shaking me impatiently. "Elspeth. Ye sleep like th' dead," she scolded.

Outside, rain was falling steadily, and thunder rumbled ominously in the distance. Hurrying across the gap separating the wash house from the kitchen I glanced up at the drear gray sky with faint apprehension.

To my surprise Emmon was sitting at the kitchen table with Kella. Seeing me, they both stood abruptly.

"What's the matter?" I asked.

"Gilaine sent me to tell ye," Emmon said. "Only ye mun nowt let on ye know or she'll be in for it."

"I promise. Now what?"

"Ye to be bonded tomorrow," Emmon said, refusing to meet my eyes.

"To whom?" I asked in a strangely distant voice.

He made a warding-off gesture with his hand. "To... Relward. The gatewarden. This is Erin's doin'," he added in a rush.

"But why?" I asked faintly.

"She's jealous. She thinks Gilbert means to request ye in bonding. He's gone off to hunt an' by th' time he gans back, it will be too late for him to protest," Emmon explained.

I blinked rapidly, fighting off an unexpected rush of tears. I had always used Rushton's stern, dark face as a talisman against despair, but this time the thought of him only evoked a fierce pain in my chest and a bittersweet longing to be home.

Then the irony of it struck me, helping me gain a measure of calmness. Here was Erin violently jealous of the fleeting and surely light-hearted interest Gilbert had taken in me, willing to go to incredible lengths to stop something I had no more desire for than she.

"I can't let it happen," I said, and in that moment a daring idea came to me. With Emmon's help, I managed to speak privately with Gilaine. She agreed the bonding must be avoided and said she would talk to the others about an immediate escape. As well, I told her I had heard Pavo was sick and wanted to make sure he would be able to walk unaided. But that night, when Gilaine and her friends damped Lidgebaby's emanations, I contacted Domick.

"Has something gone wrong?" he asked, responding to the agitation in my thoughts.

I told him emotionlessly of the intended bonding. I was surprised at the vehemence with which he said it must not be allowed to happen. "If I can help it, it won't," I sent. "Our friends here have set their plans for tomorrow night. But after we get away from here, I have an alternative to going round the mountains. It's dangerous. Rushton would never approve, but if it succeeds, we will be on the other side of the mountains in less than two days."

"Impossible. Unless your undisclosed Talents include teaching giant birds to carry us across them."

I ignored his sarcasm. "I want you to build a raft. A strong raft."

"A raft. But ... you can't mean ...?"

"We're going to raft through the mountains," I sent determinedly.

XII

Erin smiled.

A gust of wind wrenched the door from my grip and flung it shut with a resounding crash. Inside the Druid's house, it was unexpectedly quiet.

"Wait in here," Erin said. She opened the door to a small musty-smelling antechamber.

The room was dark though it was not yet evening. The day had been dreary, overshadowed by banks of foreboding storm clouds. A single candle burned in a sconce on the wall near the door, offering meager light.

As soon as Erin's footsteps faded, I crossed to the window facing the street and pulled aside a gauzy pleat of curtain.

It had begun to rain again. The wind changed direction abruptly, pelting handfuls of bitter rain against the glass. I peeped into the rainswept street. A brilliant flash of lightning gave the fleeting impression of a blighted daytime. Then it was dark again.

I hoped nothing had happened to delay the others.

There was another flash of lightning and I wondered uneasily at the building storm. Firestorms seemed to occur less in the mountains. Pavo had a theory that firestorms were increasing on the coast. He had explained that they were not real storms, despite the lightning and thunder, but an electrical imbalance in the complex forces holding the earth together, another legacy of the cataclysmic disturbance of the Great White. No one knew why firestorm rain burned, or why the flames could only be extinguished by firestorm rains. One thing was certain though— there had been no firestorms in the Beforetime. The Herders believed firestorms followed the holocaust and would continue ravaging the earth until the world was again pure. Naturally, the only way to achieve such a state of grace was to adhere to Herder doctrine.

I squinted, searching for tell-tale movements in the shadows. If there were a firestorm brewing, we could not think of escape. Firestorm flames burned even stone, but there would be more protection in the Druid encampment than in the open at the mercy of the lethal flames.

Outside, the wind muttered sullenly, echoing my inner disquiet. Erin and her traditional lecture about the duties of a bondmate were the least of my worries. Though not yet officially told I was to be bonded that night, I was already used to the idea.

Scanning the length of the street visible from the window, I wondered anxiously if Kella had managed to get a message to Gilaine. She should have contacted her as soon as I was sent to the Druid's house. Jow had decided that was the best time to make our move. But if they did not come . . .

Again lightning flashed, followed by a sharp crack of thunder. The time lapse between the flashes and the thunder was growing shorter. Rain fell in light flurries, but the heaviness of the clouds illuminated in the intermittent light indicated a deluge was pending.

Hearing a movement at the door, I dropped the curtain and moved quickly away from the window. Erin came in cautiously, as if she had thought I would be waiting to attack her. Her hand rested lightly on the hilt of a short knife she wore in a jewelled waist scabbard.

"You have been sent here so that I can tell you some wonderful news," Erin said, her eyes glittering vindictively. I was taken aback at the force of her dislike.

"Yes?" I asked calmly.

Her lips stretched across her teeth in a smile that looked more like she was baring her teeth at me. "You are to be bonded—to Relward. The gatewarden."

Knowing took the force out of my reaction, and I was glad to see her look disappointed. "This is your news?" I asked sourly.

For a moment Erin looked nonplussed, then her cheeks mottled with anger. "You are to be bonded tonight," she added viciously.

I shrugged. "What does it matter, bonding or no," I said lethargically.

"You ... What?" she stammered.

"A man, bonded or not, has no appeal for me. What does it matter to be bonded or not? It is all the same in the dark," I added crudely.

Her face reddened and she stepped away from me as if she thought I would contaminate her. "You dare speak of such things to me?"

I shrugged. "If you don't like such talk, why are you the one to tell me of this bonding?" Taking advantage of her loss of balance, I stepped toward her.

Her hand groped for the knife in her belt and she held it up between us. "Stay back." There was a loud noise in the street and we both jumped. "What was that?"

"The wind?" I said quickly, stepping forward again in my haste to distract her. She lifted the knife, her eyes narrowed, flicking to the window and back. "What's going on?" she asked, suspicion flaring in her eyes. She backed to the door, holding the knife out menacingly. Unable to think of a way to stop her, I stood still, heart banging against my ribs. If she were to catch the others and give the alarm, we would all be lost. Erin groped behind her, opening the door without turning her back or taking her eyes off me.

My knees felt weak with relief. In the hall behind her were Kella and Jik. "That is an old trick," Erin sneered. "Trying to make me think there's someone…" She stopped abruptly as Kella's arrow tip pressed into her neck.

Jik reached round and took the knife carefully out of her fingers.

"Get inside the room," Kella ordered, her face pale but determined. I was momentarily astonished to see a healer waving a knife in such a businesslike way. Erin obeyed, shock turned to fury.

"You will all die for this. My father will burn you," she snarled.

"Did you bring the rope?" I asked Jik, ignoring her. He nodded. "Tie her up."

Erin stood rigidly erect, as Jik bound her hands and feet. "What do you think this will get you?" she grated. "There are men in all the watch towers and guards on the gate. And even if you get out, he will come after you. You will be caught and then you will wish bonding were the only fate awaiting you."

I touched Jik's arm, sending a swift thought. The next time she opened her mouth to speak, he thrust a ball of cloth into her mouth, then tied another round her head to stop her spitting it out. It was a relief to have her quiet. I checked the ropes. They were tight and I guessed Erin's hissing threats had made Jik more efficient than he would otherwise have been.

I forced myself to face her. "Daughter of Henry Druid, we are gypsy folk and not meant for staying in one place. My father waits for me in Arendelft and I mean to meet him. I bear no ill will to your father, but I cannot stay. That is why you have to be tied up. To stop you raising the alarm too soon."

"Perhaps we should kill her," Jik said, obeying my covert prompting.

I pretended to consider it, gratified to see the first sign of real fear in Erin's eyes. Slowly, as if reluctant, I shook my head. "I would be just as happy to kill her, but that might make her father annoyed. Besides, we will be long gone round the head of the river and down the main road before they find her." I had no doubt Erin would faithfully relay all I had told her, sending her father off in the wrong direction.

I nodded to Jik and he opened a large chest under the window.

Erin's eyes widened with real horror. I did not like the idea of locking anyone in a trunk, even the detestable Erin, but we had to make sure she was not found too quickly. If the Druid did come home early because of the bonding, he was unlikely to think to look for his missing daughter in a spare room in a box. With Kella's help, we lifted her into the trunk, leaving the lid slightly askew, so she wouldn't suffocate. Then we went into the hall where she would not hear us.

"Phew," Jik said. "If eyes were knives we'd all be dead."

"Jow is outside waiting for the signal that she's out of the way," Kella said.

Jik went to fetch him and we went into the kitchen in case Erin could hear us talking in the hall. She must not have the slightest idea we had help from within the camp.

"Where is she?" Jow asked, coming in the back door after Jik. I told him and, unexpectedly, he grinned.

"Do her good," he murmured. Then his face became serious. "Now, you know what you have to do?"

"We go to the place where the Suggredoon goes under the mountain, then climb across the foot of the mountains, until we get to the other side. Then we make for the lowlands," I said.

He nodded. "You'll be a bit soon now. You might have to wait until the soldierguards leave. I wish we could give you more help."

"We'll be all right," I said, sorry to be deceiving him. "Gypsies know a few things about hiding." I had let them go on thinking us gypsies. I could not afford to tell them about Obernewtyn while they meant to remain in the camp.

Kella opened a bundle and handed me boots, stout trews, and a jumper and coat. I threw aside the silky red dress Rilla had made me wear without regret. Fine clothes were no substitute for freedom.

Outside, lightning cracked loudly.

"This is an ordinary storm?" I asked Jow.

He nodded. "An ordinary storm, but bad all the same. Worse for the armsmen who will have to track you."

I handed him the dress. "You could use this to lead them astray."

Jow shook his head. "When we come to your tracks on the other side, the Druid will know for certain you had help."

"What are we waiting for?" Kella asked, looking round uneasily.

"A signal from Peter," Jow said. "He should have been here, I'll go and look."

A cold blast of wind swept through the back door as he left. I shivered, less from the cold than at what lay ahead. I wondered what Jow and the others would think when they found no tracks on the other side. It would look as if we had really vanished. I wondered if anyone would suspect the truth. I thought of Matthew and Louis and prayed Domick had managed to reach Matthew. Rushton had to be warned about the Druid. He worried about the fact that most at Obernewtyn were scarcely more than children. I knew he hoped it would be years before the final confrontation with the Council. Time for Obernewtyn to grow up.

The waiting made me nervous and I began to wonder if Domick had taken my instructions seriously. My hands felt hot and sticky, though the rest of me was cold. I blew on them lightly. Going through the mountain was a gamble, but if it came off, we would be back on schedule, making up the time we had lost in the Druid camp. I had told Jik and Kella of

Maryon's prediction, and they agreed we had no choice if there were no other way to complete the aims of our expedition before winter.

The door swung open, admitting Jow, Peter, the older musician, and, to my surprise, Gilaine.

She took my hands in hers. "The others did not want me to come because I am known to have associated with you. But I wanted to say good-bye. I wish you did not have to go," she sent wistfully.

I squeezed her fingers. "We'll meet again someday. I'm sure of it." I leaned forward and kissed a cheek that smelled faintly of honey.

"Come," Jow said impatiently. "There's no time to waste."

Gilaine gave me a gentle push and waved as we followed Jow and Peter into the stormy night. Looking over my shoulder, I saw her disappear round the corner of the house.

It began to rain in earnest then, as if it had been waiting for us. To my consternation, the flashes of lightning lit up the streets. Anyone glancing through a window would see us.

Suddenly Jow stopped. "It's no good. It's too light. A group of people out on a night like this is unusual and anything unusual will be remembered after this night's work. We'll have to split up."

I went with Jow, and Jik and Kella followed Peter. I trotted to keep up, trying to ignore the pain in my feet. We met up in one of the alleys running down between the dark storehouses alongside the gate. Kella and Jik were panting, having come a longer way. Peter left at once with a terse farewell.

"I live near, so it's safest for me to be seen here," Jow explained. "I've left two horses in the front yard nearest the gate. They've agreed to run the minute they're let out." Jow was a beastspeaker.

"Your job is to break the latch on the yard gate," he was telling Jik. "Wait until a crack of thunder and smash it with a rock. Then get out of sight. As soon as I hear the noise, I'll come out and call the gatewarden to help me catch the horses. They're to run down to the other end of the camp. There'll be enough noise to attract the attention of the posted guards in the corner lookouts. Even so, you'll have to be quick. And don't leave any tracks showing which way you've gone. There must be no doubt you're making for the main road around the head of the river. You're sure you'll be able to lock the door from the outside?"

I nodded. "It'll be all right if I'm touching it." Jow looked up as a flash of lightning lit the alley. "Count five and thirty once you're in position to give me time to get back to my hut. Then bash away," he told Jik. Then he was gone.

We stared at one another, frightened and excited. "Go on," I prompted Jik. He darted off into the shadows and we edged closer to the main gate, one eye on the pens where the horses stood. The whole aim of Jow's plan was to give us a clear start. Jow hoped no one would even realize we had gone until we were discovered missing at nightmeal. And even then, the locked gates would make them think we were hiding somewhere inside the camp.

But everything depended on our getting away unnoticed.

I jumped as a loud crack of lightning mingled faintly with the sound of splintering wood. Two horses thundered past us into the street, their hooves making a great clattering noise on the stones. We watched as Jow burst out of a door in shirt-sleeves shouting for help. Two other doors flung open and men came out, wondering what was happening. A man poked his head out of the gatewarden's hut and Jow called him to help catch the horses before someone was murdered. He pulled on a coat and ran after the shouting group without looking back. A man and a woman came into the street and there was more calling and exclamations.

As soon as they were all out of sight, we hurried across to the gate, Jik running up behind us. My heart beat loud enough to drown the thunder. We were completely exposed, and my hand trembled as I reached for the lock. In the distance I could hear the babble of noise from those after the horses.

But even as my fingers closed around the bolt, a big hand shot out of the gatewarden's hut and fastened on my arm. Kella screamed and jumped back, knocking Jik to the ground.

Still holding my arm, the big-bearded man who had caught us in the first place came out into the rain, an unpleasant smile on his mouth. "What have we here?" His eyes ran over our bundles and dress. "Not running away, are we? And Relward so eager to have a maid in his bed." He laughed and rain shook from the wiry beard hairs under his chin. "What a pity, since runaways here end up as bonfire fodder."

Kella moaned in terror, snapping me out of my own trance. Anger flowed through me in a molten tide. If I did nothing, we would all burn. I gritted my teeth.

There was nothing subtle in what I did next. The armsman's bruising grip on me made him vulnerable, since it negated Lidgebaby's static net. I simply lashed out with all the frustrated power in my mind. Even so, it was less effective than it should have been. He recoiled in shock and, instinctively, tried to let go of my arm. My other hand snaked out and caught his wrist, keeping the connection. He fought me in earnest then, and when I clung like a limpet, he struck me across the face. It was too awkward a blow to have full force, but my ears sang and I felt suddenly a long way from my hands. I could feel my grip weaken. Terrified of what would happen to us if I failed to get us away, I reached inside my darkest mind for the killing power I had once used on Madam Vega. I had not used it since the night we had taken Obernewtyn. I had tried to pretend to myself it was gone. But it rose at my call like a great black snake, and only fear of that dreadful secret power gave me the strength to temper it. Even muted, I was shaken with the strength of my attack on the armsman's mind. His mouth gaped wide in a soundless shriek and he slumped unconscious at my feet. I slid to my knees behind him, retching and coughing.

Kella looked down at me, stunned. "What did you do to him?" Then her face changed. "Elspeth, you're bleeding."

I shook my head and climbed to my feet. "No . . . time. We have to get . . . away before they find him." I could taste blood and spat, but the taste persisted. Dazed, I wondered if it were my imagination that it was raining more heavily.

Kella visibly gathered herself, unlocking the gate and pulling Jik and me after her. I put my hands on the lock from the outside, and relocked it. With luck the door locked from the inside would make them think the unconscious armsman had been struck by lightning.

We picked our way with careful haste across the spine of rocks Jow had said would hide our tracks. When we had gone some distance, I decided speed was more important. "Run!" I yelled over the noise of the rain. All around us trees creaked under the weight of the downpour. It was like standing right under a waterfall. I staggered after them, my head spinning and my feet hurting badly. I was too disoriented to know which way we should go and plodded after Kella, hoping she knew.

"As long as one of us knows . . ." I said with a bubbling laugh.

Then, abruptly, we were outside Lidgebaby's range. I sent a probe to Domick. Fortunately he was waiting for me, because I had no strength left to fight his defenses. To my relief, Pavo was there already.

I stumbled over an exposed tree root and fell to my knees hard, losing mental contact. Kella and Jik helped me up. The healer's hair was plastered to her head and her face dripped with water.

I tried to speak, but my mouth refused to shape the words. Instead, I sent a call for help to Domick.

Kella and Jik half dragged, half carried me between them. I struggled to stay conscious, leading Domick to us. Crashing through the trees moments later, he ordered the other two to run, and hefted me effortlessly over one shoulder.

We reached the clearing where Pavo waited with Gahltha and Avra. My teeth felt as if they were rattling round behind my eyes. Like Domick, Pavo was still clad in the ragged remnants of the clothes we had worn from Obernewtyn that first day.

"What's happened?" the teknoguilder asked. "Kella says you killed a man with your mind."

Domick gave me a startled look.

"Not killed . . . stunned," I said groggily.

"He hit her in the face. There was blood all over but the rain's washed it off. Wait . . ." Before I could stop her, Kella reached out and touched me, drawing my pain off into herself. At once the dizziness faded.

"Hurts . . ." moaned Kella, whitefaced. I pushed her away.

"That's enough. I can think now. You've stopped the faintness."

Kella smiled wanly.

We were all huddled under an Eben tree, the only real shelter. Rain drummed down heavily on all sides.

"Did anyone follow you?" Domick shouted over the noise.

I shook my head. "No one will come after us until this storm is over. And even if they do we'll be long gone on the raft."

Something in Domick's expression struck me. "You did make the raft?"

Wordlessly he pulled me to my feet and pointed through the trees to the water.

My heart sank.

Swollen by the phenomenal rains, the Suggredoon was a roaring torrent overflowing its banks, carrying whole trees and chunks of the bank. Domick's raft was fastened to the bank by a thick, twisted rope and bobbed like a creature mad to be set free. Only a lunatic would set off on such a river.

Domick hauled the raft in and looked at me, panting. "What do we do?"

I took a deep breath. "We'll wait until daylight. Maybe the river will have calmed down by then."

Before he could respond, I heard a bark and turned to see Darga pelting into the clearing. "Many funaga coming," he sent.

I translated. Domick's face hardened. "Then we've no choice. We'll have to go now or face them." He pointed to the raft. "There are ropes. Tie yourselves down."

"Quickly," I shouted, when no one moved.

I helped Kella tie herself, and Jik tied Darga and himself down. Avra stepped into the large space in the middle obviously reserved for the two horses, and Domick bound her gently. I sat next to Pavo, trying not to look frightened.

My mind was reeling. How could anyone have followed so quickly? Unless we had been betrayed. Saul's face came into my mind.

Domick's cry broke into my thoughts. He was standing on the bank with Gahltha.

"What is it?" I shouted.

Domick waved his hand helplessly at the black horse. "He won't move."

I tried to reach Gahltha's mind, but it was as smooth and unassailable as a mountain of glass. I looked at Avra and sent an urgent query. Through the noise of the rain, I could hear men's voices and shouts.

"They come," Darga sent.

Domick threw his hands up and began to push the raft off the bank.

"Gahltha," I sent, forcing his shield. He whinnied, a high quavering note, the whites of his eyes showing. But he made no move toward the raft.

"He's afraid," Jik cried.

Domick jumped into the raft just as the water dragged it from the bank. There was a hard jerk as it reached the end of the tether rope. Still Gahltha stood on the bank unmoving, staring out at us.

"Gahltha!" I sent. "Go back to Obernewtyn."

He made no response. I saw figures running.

"They're coming. Cut the rope!" I cried.

Domick lifted his small ax.

"Gahltha. Go now or the funaga will trap you!" I sent forcefully.

He reared violently and plunged into the night. At the same time Domick let the ax fall. It landed badly and the rope was not severed. Several men had reached the bank and were attempting to reel the raft in. Domick raised the ax again and this time it fell true.

At once the roaring water carried us swiftly away from the bank. Lightning flashed, and in that moment, I saw the face of the armsman Gilbert among those who stood watching us, a look of utter anguish on his face.

Seeing me, even as I saw him, Gilbert cried out, but the sound of rain and rushing water made his words no more than a bird call.

Then the raft carried us from his sight, and within seconds we were speeding toward the dark bulk of the mountains. For one moment it seemed we would be smashed to pieces against the side of the mountains, then the black gape of a cave opened up before us.

I looked back and caught sight of Gahltha pawing at the raging water as if it were tongues of fire.

"Here we go," Domick said grimly, and we plunged into the heart of the mountain.

XIII

The Suggredoon had borne us along its ancient course at the speed of a bolting horse.

Domick stood up on the raft, slipping his feet into rope loops, and took hold of the paddle which gave him rudimentary steering. I was surprised to find a source of dim light in the cavern, instead of dense blackness. The walls glowed gently and eerily and, only when a cloud of insects stirred and rose, I saw that the light came from the tiny flying insects' bodies. A stiff, cold draught blew in my face from somewhere ahead, confirming that the tunnel was open through the mountain.

For a while it seemed we had exaggerated the dangers, then we came on the first turbulent stretch of rapids. The water boiled savagely sending the raft shuddering and careening through foaming torrents, barely missing jagged rocks. Luck as much as steering kept us from being overturned or having a rock gouge a hole in the raft.

And there were many such stretches. Each time we began to breathe easy, thinking ourselves lucky to have survived, we would hear the familiar hollow roar ahead, and tighten our grip on the raft.

At one point the entire surface of the river seemed to tilt and we were as much sliding as being swept by the current. The wind whistled past me, whipping strands of hair wildly in my face.

We had known the water must flow down to the lowlands, and I was convinced the cavern above the water would continue, but I had been afraid secretly that it might be too narrow for the raft to pass. It seemed my worst fears would be fulfilled when the walls began to close in around us. I took comfort in the breeze that must mean there was a way through, but would it be wide enough? For a moment the mountain seemed to throb with brooding malevolence.

Impatient with myself, I tried to ignore the roof drawing steadily nearer and more dim, as if the glowing insects disliked the closeness as much as we did.

Gradually, it became so low that Domick could not stand. I needed no empathy to sense Avra's fear. If the cavern became much more cramped, she would not fit. And we all knew there was no turning back.

But, just as suddenly, the way began to widen again and I shivered with reaction. In my wildest fancies, I had never imagined the trip to the coast would be such a road of trials. I had worried about the soldierguards, yet in all that had befallen us, we had not even seen a soldierguard.

Hearing a roar ahead, I prepared myself for another battering, but instead, the raft flowed round a bend and through a natural stone arch, into a huge, dark ocean. If not for the stalactites and stalagmites and the rock columns rising from the water to the roof where some had met and fused, I would have thought we had somehow got out onto the sea at night. Like the tunnel, the cave was lit by millions of the tiny insects.

The raft slowed but was still drawn along by a deeper current.

Our wonder at this sea under the mountain dissolved into greater amazement as we drew near to what we had taken as immense rocky mounds rising from the water.

Pavo realized first what we were seeing, and gasped. I was

struck by the wonder in his gaunt face. "This is a Beforetime city," he whispered reverently.

Squinting, I saw that he was right. The shapes were too smooth and square to be rocks, but the height of them astounded me. These, then, were the skyscrapers of the legends; things which I had never quite been able to believe in.

I stared about me as the current took us between two of the monstrous constructions, along what must once have been a street. There was no way of telling how far below us lay the floor of the dead city. I was silent with this evidence of the Oldtimers' abilities. Out of the distant past, I seemed to hear Louis Larkin telling me there were certain to be rare niches in the world where bits of the Beforetime were preserved.

And what wonders lay inside the buildings with their thousands of dark windows?

Up close, the surfaces were badly eroded, especially at the waterline. One day the ebb and flow would eat the foundations and this marvelous city would topple. Gaps in the rows of buildings suggested this had happened already in some cases.

Many of the smooth façades were crumbled, revealing the great black steel frames inside them, like the bones of some moldering animal. Much of the walls that were not broken were covered in a livid yellow fungus. The glowing insects either lived or fed on it, for wherever the fungus grew, they were clustered thickly, and their collective light was brighter.

I wondered if the city had somehow sunk into the mountain during the Great White, or if the earth had spat the mountains on top of it like a gravestone.

I found myself wishing Matthew could see it. He had long worshipped the Oldtimers with a glib surety that had always troubled me. The city told a story of men who were certainly great, but men just the same, with flaws that all their brilliance had not overcome.

It was a somber and sobering experience. It was not hard to think the people who had built such cities as capable of any wonder—or terror. Looking around me, I had no doubt that such a people could create a weapon that would live far beyond their span. The stark reality of the brilliance and insanity of the Oldtimers struck me then as never before.

After a while the current turned, taking us down what had been an intersecting street. Here, enough of the buildings had fallen for the rubble to rise above the water in a stony shore. Pavo asked Domick to take the raft closer. "I mustn't lose this chance," he whispered.

But Darga barked sharply in warning as we changed course. "These stones and all about us are poisonous. Only the water is clean, because it flows."

I relayed his warning. Pavo smiled faintly, and I knew he was thinking that it no longer mattered as far as he was concerned. Yet he nodded, giving Darga a speculative look.

"This is a bad place," Avra sent uneasily.

As much to distract myself as the mare, I asked her about Gahltha's strange behavior.

She whinnied forlornly. "The funaga who had him before almost drowned him when he was first brought to them. It is a funaga way of breaking the spirit of an equine, if it does not kill them first. They did not break him, for he took refuge in a savage hidden hatred, but he has a dread of water that goes beyond reason."

"I'm sure he's back at Obernewtyn by now," I sent reassuringly, thinking she was afraid he had been caught by the Druid's armsmen.

"He is proud," she sent. "Too proud to bear such shame easily."

I stared at her, puzzled. "There is no shame in what happened. No one will blame him."

Avra sighed in a very human way. "He will blame himself. I do not think he has gone back to Obernewtyn."

Unable to offer her any comfort, I turned to Domick and complimented his raft-building skills.

He smiled wanly. "I had the feeling it would need to be strong, but even I never imagined how bad it would be. We're lucky to have got through."

"Then if luck has brought us this far, let's hope we've not used up our share," Pavo said. "We have not gone down nearly far enough yet."

Hours later, we were still gliding through the ancient city. The immediate wonder having worn off, we talked about what to do once we had reached the Lowlands. The loss of our gypsy colorants meant we could no longer pass for gypsies. Kella said she might brew a new stain, but it was decided gypsies on foot would be more conspicuous than ordinary folk. But going on foot would slow us considerably.

"I still don't understand how they found us so fast," Domick said suddenly. He always wanted to know why a thing had failed so that it could be guarded against the next time.

"It was no one's fault. Remember I warned you there were armsmen out hunting? Well I recognized one of them on the bank. It was nothing more than a bad chance." Kella interrupted to explain the connection between Gilbert and my bonding. She had also seen the ginger-haired armsman.

"So, maybe he was in a hurry for another reason?" Domick said.

I felt my face redden. "This is no time to be acting like an idiot." But I could not help thinking of the way Gilbert had looked after me on the bank, and wondered what he had called.

From the corner of my eye, I saw Kella and Domick exchange a look and realized the stresses and perils that had beset us since leaving Obernewtyn had a good side too. The old enmity between coercer and healer, symbolized in Kella and Domick, seemed to have disappeared. I was imagining what effect their unexpected friendship would have on their two guilds, when we passed suddenly out of the big cave and back into a tunnel. Immediately the raft picked up speed and in seconds we were back in rapids.

Another hour passed with little respite from the ferocious white water which seemed more frequent on this side of the underground sea. Domick was swaying on his feet with exhaustion.

Then we heard a noise. At first we checked our binding ropes, thinking there was another bout of rapids ahead, but as we came nearer to the source, the roaring became louder, taking on a curious vibrating quality.

I noticed Pavo was listening intently. There was no fear on his face, only fierce concentration.

"What is it?" I shouted. "More rapids?"

"Let's hope that is all it is." Pavo answered.

I opened my mouth to ask what he was afraid of when the raft tilted abruptly sideways. Being tied on was all that kept us together. I heard Kella scream, and then we were falling as the Suggredoon became a giant waterfall, plummeting us into a black void.

∽

My face felt hot and damp at the memory of that fall.

I tried to open my eyes. A bead of sweat trickled down my face and into the hair behind my ear. I lifted my hand to feel if my eyes were open, wondering if I had gone blind.

"Shh, lie still," Kella said softly.

"My eyes," I croaked. My throat felt dry as old paper.

"Your eyes are fine. They're stuck shut by blood from a cut on your forehead. Wait . . ."

I heard footsteps on a stone floor and the murmur of voices. It was strange to hear and not see; that was how it was for Dameon. Two sets of footsteps approached and there was the sound of curtains being drawn. I felt a warm cloth on my face and gasped at the unexpected sting.

"There are lots of small cuts from the rocks," Kella explained gently. "There now."

I opened my eyes. I was in bed in a small whitewashed bedroom with sun streaming through a window and birds chirruping outside. Kella was sitting beside me on a stool, a bowl of bloodied water on her knees. Her cheek was badly bruised and her arm was bandaged. Behind her was a plump, matronly woman I had never seen before.

"I am Katlyn," she said with a warm smile.

I did not know what to say and looked helplessly at Kella. "Katlyn and her bondmate, Grufyyd, found us washed up on the banks of the Suggredoon. They know we escaped from a Councilfarm," she said pointedly.

"Don't worry about that now. You need to rest," Katlyn said. "That is the best healer of all, but first I will bring you some food."

She went out, taking the bowl of stained water, and returned in a moment with a bowl of soup.

"That smells wonderful," I rasped.

She smiled. "It is an old recipe, a special healing mixture. Eat and then sleep. You can talk later."

"Where are the others?" I asked Kella as soon as she had gone.

Kella pointed to the soup. "Eat; if Katlyn says it will heal, it will. She's incredible. She knows so much about healing and medicines. I've never seen such a herb garden."

"Herb?" I asked sharply. Herb lore was illegal.

"Katlyn is an herb lorist. She has herbs I've never even heard of, and bags and bags of dried herbs. I wish Roland could meet her. Her grandmother and mother practiced the lore before the ban on it and she has kept on with it. People from all over the Land use her mixtures."

"Does she let her name be known so freely?"

Kella smiled. "She talks about the Council and the Herders as if they were a collection of naughty boys. She knows what she does is dangerous, but she says it's her job."

"How long have we been here?" I asked, suddenly anxious

that we had stayed too long in the house of a woman who cared so little for her safety.

"Only a day, but without her help we would have taken much longer to heal," Kella said sternly, seeing my disapproval.

"I'm grateful for her help," I said. "But it's my job to keep us safe and finish this expedition without getting caught by the Council who are a lot more dangerous than bad boys. Now tell me, do these people live alone here? And where are we?"

Kella shrugged. "We're not far from Rangorn and the Ford. There's a son, but he doesn't live here. Katlyn didn't say what he does now. She talks about him as a child. She said he was always putting himself in danger, never thinking of the cost."

I reflected that this seemed to be a family trait. "Where is he now?"

"I think, it was something Katlyn said, that he lives in one of the coastal cities."

"Good. How did you come to tell them we had escaped?"

"Domick insisted on telling them something. No one would have crossed the Suggredoon so high unless they were trying to avoid being seen. There was no way of hiding that we had been in a boating accident. I couldn't tell them we came out of the mountain, so the Councilfarm runaway story seemed best."

"You are certain they didn't send word to the Council? There is a reward for information leading to the capture of runaways."

Kella shook her head emphatically. "I don't think it occurred to them."

I frowned. "If Katlyn is a herb lorist, she wouldn't want soldierguards here, so we're probably safe enough for now."

A flicker of anger crossed Kella's face. "You're too cynical, Elspeth. It makes you blind to things right under your nose," she added obliquely. I seemed to be hearing that a lot.

"What about the others?"

"Everyone's fine except for a few bruises and bumps. Pavo is not too good, but that has nothing to do with the accident."

"Jik?" I asked.

She smiled. "A cracked rib. He's milking the goats with Grufyyd. Domick has gone off to scout the area. Once a coercer..." I was astounded to see her eyes soften and wondered if friendship was all that had grown up between them.

Kella stood, taking the empty bowl from my fingers. I could not remember drinking the soup.

"Sleep and get better. The world will wait," the healer said.

Weary as I was, I could not rest easy. The expedition seemed to be in tatters, without disguise or papers, two all but unfit to travel. Would we ever get home again?

Domick returned late that night.

"Elspeth?" he whispered outside the window.

"I'm awake," I answered softly, sitting up. "Come in."

He climbed through the window. "I am to sleep in the stables with Jik and Darga, but I wanted to talk to you while it was quiet. Katlyn and Grufyyd are good people," Domick said. "Kella believes it and so do I. I don't like lying to them."

I hid my amazement at these uncoercerlike sentiments. Domick went on. "They seem ... accustomed to people like us— people on the run, scared, and without anything but a flimsy cover story. The medicines, the food, the lack of questions ... makes me think they have done this before—sheltered runaways."

"What are you trying to say?" I asked.

He frowned. "Something Katlyn said, right at the start makes me think this son of theirs, Brydda, might be mixed up in Sedition, rescuing other Seditioners. It's my guess he sends people here from time to time."

"Are you sure? How do you know?"

He shrugged. "Instinct as much as anything. Remember a while back one of the Misfits we rescued spoke of rumors in

the lowlands of a Seditious organization where escapees from
the Councilfarms could find help."

I nodded thoughtfully. "If you're right, it means we're safe
enough here. But we have to get going again soon, or we'll waste
the time we gained coming through the mountain. The expedition must go on, even if some of us are to be left behind."

Domick's face was impassive, and I knew he had come to
the same conclusion.

"We're close to Rangorn, but we can get to the Ford
without being seen. It's unguarded, though Grufyyd says there
are guards further down at the ferry. I'll get some papers before
I have to go across, but what about the rest of you?"

"We'll manage without them. I think the best thing is for
you to try to get hold of a cart. That way Pavo and I will be
able to move more quickly." I touched his hand. "Go to bed
now."

He left as soundlessly as he had come.

Later Katlyn came in to change the bandages on my feet.
"Poor ill-treated feet," she said gently, unwrapping them. "I put
on a salve to numb them so you could sleep. The scars are deep
and have not healed well, though they are old."

"I have to walk," I said.

Katlyn nodded. "If you must, these will carry you. But
walking will increase the pain. If they are ever to heal properly
you must rest them completely for many months, perhaps even
longer."

Katlyn looked up at me, her expression serious. "Child,
there is something I want to say to you. By the look, you be
th' leader of these bairns. Kella told me you are making for the
outland coast regions, in search of sanctuary. I tell you, I do
not think you will find any safe place on the coast. I want you
to think of staying here with us."

"Here?" I echoed, astounded.

Katlyn reached out and touched my hand. "This is truly
a safe house, a refuge for runaways . . . and for others. You could

help us in our work. Help others like yourself..."

I stared at Katlyn, my heart beating fast, for her eyes told me clearly that she knew we had not told her the truth about ourselves.

"Think on it. Talk with the others. Let us know tonight what you decide," Katlyn said softly.

XIV

"What will you tell her? Won't she find it odd that runaways refuse refuge?" Pavo asked, when I told the others of Katlyn's offer.

"I have decided to tell them the truth," I said. "I think we owe them that or as much of it as we can tell."

Grufyyd turned out to be a big, silent man with a brown beard and somber, smoke-gray eyes. After we had eaten nightmeal, my first that day, I asked if I could retell our story.

"We have had to lie so often that it's hard to see where the truth can be told," I began. "It is true we are escapees, in one sense, but that was a long time ago. Now we, and others, have a secret . . . place in the high country. There are a lot of us now, mostly no more than children, and mostly runaways. Some came to us, more we helped get away. Until recently, we thought our existence a secret. Then we started to hear rumors of a Seditious organization rescuing people from the Council and we were afraid it might mean us."

Katlyn and Grufyyd exchanged an odd, tense look.

"We also heard the Council meant to investigate the highlands, and that meant we were in danger. So it was decided to send us down to see what we could find out. And at the same time, we mean to search for a friend we think is hiding somewhere near Murmroth and Aborium."

"How did you come to be half-drowned on the banks of the Suggredoon?" Grufyyd asked in a rumbling voice.

"We came across the White Valley looking for an Oldtime pass through the mountains. We didn't want to use the main roads. But we stumbled on a secret camp run by Henry Druid. He takes prisoner anyone who gets too near, and they have to join him. He makes all the men join his armsmen."

Katlyn cast an appalled glance at Grufyyd. "Armsmen. Then he still means to get revenge?"

Grufyyd shook his head sorrowfully.

"We managed to escape, but the Olden way proved impassable. We were desperate with the Druid's armsmen close behind us, so we rafted the Suggredoon through the mountain."

Katlyn gasped. "But is it possible?" No one answered, since we were the living proof of our story.

"Looked overmuch damage for an overturned boat," Grufyyd observed dispassionately.

I continued. "Now . . . all I have told you is true, but I have not told everything, mostly to protect the ones we left behind. But I would not have said this much unless I trusted you, and because we want you to understand that we can't stay here."

"We are no strangers to necessary secrets," Katlyn said gently. "I spoke impulsively this morning, though I guessed you would not stay. But we would like to offer you further help, in return for a favor."

"What favor?" Domick asked.

Grufyyd rose suddenly and decisively. "You have heard enough, I reckon, to guess our son Brydda does not live strictly according to Council lore. In short, he is a Seditioner. He helps people who are to be burned for Sedition to get away and start afresh. It is possible his organization is the one your rumors spoke of. Our problem is that we have lost contact with him. Brydda has neither visited us nor sent people to be hidden for two moons, and we are afraid something has happened to him.

No one would send word to us, because no one else knows about us. He keeps us secret for our own safety and for the safety of the people he sends."

"We are too old for intrigue, and we ask that you will go into Aborium and bear a message to Brydda from us."

Domick looked at me. "No," he said decisively. I was startled at his brusqueness after his words the previous night. "If I were with you . . ." he said.

"We mean to part before Morganna, you see," I explained. "Domick will be going to Sutrium alone. We have no papers and had meant to stay away from the towns. And Aborium does not have a good reputation, even in the highlands."

Grufyyd nodded. "It is a bad place."

"You spoke of help," Domick said belligerently. "I don't see how delivering a message to a dangerous city can be called helping." He was looking down at Kella, and suddenly I understood his agitation.

Grufyyd nodded with grave courtesy that made Domick seem rude and brash. "I meant to offer you the use of our cart, which your horse can pull."

"We will be happy to deliver a message to your son," I said, deciding. I gave Domick a hard stare. "It is the least we can do after all you have done for us."

Grufyyd's face broke into a beguiling smile. He crossed abruptly to the door, gathering up his coat. On the threshold he turned. "Soon the rains will come. It will be best for you to go soon. Tomorrow morning." Without waiting for a response, he went out, leaving a startled silence behind him.

I looked around to see Katlyn looking at Domick. "He has been frightened for Brydda; we both have. Do not fear for your friends, Domick. No one checks papers in Aborium. And it is even possible Brydda can help you."

Katlyn looked at me and smiled. "Now . . . food and drink to travel." She turned to her store cupboards.

"How are we to find Brydda?" Jik asked timidly.

Katlyn smiled over her shoulder at him. "You must go to the Inn of the Cuttlefish and ask for Brydda Llewellyn—that is what he calls himself, but it is also a password. Wait then, and he will come to you."

"And if he doesn't?" Domick asked.

Katlyn's back was toward us, but it seemed to shrink. "Then that will mean he cannot come. The journey takes three days. If you leave very early tomorrow morning and travel steadily, you will arrive at Aborium at daybreak, and that is the best and safest time to enter the city. Tradesmen from outlying regions come then, when the gates are opened."

"It is a walled city?" Domick asked sharply.

"The gates are open freely and unguarded in the daylight hours," Katlyn assured him.

She turned to us suddenly, her face serious. "I would not ask this of you unless there were no other way. But remember the rumors you have heard about Aborium, for all its open gates. Do not linger more than you need. Many disappear and are never seen again."

"Slavers . . ." I murmured.

Katlyn's expression altered subtly. "You have heard of such things?" Domick and Kella gave me a wondering look.

"I heard a story while we were in the Druid camp. I didn't know if it were the truth or not."

"Many things that seem impossible are true of Aborium. In its own way, it is worse than Sutrium. There the Council rules, but Aborium belongs to the Herder Faction."

Jik paled.

"It is a bad place, bad and dangerous, and I fear for my Brydda," she added in a whisper.

XV

We arrived at Aborium three days later.

Bypassing Morganna on Grufyyd's advice, we traveled on a lesser road. Only when we were near Aborium did we venture near to the coast.

From the distance the town was curiously ugly. Sprawled along the shore, it seemed to be made up of smaller versions of the square skyscrapers we had seen under Tor. Above the city hung a dense, bleary mire of smoke.

"I don't like the look of this place," Kella said.

Avra was uninterested in the city. "All such places where the funaga live like rats in a nest stink," she observed with disparagement that would not have shamed Gahltha.

She was more interested in the sea, which provided a dazzling setting for such a grimy jewel. Being mountain bred, she had never seen the great sea and was fascinated by it.

We had meant to arrive outside Aborium at dawn, but the loss and slow repair of a wheel delayed us half a day. In the end we had our first glimpse of the city just before dusk. I did not like the idea of going into the city by night, so we made camp on the shore. We would enter Aborium as Katlyn had suggested: at dawn with the tradefolk.

Sheltered from the city and the road by a lump of rock,

we used the wood Grufyyd had somehow known we would need to make a fire. We watched the sun fall into the sea in a blaze of colored glory.

Suddenly it was night.

Kella set a cauldron of Katlyn's herbal soup to warm and made some damper bread to cook in the coals. Pavo and Jik reorganized the cart, concealing the all-important maps in a pocket in Avra's harness.

There was a slight breeze, but it was a warm night and the air smelled fresh and salty. Moved by impulse, I went to the water's edge, barely visible in the moonless night. I stared into the shadowy waves for a moment, then took off my boots. The water was surprisingly warm after the initial chill. I stood there letting the rim of the Great Sea break over my feet and wondered what lay ahead of us.

I started to find Avra beside me.

"There is a story among the equines that there are many Lands beyond the sea which leads to the sky, where there are no funaga, and beasts rule themselves," she sent. We stood awhile in silence, half-mesmerized by the murmurous sighing of the waves on the shore.

Returning to the fire I found the others seated, staring into the flames with the half-dreamy expressions a fire always seems to evoke.

"I have never seen the sea before," Kella said softly. "I did not imagine it would be so beautiful, or so frightening." Her voice fell nearly to a whisper on the last word.

"Frightening?" Pavo took up the word as if it were a curio.

Kella nodded without looking at him. "It reminds me how big the world is, and how small I am to be pitted against it." She nodded at the sea, where the ghostly reflection of our fire glinted on black waves. "I wonder how many people are like that, with their own dream, thinking it's the right way, the right dream for the world. Perhaps all lives are little and meaningless, really."

Pavo regarded the healer silently for a moment, then a smile lit his pale, bony face. "The world is large, but each life is important to the liver. Think of the Beforetimers making the city under Tor. If they had let themselves feel small and insignificant, they would not have bothered. Such a city is the end of a thousand dreams." He stopped, panting faintly. Jik and Kella looked impressed, but I could not help thinking that their illusion of greatness had also led them to the making of death machines.

"Once, I heard a priest talking of a machine that flew men to the stars," Jik said, sidetracked.

I smiled because he reminded me so much of Matthew in that moment.

But I was surprised to see Pavo nodding seriously. "There are records that suggest such a thing, but it is hard to be sure. The Oldtimers were great storytellers. Sometimes it is hard to tell stories from fact in their writings. But perhaps this hidden store of books will tell us more of them and the old world."

We ate the soup and bread hungrily, and talk turned naturally to Katlyn and Grufyyd.

"I wonder what this son will be like," Kella said, packing away the washed utensils.

"Like Grufyyd. Big and soft spoken. A man of few words," I guessed.

"Perhaps he will be like Katlyn, short and plumpish and always smiling and singing," she suggested.

Pavo smiled. "More like a bit of both. And what will he make of us? I doubt he'll be as free and easy as his parents. He couldn't afford to be." We all looked at the city, no more than a shadow in the night.

I felt my own smile fade. "I trust them, but we know nothing of him. You notice they did not say why Brydda helps people. Why would a man risk his neck like that?"

"He is a seaman," Jik said.

I nodded. "Perhaps he's more than that too. I'll keep my judgment until we meet."

Kella bridled angrily. "If he is Katlyn's son, how can he be other than honest?"

Pavo gave her a reproving look. "The guildmistress is wise to be cautious," he said, with faint emphasis on my title. I caught his behind/thought that the trip had made Kella too outspoken.

Jik shifted uncomfortably beside me, disturbing Darga, whose head rested on his knee.

"Would Domick be in Sutrium yet?" Kella asked, revealing the reason for her melancholy mood.

I was tempted to tell her what I had seen in Domick's mind when he bid us farewell, despite his coolness with her. Then I realized the knowledge would only intensify her regret at his departure. Better not to meddle.

"Much better," Darga sent laconically.

I started. He had read my thoughts with an ease that astounded me.

"My mind grows stronger," Darga sent.

I was about to answer this when a blinding realization struck me. In my excitement, I shouted. "What if the Talent is not human?"

"What?" Kella asked, looking at me as if I had gone mad.

"I meant, what if the Talent that registered on the Zebkrahn isn't human. What if it's a dog, or an equine?" I said.

"Does it matter?" Avra inquired coolly.

I was taken aback. Did it matter? If we were to accept animals as equals and allies, this must lead eventually to animal rescues. Sobered, I shook my head.

"I'm an idiot. Of course it doesn't matter," I sent.

"Gahltha hoped it would be a beast to break the funaga prejudice," Avra sent, mollified.

"Prejudice?" I said.

"The worst prejudice is unknowing. You think you treat

us as equals but, in your deepest heart, you regard the funaga
as superior. In part this is because you yourself are powerful.
But that does not make the race of the funaga better than that
of dog or equine." Darga's gentle criticism cut me like a knife.
I was not certain I believed the funaga admirable as a race, but
there was some truth in his accusation. And how could one fight
such an insidious prejudice?

"You are less prejudiced than most of your race," Darga
sent. "But Gahltha hoped we would find a beast mind to rival
yours. He believes that is the only way to alter the funaga's
deepest attitudes, even at Obernewtyn. Perhaps he was right."

"It might be a girlfriend for Darga." Jik giggled. The others had not been part of our silent dialog.

I leaned over to Pavo. "Do you think Domick is there
yet?"

The teknoguilder shook his head. "He had the same distance we had to travel, but on foot. Tomorrow night is my
guess."

"How many hours do you estimate from Aborium to the
hidden library?"

Pavo considered. "Under a day, but it's hard to tell. Nothing is exact because the Land itself is changed. I hope we will
not be delayed too long in Aborium."

Coming to one of the city gates just after sunrise, I was
startled and unnerved to see soldierguards posted, but though
they looked searchingly at our faces, they neither spoke nor
sought our papers. We had expected neither the guards nor the
huge crowd of people and carts clamoring to be let in the gate.
Many of those waiting were laughing and singing, and one girl
did a cheeky jig, to the calls and encouragement of her friends.
Some way back I caught sight of a real gypsy rig, being driven
by a handsome, surly-looking boy. He appeared to be alone in
his bad temper. The rest of the crowd were full of merriment.
I was puzzled as much at this as anything else. Surely a city

that had so many eager visitors could not be such a bad place. It took some hours to get through the gate because of the throng.

Once inside, we made directly for the seafront and the Inn of the Cuttlefish. Grufyyd had given us directions, but it was harder than we had expected to follow them, for we were swept along by the crowd past the turns we had wanted to take. As well, the city was of a tortuous design, so there was no working our way back. Streets ran off in all directions, bisecting, curving and turning back on themselves.

"If we can find the water, we can work our way along," Pavo suggested. We were loath to mark ourselves strangers by asking the way, but morning passed into afternoon and still we were lost. I did not even remember how to get back to the gate. "No wonder people come in and never come out," I said wearily. "They probably can't find their way out."

"We'll have to ask," Kella said.

I asked a woman, then a boy and another woman. All claimed not to know the inn. That struck me oddly. Aborium was large, but not so large to have more than a few well-known inns. Still trying to decide what to do, we continued to be carried along within the milling crowd. Jik sent a brief message that Avra was on the verge of panicking at the way people were pressing all around her.

"We've got to get out of this," I shouted. I directed Avra to force her way to the edge of the crowd and take the next turn away from the main flow.

"I didn't know there were so many people in the world," Kella said in a shaken voice. "Where are they all going?"

I looked at Jik who wore a puzzled air. "There were not so many when I was here."

Suddenly the broad road down which the crowd pressed opened into an enormous central square. Here people swirled and butted one another like goats in a pen. I could hear laughter and strains of music, and the smells of food and warmed drinks wafted to our noses.

"It's a moon fair!" Pavo said, slapping his forehead. I laughed aloud in relief. That was the reason for the number of people waiting to come into the city. And the people we had asked directions of were strangers too.

Avra managed to take a turn just before the square and we halted the cart in a quiet byway. A foul stench filled the air.

"What is that?" Kella asked in a disgusted voice.

"Seaweed," Jik said with a grin. "We must be near the wharves."

"Fancy having an inn near such a smell," Kella muttered. Then she gave me a startled look. "Where are you going?"

"I'll have a look for it on foot. It will be easier in these crowds."

"I will go with you," Darga offered, and jumped down.

"Darga will come back alone if anything goes wrong. If he does come back without me, go straight out of the city and wait for me where we camped last night," I said.

Kella and Jik paled at my words. I laughed. "Nothing will happen, but we have to have a plan just in case." They looked only slightly reassured.

I set off, ignoring the slight pain in my feet. The gypsy caravan, the raft, and the cart meant I had done little walking, and though they were still tender, they were much better. I hoped I would not have to walk too far. I was glad of Darga's company though, once or twice, I noticed people staring at him oddly. I wondered if I were breaking some city law, letting him walk unchained.

I looked around, trying to see someone who looked like they belonged in Aborium. A rough brown seaman approached. I stopped him and asked the way to the inn. "Never heard of it," he said abruptly. "Blasted moonies," he muttered.

I spotted an old woman struggling with a load of washing

down another alley and hurried to catch up, hoping kindness would beget kindness.

"Mother, let me help you," I offered.

She gave me a long measuring look before letting me take one of the handles. " 'Tis good of ye, sure enough," she said in a broad highland accent. "I dinna mean to be so slow at takin' ye offer, but a moon fair dinna improve manners an' a helpin' hand is rare at any time. What be ye name, lass?" she asked, squinting at me.

"Elspeth," I said.

"Well, I'm Luma," she said cheerfully. "I live just round th' next corner. I went out to gan th' wash an' were near swept away wi' moonies. It gans worse every year," she added despondently. She prattled on, as we walked, complaining bitterly about the damage done to the city during the fairs. At a narrow door, she set down the basket to find her key.

"No doubt it's been picked from me," she said, searching in a haphazard way in all her pockets and folds. "I'm from th' highlands. There ye dinna have to lock ye door, but in a city, leavin' it open is a right invitation to any robber." At last she found the key. Bidding me help her a little further, she told me to call Darga in.

"Things have a way of disappearin' in Aborium," she said confidingly. Stone steps led down directly from the front door. We carried the basket awkwardly between us down them and through into a large rustic kitchen.

"What an effort," gasped Luma, panting and fanning her red face. "Ye'll have a glass of cordial to wet ye whistle? 'Tis th' least I can do." Taking a squat jug from the cooling cabinet, she poured two mugs. " 'Tis me own brew I'm givin' ye, though I'll thank ye nowt to speak of it after. We are bound by lore to buy th' Herders' bitter cordials an' makin' it is an offense." She drained her glass with relish and watched me drink mine.

"Ye be a moonie? I'm sorry for all that I were sayin' of them, but it gans on a body's nerve to have so many at once."

"I'm a traveler on my way to Murmroth. I only called into Aborium to deliver a message. I didn't know there was a fair," I said.

Luma beamed. "An' I might ha' guessed it. Ye look to have too much sense to be part of that nonsense. Who do ye carry a message to? 'Tis nowt of my affair or care, but I know most folk hereabout, an' might save ye some trouble."

I took a deep breath. "He's staying at the Inn of the Cuttlefish."

She nodded thoughtfully, her eyes on Darga. "A fine creature that, for all he puts me in mind of th' Herder breed."

"I've heard they breed dogs for the Isle," I said.

"An' for th' cloister in Aborium. They are supposed to protect th' cloister, but who in their right mind would want to break into one?" She looked at Darga again with faint unease. "Yet he's a match, though small an' th' wrong shape. Well, th' inn is just a step from here. Ye could follow ye nose when the wind is t'other way, but it blows off today. Ye dinna say who ye were lookin' for."

"A seaman," I stalled.

She cackled. "A seaman? Ha! Well, what else would ye find a man doin' in a seaport? I myself ha' two strappin' sons an' my bondmate Arkold were a seaman too, Lud rest his head."

"The man I'm looking for is called Brydda Llewellyn," I said.

The color drained from the washerwoman's face.

"What is it?" I asked quickly.

She smiled, a horrible false twist of her lips. " 'Tis nought. I were thinkin' somethin' else for a minute. I hardly heard ye. Now. Llewellyn, ye said? I dinna know th' name!"

"She is afraid," Darga sent.

She took me onto the street and pointed the way I had to walk to get to the sea. I felt her eyes boring into my back until I was out of sight.

"What happened?" Darga asked. We were walking quickly now.

"I don't know. One minute we are talking like two sisters, and the next she looks as if I murdered her best friend. And all after I mentioned the name of Katlyn's son."

"He is well known?" Darga suggested.

"I don't know what it means, but I don't like it. Yet I promised to try delivering this message."

The inn was only a few minutes away from Luma's house and set on a side street whose front windows faced the open sea. It was a modest place with a faintly dingy air and peeling paint. Along the front was a stone veranda where men sat in the fading dusk light talking in low voices. Wishing I had reached the inn before dark, I told Darga to wait in the street. "If I don't call or come out within an hour, go back to the others."

"Better not to go in," he sent.

I glanced down at him, wondering what he sensed. "I don't want to, but I promised."

The men on the porch fell silent as I approached. I asked for the manager of the inn in what I hoped was a confident voice. One of the men jerked his head toward the door.

"Thank you," I said, and hurried through.

The reception room was dim and cool. For a moment could see nothing, and blinked trying to accustom my eyes to the dimness.

"What do you want?" asked a sharp voice. I jumped and heard a snicker of laughter. A woman and two men were sitting near the window, silhouetted against the fading pink sunset.

"I . . . A room," I said, losing my nerve. There was a subtle air of menace about them, and I was sorry I didn't have Darga to gauge the emotional state of the room.

"No rooms for moonies," the woman said tensely.

I swallowed dryly. "I . . . I'm also looking for a man. I have a message to deliver."

"What is his name?" the woman asked coldly.

I made myself speak. "Brydda Llewellyn."

A match flared and a lamp was lit on the table illuminating the narrow, ratty face of the manageress and the hard wary faces of the men.

The woman smiled, a folding rather than a curve of thin lips. "Brydda lives at the inn, but he has been on his boat this last moon. He will be here tomorrow morning. I will let you have a room for tonight."

Again the sour smile and, as she rose, dark satin skirts rustled around her feet like a nest of snakes. "Come with me," she commanded, and I dared not refuse. The inn was larger than it looked, and I was filled with unease as she took me downstairs where there were a number of bedrooms. The room she gave me was halfway down a hall, and had a narrow window level with the street. It was sparsely furnished containing a trundle bed with a blanket folded at the foot, and a bedside table with two towels on it.

"This is the only room we have free. I'll send water for you to wash and some supper. Best if you keep to your room. The men who stay here are not used to having women here."

Forcing a smile, I went across and tested the springs of the bed. "It's a while since I've slept in a bed," I said casually. "I don't mind a bit of rest."

"I'll lock the door so you're not disturbed. Ring the bell if you want anything." She nodded smugly and departed.

My own smile fell away the minute the door closed, for I had no doubt I was a prisoner. The moment I tried to leave, the thinly veiled pretence would end. I was almost certain one of the silent men at the table would be lurking outside. But where was Brydda Llewellyn?

I lifted the bench to the window and climbed up to peer out. There was no possibility of getting out that way. I could fiddle locks, but I could not magic myself through the ground. I sent a call to Darga, telling him where to find me.

"Can you get out?" he asked, as soon as he appeared.

"Not through here. I think I can get out, but it might take a while. I want you to go back to the cart and get the others out of the city."

"Why have they locked you up?" Darga asked.

"I don't know, but there's no sign of Brydda Llewellyn." I wondered what Rushton would do in such a situation.

"He would not risk you," Darga sent.

I stared. "What do you mean?" I shook my head. "Look, there's no time for this. You have to be out of the city before the gates are closed for the night."

When he had gone, I felt calmer. I did not want Kella and the others to spend a night in the city after what Katlyn had said about people disappearing in Aborium.

The door lock was a simple device and easily opened. I tampered with the mechanism so the lock would seem to be broken. After a moment of thought, I wrapped a towel round my hair and stuck my head out into the hall. The man outside started up in astonishment at the sight of me. "How ...?"

I interrupted him. "I've rung the bell three times and no one comes. I want some water for a wash," I demanded. Amazement gave way to confusion and then indecision. He had obviously been told to guard the door, but I was not acting like a prisoner. My querulous demand for water and the towel on my hair had confused him, and I sensed him wondering if he had somehow got his instructions muddled.

"Go on then, tell her," I snapped, and shut the door.

Shaking, I listened to his footsteps receding. Then I threw off the towel and slipped back into the hallway. I had barely taken two steps before I heard voices. I dared not go back to the room. Turning, I hurried in the other direction, trying the doors frantically. A locked door meant they were occupied.

My heart leaped as I recognized the manageress's voice. "What do you mean the door was unlocked? I locked it. ..."

The last door was also locked, but I had no choice. If

there were someone in the room I would have to stun them. I bent my mind to the lock, but before I could do anything, the door opened and a young, bearded man looked out. We stared at one another in astonishment, then he reached out and pulled me through the door, shutting it quickly. He made a sign for me to be quiet and we listened intently. I heard the manageress shriek in rage at finding me gone.

"Find her! She can't have gone far. She has a limp. Search the rooms on this level."

The young man turned to look at me. He was not much older than Rushton, and his skin was the clear smooth brown of a seaman. He wore trews, but his wet face and bare chest told me I had caught him in the middle of a wash. On the floor was a big trunk. Either he was about to leave or he had just arrived.

"You are the girl after Brydda Llewellyn?" he asked in a low voice.

I had thought myself beyond surprise after all that had happened, but my mouth dropped open at his words.

"Quick. Answer me. We have only a moment," he said urgently.

I nodded dazed.

There was a loud knock on the next door and I looked at him in a panic.

In two strides he crossed the floor and flung open the trunk. "Get in."

There was a knock at his door. I climbed in the trunk and heard him turning the key slowly.

"Why did you take so long to answer?" It was the manageress. I held my breath in terror.

"I was washing. What's going on?" he asked crossly.

"Ah... well, we have had a girl staying, as a favor to her father who is a seaman. She is subject to manias and brainstorms. For her own safety she was locked in, but she has got away."

"Is she dangerous?" asked my rescuer seriously. Despite my fear I grinned at his anxious tone.

She grunted.

"Well, I heard this was a respectable place, but with all the noise and murdering madwomen running around, I will not be back. Send someone to bring up my trunk."

My heart thumped in fear that she would demand to see what was in the trunk. "Carry your own bag." snapped the manageress rudely. She flounced out, slamming the door behind her. There was silence and some movement, then I felt myself lifted. I slid to the bottom of the trunk, half-suffocated by clothes. I could tell from the movement that he was carrying the chest on his back.

"Don't make a sound," he hissed.

In the hall, I heard enough to chill my blood.

"The Council won't like this," said one voice.

" 'Tis nowt th' Council troubles me but th' priests. They're th' ones he's plagued," said another voice. The two voices faded and I realized we were climbing the stairs.

Suddenly there was another voice. "Ho, Reuvan. Where are ye goin' at this hour?"

"I'm for the sea tonight," said my rescuer.

"Tonight?" There was an edge of surprise in the other's voice.

"The Herders have given permission to my Master," Reuvan said. "But I don't know why he can't wait till a civil hour to set sail."

There were no holes in the trunk and the air was beginning to foul. I felt sweat trickle down my spine.

At last the other laughed. "Better you than me. I'll see you."

"Not here you won't," Reuvan said easily. "It's a damn sight too noisy and that sharp-tongued manageress is no enticement."

The other man laughed and we moved on. Finally I felt

myself being set down, and the distinctive sound of hooves scraping over cobbles told me we were in the street. I felt sick from tension.

The chest jerked and I realized I was in a cart, moving. After an eternity, the latch was undone. "Stay down. It's not safe yet," the seaman whispered softly.

"Why are you helping me?" I asked in a low voice.

There was a pause. "You wanted to talk to Brydda Llewellyn, didn't you? Well, I'm taking you to him."

XVI

Brydda Llewellyn was a giant of a man, towering above the men around him by a head and shoulders. His face, illuminated fitfully in the guttering candlelight, was as stern and craggy as weathered rock.

Reuvan gave me a slight push. "Brydda, here is the girl who asked for you at the inn. I caught her trying to escape the old crow's clutches."

The buzz of talk from the press of men in the room ceased. My heart thumped unevenly under their hostile scrutiny.

"You have taken your time in coming," said Brydda, for all the world as if he had known. "What have you to tell me?"

"You are Brydda Llewellyn?" I demanded. "If you were where you were supposed to be, I would have been quicker."

An astounded silence followed my words, then the giant roared with laughter. "Well, well, so they have sent a kitten that snarls and spits. I could crush you with one hand, sad eyes, but I don't. Let that be a sign of my good faith. Now what is your message?"

I was less intimidated by his threats than reassured by his laughter, for I had seen Katlyn in it. But I was puzzled by his seeming to expect me. "I come from Rangorn. I bring a message from your—"

To my surprise, the smile disappeared and Brydda held up an imperious hand. "Speak no more of that for a moment." He glanced around and silently the men filed out, giving me curious looks. Then, we were alone except for Reuvan, who went to stand by the door.

"Don't be afraid," Brydda said in a softer voice. "I thought you were a different messenger. One that I have been awaiting eagerly. I did not think ... You come from my parents? Are they well?"

I nodded. "They are worried because you haven't written or sent word to them in so long. I think they feared something had happened to you."

Brydda ran a massive hand through the dark, springing curls on his forehead. "So it has. I suppose they told you about me?"

"They said you help Seditioners."

He smiled faintly. "Well, that is as good a way as any of putting it. How did you come to meet my parents? You are not from Rangorn."

"We had an accident and your parents helped us. We offered to bring a message to repay their kindness."

"You are not alone?" Brydda said sharply.

I shook my head, hoping Darga had got the others away. I felt I could trust Brydda, but I did not want us all in his hands. "When I left them they were in an alley not far from the inn."

Brydda started up, a look of concern on his face. "They were in the street? At night? Quickly, Reuvan, go and take some of the others. Bring them back." He turned to me. "What do they look like?"

"A girl, younger than I am, a boy, and a youth," I said.

He nodded and Reuvan hurried away. "It is dangerous at night, though less than usual because of the moon fair. Is there no one full grown among your companions?"

Slightly indignant, I told him we were perfectly able to

look after ourselves. Changing the subject, I asked why I had been locked up at the inn. "Your parents told us to mention your name. I didn't reckon on such an unfriendly reception," I said resentfully. Brydda only laughed and gave me a slap on the back that winded me.

"Much has happened since I last spoke to my parents. I was betrayed by one of my men. The inn was once a place where messages for me could be safely delivered. Now it is watched, and the manageress is under instructions to hold anyone who mentions my name. Once I could go to and from the inn openly, an ordinary seaman, but now I am known to be the notorious Seditioner they call the Black Dog. You are lucky I had friends keeping an eye out at the inn for the messenger I mistook you for. Once the message comes, I will leave Aborium. I dared not send word to my parents because I was afraid of having their connection with me exposed. But I am glad to hear they are safe."

"Those soldierguards at the gate," I said in sudden realization. "It was you they were looking for."

He nodded. "The Council would like to catch me, and so would the Herder Faction. My name has been well advertised, and there is a reward. But I will slip through their fingers like snow during the moon fair."

"They must want you badly to post soldierguards at the gate. What can you have done that makes you so terrible?" I said unthinkingly.

Brydda looked at me for a long moment. "Few would dare ask that question of the Black Dog, for I have a very bloodthirsty reputation, and I would give fewer an answer. But I believe I can trust you. Does it seem strange to you that a man who commands a secret army and plots the downfall of the Herder Faction trusts his instinct over an unknown girl?" He smiled when I did not answer. "I have a kind of infallible knack at judging people."

"Yet you say you were betrayed. . . ."

He nodded grimly. "By a man I loved like a brother. But I did not misjudge him. He was tortured and made to speak, and there will be a payment for that. Come, tell me the truth. Are you not a Seditioner yourself, that my mother should tell you my secrets?"

I stared at him in fright.

"I told you. I have a knack at guessing. But don't look so unnerved. It makes us allies, not enemies," he said.

I nodded, shaken, filled with an odd notion about this uncanny "knack" of his. "My parents were burned by the Council as Seditioners, and my brother was killed by soldierguards," I said.

Brydda nodded triumphantly. "I thought as much, though I think there is more to your story than that. But it is enough to know we fight the same fight. It is my aim to rid this land of the Herder Faction and its tyranny. One day, we will fight them openly, but for now I and my friends oppose them in a thousand small ways. I have many allies who think as I do, and the time is not too distant when we will challenge the Herder Faction openly."

I was filled with excitement for his words were almost identical to Rushton's, except Brydda seemed to think the Herder Faction worse than the Council. "But you said you had been betrayed . . ."

His face darkened. "How you do harp on that. You think I don't know it? But useless revenge is no tribute to my friend's memory. The message I wait for is to ensure there are no Herders waiting for me in Sutrium. I have friends in many places, not just Aborium. It is too dangerous for me here now, so I will go elsewhere and harass them anew. Sutrium. They will not expect me to be so bold."

Reuvan came in, grim faced. He bent and spoke into Brydda's ear.

"What is it?" I asked.

"Your friends are gone," Reuvan said.

I sighed in relief. "They will have gone outside the city when I didn't come back. That was what we planned. Besides, you couldn't possibly have got there and back so quickly."

"There was no need," Reuvan said softly.

Brydda said, "He means they have been taken prisoner. I have friends who let me know who has been taken by the Herders and the soldierguards. It seems your friends were among today's intake."

I shook my head in disbelief.

"Rumor says the boy was a runaway Herder novice," Brydda went on.

"No!" I whispered in horror. "Where have they been taken? Who has them?"

"The Herders," Reuvan said. "They'll have been taken to the cloister cells on the other side of town for interrogation."

"I have to help them," I cried, blaming myself for leaving them alone. And what had happened to Darga?

Reuvan shook his head. "No one escapes the cloister cells. There are priests everywhere and killer dogs. And the place is built like a labyrinth with the prison cells underground."

Brydda scratched his head. "Only a madman would attempt such an impossible rescue."

There was another commotion at the door and a girl dressed in rough trews entered. Weary and travel-stained, she half-staggered into a chair. "You are the messenger?" Brydda asked.

The girl nodded. "Sutrium and all the other branches are safe. It seems he died before they could make him tell any more..."

Brydda's shoulders slumped. "I should be glad..."

I did not wait to hear any further. Taking the chance offered by the momentary confusion, I slipped into the street.

It was dark and very cold. I shivered and wished I had not left my coat on the cart. I had delivered my message, I thought bitterly, but at what cost?

When I had gone a safe distance from Brydda's hovel, I stepped into a darkened doorway and closed my eyes, sending my mind to the other side of the town. My mind played back and forwards, seeking Jik's familiar pattern. It seemed hours before I spotted a dull glimmer at the farthest edge of my reduced lowland range. I sent the probe gratefully.

"Elspeth?" Jik's thoughts were faint.

"Jik, are you in the Herder cloister?" It was a strain communicating at that distance.

"Yes," he sent.

"Are you all together?"

"I'm on my own in a cell underground. I think Kella and Pavo are together somewhere else. Avra is in the stable," Jik sent. I was filled with loneliness and apprehension, but realized Jik was empathizing his own emotions to me.

"What happened?" I asked.

"One of the priests recognized me from Darthnor. I tried to tell them Kella and Pavo didn't know about me, but I don't think they believed me. They want to know how I got here, and how I made it look like I died. They want to know where I've been and if I had help. I'm scared. I think they mean to take me out to the Isle." Jik's terror spilled over into my own mind, and for a moment I saw his nightmarish vision of the interrogation methods awaiting him.

"I won't let that happen. I'm coming," I sent, but the contact had begun to fade.

I found myself slumped in the doorway, gritty water seeping through the knees of my trews. Sweat was freezing on my cheeks and my teeth were chattering violently.

I had meant to try reaching Darga as well, but that would have to wait. I had to get to the cloisters as fast as I could.

The night had grown steadily colder and my stomach echoed with hunger, but there was no time. I had to get Jik away before he was taken to the Herder Isle. Get him away, or turn him into a mindless idiot, a darker voice reminded me. I shuddered and walked faster.

I was certain the scars on my feet were open again, and all Kella's good work undone, by the time I reached the other side of the walled town. It was not hard to tell which building was the cloister. Set apart from the other buildings, it had its own high wall. Branches of trees and leaves visible at the top told me there was a garden inside. I made my way carefully around the perimeter, looking for a weak point. There were two small gates, barred and guarded, and one larger gate open, but heavily guarded. The contact with Jik had left me too depleted to coerce a guard, let alone more than one. Somehow I had to find another way in. I decided I would have to climb over the wall and try to find them.

Leaning against it, trying to gather my energy for the climb, I realized there was someone on the other side: a dog about to bark. I sent a quick greeting, and its urge to bark became curiosity.

"Who/what are you?" It was a dog named Kadarf.

"I am a funaga. I mean no harm. I want to come over the fence and visit a friend," I sent. Forcing back a wave of nausea, I pushed the dog's mind, forcing its acceptance. Fortunately it was not smart like Darga. I climbed the fence with the help of a spindly tree growing up the side. Sitting on the top, I could see the Herder cloister through the trees, a dark, squarish building with few windows and no visible doors.

At the foot of the wall, a muscular, brindle-colored dog watched me slither awkwardly to the ground. He bore a strong resemblance to Darga. I closed my eyes and reached out my mind for Jik. Finding him, I was almost paralyzed by a wave of emphathized terror.

"What is it?"

"Elspeth!" Jik sent. "They're taking me to the Herder Isle tonight."

"I won't let them take you. I'm right outside. Now, how long before they come?"

Jik made a concentrated effort to control his panic. "In ... in an hour, they said. But that was a while ago. Is Darga with you?"

I sent a gentle negative. "I was delayed at the inn and sent him back to the cart, but you must already have been taken. He's a smart dog. Remember when he disappeared in the Druid camp? He'll turn up."

I left Jik for a moment to locate the others. Kella and Pavo were in a cell together, but I could not farseek either of them easily, since both lacked coercive or farseeking abilities. I found Avra in a stable near the perimeter of the grounds.

She responded with relief to my probe, and I realized she had been afraid we would abandon her. She had been unharnessed, but the harness containing the all-important maps had been set near her. Quickly she outlined the arrangement of the stables. I told her Kella and Pavo would come to get her shortly.

Returning to Jik, I was glad to find him calmer. "I've found Kella and Pavo. I'm going to free them first because they're on the top level, then they can free Avra," I sent.

"If the Herders come ..." Jik sent fearfully.

"I'll get back in time," I said.

"Promise you won't let them take me to the Isle," Jik said urgently.

"I promise," I sent, feeling sick at the knowledge that it was a promise I might be unable to keep.

I looked down at Kadarf and probed him to locate a lesser house door.

Following me, Kadarf stretched himself outside the door to wait.

Inside was a short hall branching in two directions. I took the left way, leading to Kella and Pavo, noting the other way would bring me to stairs leading down to Jik's level. Passing numerous closed doors, a slight amplification of my senses was all I needed to warn me if anyone were coming the other way, or about to enter the hall.

I was limping badly by now, but there was no time to rest. Turning warily into another hall, I jumped at the sound of voices, but no one came out.

I could hardly believe I was creeping through a dread Herder cloister. I would not have imagined I would have the courage, but Jik's fear of being taken to the Isle and my own fear of having to erase his mind spurred me on. I did not have the reserve to handle an open coercing if I was seen, but I kept my powers in readiness.

I stopped abruptly, realizing I had found them. A brief straining and the lock clicked. Kella and Pavo looked up, mouths falling open in astonishment.

"There's no time to talk," I said, forestalling their questions. "Jik is about to be taken out to the Herder Isle for questioning. I'll take you to an outer door. There is a dog there who will take you to the stables where Avra is kept. Make sure you get the harness with the maps in it. Avra said you can get out of the stable to an exercise yard. You can get out into the street that way. Leave at once, and get straight out of the city. You might have to bribe the gate man. Head for Murmroth until the lights of Aborium dim. Camp on the beach. I'll find you. Now let's hurry."

"I will slow you down," Pavo said faintly. I was shocked by his ravaged face. He seemed to have aged years in a few hours.

"Help him," I said to Kella brusquely. She looked hurt at my tone, but some of the dazed horror faded from her eyes. Moving back down the hall, I was puzzled to note how awkwardly Pavo moved. Had the disease begun to affect his limbs? I noticed a bloody streak on one ankle and then I understood. He had been questioned.

I felt sick with disgust. I had heard much of Herder interrogation and torture, but I had never been confronted so brutally with the evidence.

For a second, I was overwhelmed by a black tide of hate. This dissolved into fear as my senses told me a priest was approaching. There was no door near enough to offer refuge, and the hall was long and straight with no turnings behind and in front of us. Neither Pavo nor I was capable of running fast enough to go back to the cell before he came round the corner.

Desperation gave me an idea.

"Get close to the wall and don't move, no matter what happens," I whispered. I blew out the candles on either side, throwing a small section of the hall into shadow. Flattened to the wall in the dimness, I mustered my strength.

I could feel my legs shaking as I sent out a fine coercive probe and let it mesh with the priest's mind. The alignment was perfect and, for a time, I simply mirrored his thoughts about the power-hungry manipulations of a fellow priest. Then, gently, I began to exert my own force beneath the conscious level and into the semiconscious region of the mind.

My brother Jes and I had played hide and seek as children, and I had always won when he searched, no matter how bare the boundary we set, because I could make his mind look everywhere but directly at me. Our only hope was that a child's trick would work on the priest.

He came around the corner and Kella hissed in fright. I willed her to be still as he came nearer. It would only work if we were completely motionless. Pushing him fractionally, I made him turn his head absentmindedly to the wall where the candles were extinguished. He passed us, looking steadfastly the wrong way, entirely unaware of us or my subtle coercion. I did not dare release him until he had turned the corner, then I slumped back, exhausted.

"He didn't see us," Kella said incredulously. "How could he not?"

"Quickly," I snapped.

Outside Kadarf agreed to take them to the stables and prevent their harassment by any other dogs. I did not stay to see them go. Time was running out for Jik. Nearly hobbling now, I sent my mind ahead.

To my dismay, he was not alone. There were two priests in the room with him. I was too late!

Agitation made me careless and Jik perceived me. "Elspeth?" his mind cried out in hope. I was filled with remorse at the terrible duty that lay before me. I knew I could not let them take him without a mind lock to stop him betraying Obernewtyn. No matter how brave he was, in the end they would make him talk, even as Brydda's friend had been made to talk. But as I tried to rouse my sluggish thoughts, I knew I had neither the heart nor the strength for such an operation.

I had another idea.

Retracing my steps painfully, I came back into the garden. Kadarf was waiting. He followed me back to the fence and watched me struggle to climb it. "I'm sorry you are going," he sent.

I waved a brief salute then dropped to the path on the other side. The jarring filled my head with stars for a minute. Kella and Pavo were nowhere in sight. I hurried around to the ornate double gate Kadarf said was used for most coming and going among the priests. I prayed they would bring Jik out that way.

I waited, kneeling in the shadows beneath a bush to give my feet a rest. It was some minutes before I saw any sign of life. One of the guards brought a large cart out and harnessed up two white horses. Then a group of priests came out, carrying boxes and parcels. Peering from my hiding place, I saw Jik between them looking small and frightened. My heart ached for him, but I turned my mind resolutely to the horse. My only hope was to create some sort of diversion to give Jik the chance to run.

Suddenly a hand touched my arm. Whirling, I stifled a scream of fright as I looked into Brydda Llewellyn's face.

"How..." I began, only to be interrupted by the sound of horses and a carriage. Frantically I tried to collect my thoughts, but I was too slow. With a cry of despair I saw the carriage draw away and knew I had failed. I had a brief glimpse of Jik sitting upright among the grim-faced priest masters.

Then he was gone.

XVII

I stared down the empty street, knowing I had failed Jik and Obernewtyn.

"Quickly," Brydda said urgently. "We will have to move fast if we are to catch them."

He half dragged me across the street and around a corner, where a grinning Reuvan sat behind the reins of a carriage embossed boldly with the gleaming Herder seal.

"Courtesy of the Herder Faction," he said with a mock bow.

Dazed, I let myself be lifted in behind him. The cart lurched as Brydda climbed in. Reuvan shook the reins, urging the horses on to a wild pace.

"You are hurt?" Brydda shouted over the clatter of hooves on the cobbles. He nodded at my feet.

"Old wounds," I shouted back. "How did you know I was inside?"

"I didn't," Brydda said. "You were gone before I realized, before we could talk of ways and means to rescue your friends. But I knew where you had gone."

"You said helping them was impossible," I protested.

Brydda shook his head. "I said only a madman would

attempt such a rescue. I forgot you did not know me well enough to know that I am just such a man."

I was struck dumb at his words.

"Besides," Brydda said, "you had not meant to come to Aborium, except to deliver my parents' message. Therefore I am the direct cause of your troubles and honor-bound to help you. And if the Herders are so keen to have your friend, I am just as eager to stop them." He grinned. "We were waiting to see you arrive, never dreaming you had already magicked yourself inside. . . ." He hesitated, obviously curious, but I said nothing. "A lad and a girl came out stealthily, leading a horse. They fit the description you gave, so we stopped them. It took us a minute to convince them we were trying to help, and then they told us you were inside and the Herders about to whisk the boy off to the Isle. I sent one of my people to show them a safe way out of the city. I wanted them to take the cart, but I have never seen a pair more attached to a horse."

"I don't know how to thank you. . . ." I began, but again Brydda held up a hand.

"No need for thanks among allies. Now, the Herders will be going to the wharf. The girl said they want to question the boy. . . ." For a moment his face really did look like stone, and I understood that Brydda Llewellyn would be a savage enemy.

"There's no time for subtle planning. I meant to leave the town tonight anyway, so it does not matter if the Herders think I freed the boy. It will madden them trying to understand the connection. Is he really a Herder novice?"

I nodded. "What can we do? There are about five in that cart," I said as Reuvan suddenly reined the horses to a slow walk. I could smell the sea and the sour smell of old seaweed. "We're nearly to the wharf," Reuvan said over his soulder.

"Go softly then," Brydda said. "We can handle five between us, six counting the ship master."

I nodded, praying they would succeed, for I knew I didn't

have the strength to wipe Jik's mind clean of his dangerous knowledge.

The clatter of stones ceased as the wheels ran onto board. We had reached the wharf.

The waning moon shed a feeble light and all was darkness, the smells of oil and spices mingled with sea and fish scales. Moored vessels bobbed in the dark, gurgling water, bumping occasionally into their mooring posts with a dull thud.

"The Herders cast off from there," Brydda whispered, pointing to the very end of the wharf. Lanterns swung from either end of a long slim boat moored there. Illuminated fitfully in the gritty, shifting light was the carriage that had brought Jik. It was empty and there was no sign of him. Priests were moving between the ship and the carriage, transferring boxes to the vessel.

"Why do they travel at night?" I whispered, as Brydda made a sign for Reuvan to draw the carriage into a shadowed corner.

"They are a secretive lot and night suits their fell purposes. Most ships go out at dawn or just before. Folk know the Herders come here at night, and that is enough to discourage anyone else. People who seem too interested in Herder business have a way of disappearing. There's the boy."

Jik was standing between two priests, half obscured by their flapping cloaks. His hands were bound behind him and his shoulders slumped hopelessly.

"Jik," I sent.

His head jerked in surprise, but he subsided when one of the priests gave him a hard look.

"Careful," I warned, and sensed him make an effort to maintain his dejected pose.

"Elspeth," he sent in a powerful wave of gladness that twisted my heart.

"We are at the other end of the wharf in the shadows.

We're going to help you. Be ready to run when you get the chance."

I started and broke contact, feeling Brydda's hand on my arm. "It's no good. There are at least seven priests down there. Some must have come earlier. And there is the ship master. Two of us might barely overcome the lot, and I'd take the risk, but for the dogs. They are trained by the priests to tear a man's throat out on command," Brydda said.

I blinked at him trying to equate the savage picture his words evoked with Kadarf. "But you said... we've got to get him away from them. I...I..." I stopped, gulping back tears.

"It's not possible, lass. You see that, don't you?" Brydda asked.

"You don't understand. He...he can tell them about me, us. About everything."

Brydda shook his head. "Getting ourselves killed or caught won't help the boy or your cause."

I threw caution to the winds. I had no strength left to wipe Jik's mind, so we would have to save him. I could not let him be taken to the Isle.

"Brydda, I am a Misfit," I said.

Brydda sighed. "Ahhh. I thought there was something. And the boy?"

"Listen," I said urgently. "The reason I'm telling you is because I can stop those dogs from attacking. You think— everybody does—that Misfits are only true dreamers and defectives. Useless. But there are other kinds too. Misfits like me and my friends. I can make those dogs do what I want, and I can talk to Jik from here, inside his head. If you can handle the men, I can deal with the dogs."

I could hardly believe myself revealing so much. Reuvan was staring at me as if I had gone mad.

"I'll prove it," I said desperately. "Watch Jik. I'll make him look toward us and nod." I sent a message to an astonished Jik, asking him to respond as obviously as he could, without alerting his guardians. He turned his head slowly and nodded with a faint but obvious wink. Reuvan hissed in astonishment.

"You can hold the dogs?" Brydda asked.

I nodded, hoping they would be as easy to convince as Kadarf. "Help me save Jik. Please."

After a long tense moment, Brydda grinned. "Well, I'm probably finally going mad, but we'll have a go at it. Seven men—we can handle that many between us, eh, Reuvan?"

"Seven men, yes. But those dogs..." he said doubtfully.

Brydda clapped him on the back. "Come, man, you saw the boy. Those dogs will be all bark and no bite."

Reuvan looked at me warily, as if I might bite, but such was the strength of Brydda's personality that he nodded.

"Good lad. Now, Elspeth, tell the boy to run for it as soon as he gets the chance. Don't wait for us. As soon as you have him, get out of the city as fast as you can. There is a gate back near the cloister. Go out that gate and no other. Wait with your friends and I'll find you."

"What about you?"

"I'll worry about me. Make sure you do as I said."

I reached out and touched his arm. "It was a glad day when I first heard the name of Brydda Llewellyn," I said.

He smiled. "Life is an adventure, is it not?"

At a signal from Brydda, they melted into the shadows and began making their way toward the Herder vessel.

I groped about until I found the mind of the ship master. He was in the hold organizing the laying of the cargo. I pinched a nerve experimentally and sensed him groan and double over. I grinned, catching his thought that he must have eaten a bad fish stew.

I tweaked the nerve again, more firmly, and this time he groaned loudly enough to be heard by the priests on shore. They looked at one another. One stepped onto the deck and climbed down into the hold.

Taking advantage of their preoccupation, Brydda and Reuvan attacked with wild cries, brandishing knives. One of the priests standing on the edge of the vessel fell overboard in fright. Another Herder, with stronger nerves, reached down to unloose the dogs he had on leash. Quickly I beastspoke the dogs, asking for help. I had no strength left to coerce more than very slightly, but to my surprise, they agreed to help. I saw that the dogs had no love for their masters, for all their savage training. As soon as they were loose, they began to bark wildly and snarl, jumping and running in circles. The look on the Herders' faces would have been funny if there had not been so much at stake.

Then Reuvan jumped onto the deck, delivered a stout blow to the emerging priest and slammed the hold shut. That left five. One of the priests held onto Jik while the others divided into pairs to attack Brydda and Reuvan. Brydda was more than a match. A blow from his fist and the first priest crumpled at his feet like a wet cloth. The other had drawn a knife and tried to sink it in Brydda's belly, but the big man was agile for all his size, and whirled on his toes like a dancer before dealing a blow with the haft of his sword. He stepped over the unconscious priests and turned around.

Reuvan had dispatched one of his attackers and was busy with the other. Brydda turned menacingly to the priest holding Jik. Calmer than his brothers, he drew a long knife from the folds of his cloak and let go of Jik's arm.

"Run!" I sent.

Jik lurched forward, stumbled, righted himself, and stumbled again, hampered by his bound hands. Panting, he fell again as he reached the cart.

"Quick, get in," I whispered. His nose was bleeding and his breath coming in sobs, but he clambered awkwardly into the cart and fell across my feet. I gathered up the reins. I hated to leave Brydda, but he had struck me as a man used to having his orders obeyed.

Reluctantly, I beastspoke the surprised horse, and we rode away from the wharf.

I was afraid someone would spot us crossing the dark city in the Herder cart, and slung a bag over the side to obscure the insignia. As we drew up to the gate, my heart was thundering, but the gate man barely looked at me before letting us through. There was not a soldierguard in sight.

Incredulous, we found ourselves outside the city.

Sheer relief made us both hoot and laugh like madmen the moment we were out of hearing. I laughed till my stomach hurt and tears rolled down my face.

"Who were those men?" Jik asked, when the laughter had died away.

I sobered quickly. "The big one was Brydda Llewellyn."

I beastspoke the horse again, telling her where we wanted to go, and promising freedom once we arrived. She was a beautiful creature to look at. I was interested to learn that she thought of her masters as jahrahn, the cold ones. She appeared unconcerned at the strange events of the night, and even at leaving the walled city.

It seemed the Herders often rode out at night beyond the city limits to meet with funaga on the seashore. Sometimes they brought men and women and children, bound as Jik was. These were always left behind. Slavers, I thought bleakly.

I thought I saw a faint flicker of fire in the distance. Closer, we could see it was a shore camp, but we were almost on it before I saw a figure jump up and Kella's voice rang out gladly.

After the first excited greetings, Kella introduced me to a tall blond youth called Idris, who cut Jik's bonds and left us to unharness the horses. Jik and I warmed our hands, and related the details of our escape. Kella and Pavo were amazed to hear that I had told Brydda so much.

Pavo, looking pale and fraught, told me their side of the story, meeting Brydda and then leaving the city with Idris. His feet were freshly bandaged, but he refused to talk about what had been done to him, save that they had made no real attempt to make him talk.

Our talk reminded Kella of my feet, and she insisted on looking at them.

The shoes and stockings had to be soaked and cut away from the scars. I was dizzy with pain before a grim-faced Kella had finished her ministrations. Then she looked up, not with the reproof I had expected, but with tears in her eyes.

"I don't know how you walked so far on them, yet . . . if you had not—" She stopped abruptly and hurried down to the sea to wash her instruments.

I looked at the others with faint embarrassment. "Anyone would have done the same."

Pavo smiled wanly. "*Would* do and *have* done are two different things."

I felt my face redden and was glad of the darkness. To turn attention from myself, I asked Idris how he had come to know Brydda.

The boy said his father and two sisters had been taken by the Herders. One night he, the babe of the family, and his mother, had returned from a visit to find their house a charred ruin. Neighbors said the Herders had come and taken the husband and daughters away, but the priests claimed Idris's mother was mad with grief, and that her husband and children must have burned to death in the fires.

Idris had never seen his father or sisters again. He met Brydda after his mother went to the rebel for help. She had died shortly after learning her husband and daughters had been sold to slavers. Brydda had taken the shattered boy in, and though Idris did not say it out loud, it was clear he worshipped the big seaman.

It was near midnight before Brydda and Reuvan found us. They had dealt with the Herders quickly, binding and locking them into their own hold, before setting the ship adrift. Brydda said in casting off he had offered up a fervent prayer that the ship would be seized by slavers. They had gone back to Brydda's hovel for supplies since they would not be returning to Aborium.

Hearing my amazement at the ease of getting out of the city, Brydda grinned and said the real gate man and three soldierguards had been tied up securely and uncomfortably in the watch hut for the night to ease Brydda's departure. All we had to do was wait for a message from the city to tell us how the Herders had reacted, and if it were safe to move.

We were all weary, but Brydda's suggestion that hot food would do us more good than sleep was met with enthusiasm. We deferred serious talk until after we had eaten. "It is bad for the stomach," Brydda said with a comic roll of his eyes. Kella and Idris unpacked and prepared a meal, and Brydda regaled us with stories of his travels on the sea and his adventures as a Seditioner. He made it sound like a game. I suspected he was telling only the brighter side of the tale, but even Pavo laughed at some of his more absurd tales and we sat to eat at last in good spirits.

With shining eyes for his rescuer, Jik asked shyly how Brydda had come to spend his time rescuing people. Brydda said it was a long tale, and refused at first but, finally, when we all pleaded, he agreed to tell his story.

"I traveled to Aborium as a lad to get a trade as a seaman. I lived in the mountains but, like many a boy, the sea called me. While I waited in Aborium for a chance to go to sea, I heard rumors of slavers. I thought them no more than another salty tale at the time, but as I grew and worked the sea vessels, I learnt that there were slave boats which called at our shores. No one said openly how the slavers got their cargo, but it was whispered that the Herders filled their moneybags by selling prisoners and innocent folk they brought in for questioning."

"I pitied those taken, but I thought it was none of my affair and meant to mind my business," Brydda said.

"Then a lad who was the son of my landlord, and very

dear to me, was taken. He had simply been in the wrong place at the wrong time. I had no hope of doing anything, for I did not learn of it till days after, when I came back from a fishing trip.

"I swore then that I would never again stand aside and let some injustice happen, simply because it was none of my business. From that, it was not far to the next step, finding others who thought as I did, and were prepared to fight the Herder Faction.

"And so we have done these long years past, stealing their cargo and silver when we could, disrupting their festivals and plans, rescuing prisoners, and spiriting them away. And we have bided our time."

Brydda looked into my eyes. "You asked once why they wanted me so badly. That is why. They are afraid that if I grow too strong, I will revolt openly, and that people might follow me."

He looked at me speculatively. "If I had a hundred like you, I would dare to try it today."

"Don't you despise me for my deformed mind?" I asked so coolly Kella gasped.

Brydda spat into the flames. "If the Herders are normal, then let me also be called Misfit. As to fearing you, I fear no man——or girl. Even if she can talk to dogs."

Pavo and Kella exchanged a quick look, and Idris looked at Brydda in confusion. I took a deep breath. "Then maybe one day you'll have your wish."

Brydda's eyes flashed. "What do you mean? Your people might fight with me?"

I shook my head. "You go too fast. I'm not the one to decide."

Brydda looked angry, then he laughed aloud. "That's me all over. My mother always said I was like a wild bull at a fence. Yet I think we will one day be allies." His eyes had a familiar faraway look.

I was more than ever convinced Brydda had some sort of Misfit ability, a combination of empathy and futuretelling, just enough to make him an infallible judge of character and a lucky guesser. But if he wanted to think of it as a "knack," past experience told me to say nothing of my theories.

"I have always thought of Misfits as unlucky mutants. Now I see there are Misfits and Misfits," Brydda mused. "Life is too short for all there is in it. A man with his eyes open learns something new every day," he added so ironically we all laughed.

Gradually, the others fell asleep, but Brydda and I stayed up talking far into the night.

His organization was very large and he agreed his was the organization the rumors we heard had indicated. "But I have no people in the high country." He frowned. "You do come from the highlands?"

I nodded.

By comparison, Obernewtyn was very small fry. But Brydda disagreed, saying more like myself might shift the tide of a battle. He was taken aback to discover how young we were, but still believed we could help one another. I agreed to try to organize a meeting between him and Rushton, but I was not sure our aims coincided.

"At the bottom of everything we are Misfits, and few men would have reacted as you did. Can you say for certain all your people would think as you do? Not be disgusted by us, or frightened?"

Brydda looked thoughtful at this. "I don't know. Maybe the thought of someone who could talk inside your head, or make animals do anything they want... would seem frightening."

I had told him little about our abilities, letting him assume he had seen all there was.

"If people are frightened, it is because of their ignorance

and Herder lies about mutations. They could learn," Brydda said at last.

"Maybe, but we have to be sure," I said. "There is no good in our exchanging one kind of tyranny for another."

∽

We had decided it was safer for us all to travel together until we reached Rangorn. Brydda knew we were looking for a Beforetime library, but this interested him less than our hope that we would find an unknown Talented Misfit in the same vicinity.

Brydda asked Pavo where he thought we would find the library. At the mention of ruins, he frowned.

"I don't know about a library, but there are ruins of an old city near here."

Pavo looked excited. "That must be it," he said, then his face fell. "But if it is near and common knowledge, the library is sure to have been found and ransacked."

Brydda shook his head. "No one goes there."

"Why?" Pavo asked in a puzzled tone. "It's not in Blacklands territory. It is not even tainted badlands."

"It is haunted by ghosts of the Beforetime," Reuvan said.

Pavo gaped at him, then burst out laughing. "But there are no such things."

Brydda looked at him without smiling. "So I once thought, but these are real enough. I have seen them."

"And I," Reuvan said with a shudder. "Terrible monstrous faces twisted in mortal agony."

"Ghosts?" Pavo echoed, confounded by their joint evidence. I stared from one to the other, just as astounded.

"Ghosts," Brydda said decisively.

XVIII

In the early hours, a man rode out from the city with news for Brydda. The attack on the Herder ship and the escape of three dangerous Seditioners aided by the notorious Black Dog, Brydda Llewellyn, was the talk of the town. Huge rewards were being offered for information leading to the capture of Brydda, Kella, Jik and Pavo. There was also a reward for a girl seen escaping from custody at the Inn of the Cuttlefish, believed to have been an associate of the Black Dog.

The Herder ship had been found floating aimlessly, empty but for the wounded ship's master. He had described Brydda's attack as ruthless and bloody, claiming thirty cutthroats had descended without warning.

"Now you see where I came by my terrible reputation," Brydda said.

According to the ship's master, the priests had been set adrift by the villainous Black Dog, after freeing an important prisoner, and had been taken by slavers.

Brydda was delighted with the way the Herders had linked the events. "How they will sweat wondering what a Herder novice had to do with the Black Dog," he crowed.

More disturbing was the messenger's report that a search party was combing the town. "It will only be a matter of time before they come on the unguarded north gate and realize you have gotten out. Then they will begin to search the plains," the messenger said grimly.

After the messenger had gone, Brydda said, "They want me badly because I stand as a symbol to all those who, though they don't fight openly against the Herders, wait and long for us to rise."

"For their sakes I can't take the risk of being caught. There are four watch towers in Aborium with a clear view together of the plain from the Blacklands to the great sea. They will be watching for any movement away from the main roads, and all roads will be guarded. We must go at once, while it is dark. I have no desire to go to your ruins, but right now it is probably the safest place."

We packed up the camp quickly. Reuvan and Brydda rode the two horses they had stolen to leave the city, I rode on Avra, and the rest went in the cart with Idris at the rein. Fortunately it was a black, moonless night, but the darkness made it impossible for us to move quickly.

To while away the time, Brydda made me help him devise a method of signaling that would let him communicate directly with the horses. He was intrigued by their intelligence. "I always liked animals better than people," he confided.

Later he asked Jik and myself to demonstrate our abilities. He was amazed to find his emotions swayed by Jik. "Imagine such an ability in battle. He could shatter the nerve of a dozen good men without firing an arrow. He and more like him could mean a nearly bloodless victory."

"It wouldn't be very fair to make brave men act like cowards," Jik said.

Brydda gave him an incredulous look.

Pavo spotted the ruins first.

He had always seemed ageless to me, but now he looked ancient, shrunken with pain; Kella told us the illness raged freely through his frail body. His hair and teeth had begun to fall out, and this made it look as if he were aging at an accelerated pace. Yet he seemed untouched by his outward transformation, in better spirits than anyone, apart from his perplexity over Brydda's ghosts.

We had been riding in silence, each busy with his own thoughts, when Pavo stiffened and pointed.

"There it is," he said, his voice a triumphant sigh.

At first we could see nothing. Then I saw the square shapes of buildings barely distinguishable from the dark night. Up close, they were in far worse condition than the ruinous buildings we had seen under Tor. Here the walls rose only slightly above our heads, the stone cracked and grown over with a weedy beard of green scrub and moss. The faint moonlight gave the buildings an intangible look, as if they were a mirage that might dissolve any second.

We were within two lengths of the first building when Brydda called a halt. "We'd better stop here. The ghosts will rise if we go nearer. I think it will be safe enough. No one would dream of us taking refuge here."

I looked at Pavo's determined face. "Pavo and I will be going in to look for the library. The rest of you may wait here with Brydda, or come as you please," I said.

Idris said he would wait with Brydda, but the rest, even Reuvan, said they would come. We left all the horses except Avra, who would draw the cart to bring back the books we found. Reuvan, Kella, and Jik elected to walk, while Pavo and I rode in the cart. Pavo was holding his precious drawings and maps tightly on his knee. He did not look at them, knowing them by heart, as he had studied and pored over them so often.

"I know where we are now," Pavo said suddenly. From that point on, he directed us. Occasionally he led us to a road that rubble had made impassable, then he would frown and take us another way. Without his guidance, we would never have found the hidden store of books.

I did not believe in ghosts, but the deeper we went into

the dark maze of stone and crumbled walls, the more uneasy I became.

It was clear some disaster had befallen the ruins, for there was far more damage than to other ruins I had seen on the Blacklands fringes. In one place, pale moonlight glimmered on a charred wall, showing the shape of a man running. I did not know what it could mean, but I felt a deep chill in looking at it. Jik stared at it, his eyes bulging.

I began to think of all the stories I had heard of ghosts, how vengeful they were supposed to be when their territory was invaded. If there were ghosts, the ancient ruin would be the perfect place to find them. I wished we had waited until dawn to begin searching.

Though the previous day had been cold, the early morning was icy, and when a faint breeze blew across from the sea, smelling of damp stone, the cold began to seep into my bones.

My apprehension increased with each step, yet there was no overt reason for it other than the strangely compelling atmosphere of the city, as if it were alive and watching us pass. The others were showing signs of disquiet too.

Kella's breath was coming fast, though she was walking quite slowly, and Jik stayed very close to the side of the carriage. I was surprised to see even Pavo looking about himself with a faint distracted frown.

"I'm frightened," Jik said suddenly, his voice quavering in the stony silence.

"So am I," Kella admitted.

"Something is going to happen. Can't you feel it?" Reuvan said, in a voice made flat with suppressed fear.

There was a faint moaning noise and we all froze, staring around nervously.

"What was that?" Kella whispered.

"The ghosts," Jik said in a high, frightened tone.

"The wind," I said, but my voice sounded uncertain. I looked at Pavo.

"I don't understand it," he said. "I am afraid too, but what have I to fear?" He reached out and took up a brush torch and set a flint to it. The flame flickered and blazed, throwing light onto his bony face. "We are not far from the library now. Just down here."

The lane ended in a mass of twisted metal and rubble.

"We'll have to clear this," Pavo said.

I looked at him in dismay. "It will take weeks."

He frowned then climbed out of the cart with an energy that belied his illness. Taking the torch, he began to clamber over the rubble.

"It doesn't matter about the light," Reuvan said gloomily, mistaking my look of concern. "We often see ghost lights moving around the city. No one will come to investigate."

Watching Pavo peering about, then scrambling higher, I found myself unable to believe anything could have survived the devastation that had overtaken the city. Nothing was left but enduring stone weathered with time. Paper was a thousand times more vulnerable. But Pavo seemed undaunted by the look of the city.

My neck prickled and again I had the queer feeling we were being watched.

"I think we should leave while we can," Reuvan whispered. Kella and Jik said nothing, but looked as if they felt the same. With shaking hands, I lit another torch.

"Here!" Pavo shouted, disappearing over the crown of the rubble mound. "The entrance is over here."

I had no desire to go into the dark alley waiting like a toothless mouth. But Pavo was alone and calling for me. The pain in my feet was a welcome distraction from the fear creeping into my veins as I climbed after him. The mound did not extend very far into the alley, and Pavo was kneeling on the ground beyond it, scrabbling in the dirt and muttering to himself.

He looked up excitedly. "This is strange. I understood the lock worked from the outside, but it seems to be locked from the inside. Do you think you can open it? It will be complicated." He described the mechanism, which was so complex I wondered why such a lock would be wanted to protect books which were supposed to have been plentiful.

I looked around, not liking the way the dark seemed to crouch just outside the wavering circle of flame light. Pavo's scratchings had marked out the squarish shape of a door. There was a great deal of earth layered over it, but Pavo assured me it would make no difference. I let my mind feel out the lock until I understood how it worked. It was as much a seal as anything, but somehow, it had been activated from the inside, jamming the mechanism so that it could not be opened except by force. After a long moment, there was a distinct whirring sound. The ground trembled, and a section of earth seemed to drop and slide away into a concealed space, showering dirt onto the metal steps running down from the opening. I had expected the air to smell bad, but it was very dry and cool.

I knelt and peered in. Fear struck at me with the almost physical force of a blow and I fell back, instinctively raising my hands in defense, certain something was about to leap out at me.

"I'll go first," Pavo said impassively.

"Wait," I said.

Climbing back to the top of the mound, I told Reuvan to stay with Avra. Kella and Jik came to help, carrying their own torches.

"Warn us if there is any danger," I sent to Avra.

We descended into the dark with as much joy as if it were our grave, except for Pavo. He went first, fearless. I came next, and behind me, Kella and Jik holding hands. As soon as my head was below ground level, I realized the ground was tainted slightly—enough to prevent me from reaching Avra.

The steps took us down to a long dark corridor.

I was struck by the smooth sameness of all the surfaces. There was no hint of the owner's personality, no feeling that human beings had ever been there. Now that we were inside, my attack of nerves had faded, and I found myself curious about the library. Why would a library be built like a secret fortress?

"What is this place?" Jik whispered.

"Why are you whispering?" Kella whispered. They stared at one another, then exploded in a fit of nervous giggles.

"We believe it was a storage place," Pavo said in a normal voice. "The Oldtimers eventually used machines to store their knowledge, and books became less important, even old fashioned. Luckily for us they never fell completely out of favor. This place was a historical storehouse. Among other things."

I did not like his tone, but before I could ask what he meant, we rounded a bend in the corridor.

Pavo stopped dead ahead of us with a hiss of indrawn breath. I looked over his shoulder and gagged. Kella screamed and Jik looked close to fainting.

"They're dead. They can't hurt you," Pavo said, but he sounded shaken too.

Before us, leaning against the side of the hall, were a number of human skeletons. One was small, the size of a young child. Almost certainly the skeletons of Beforetimers.

"What . . . what happened to them?" Kella whispered.

Pavo sighed. "There was evidence that this storehouse . . . was meant to store more than just books. The Oldtimers actually wrote about the possibility of the Great White which they called First Strike. There were lots of places listed as possible shelters. This place was supposed to be one of them, because it could be completely air sealed. But I guess they locked themselves in, forgetting they wouldn't be able to get out. Or maybe they hoped someone would be alive to let them out."

"They . . . they were hiding?" Kella said, aghast.

Pavo patted her on the arm, and we passed single file and ashen faced.

There were no other unpleasant surprises, although we walked down the corridors leading to the main storage with as much trepidation as if skeletons might wait around every turn. Eventually we came to another series of solid and immovable doors. Pavo showed me the locking mechanism. I rested my hands on the cool metal and worked the lock. Each time a door opened, there was a hiss.

Opening the last door, we found ourselves in a gigantic storage room filled with endless rows of books on shelves reaching high above our heads and running away into the shadows.

For a long time we simply stood there and stared. Even Pavo, who must have anticipated such a find, was struck dumb by the scale of the storehouse. Surely all the knowledge of all the ages of man before the holocaust must be contained in the thousands of books we saw before us.

Then Pavo stepped forward and laid his hand reverently on one of the books. "Just think of it," he said in a voice that trembled with excitement. "We are the first in hundreds of years to come here. The first since the Oldtimers." He gathered himself visibly.

"The books are old and frail. Only the dry air has preserved them so well. Handle them lightly and as little as you can. Look for books on Oldtime machines like the Zebkrahn. Also books showing maps of the old world. The Beforetimers were very orderly. If you find one map book, you will have found all such books. Also books on healing," he said.

"We will take a different section each," he decided. "I'll start here; Kella, you start to the left; Jik to the right, and Elspeth down the other end. Bring anything worth looking at up and lay another book on the ground so you don't forget where it came from."

I padded to the far end of the vault, amazed at how quickly my fears had gone. I was not easily frightened, but there was something about the ancient city that worked on a person's mind. That was probably the real truth behind Brydda and Reuvan's ghosts.

Despite the arrangement of the books, the sheer volume

made it hard to find what he wanted. Though I understood the words, many of the books made no sense to me, being filled with references to things I did not understand. Some of the books I could piece together offered up bizarre notions and ideas.

One book claimed there had once been midget races of various kinds—squat wizened men with huge axes, and tiny men and women with wings. Another book talked of a land where there were men and women taller than skyscrapers. Kella came hurrying down to show me a book she had found showing drawings of men and women with fish tails instead of legs.

I began to feel bewildered. If there had been so many different kinds of races, what had happened to them all?

Jik gave a shout. He had found a book showing wonderfully clear pictures of a Beforetime city. Pavo stopped his sorting to explain that the remarkably lifelike pictures had not been drawn by artists, but were actual images of reality, somehow preserved by a process designed by the Oldtimers.

Jik's book seemed to be composed entirely of such images, showing a number of Beforetime cities in all their glory. Here were the dark towers we had seen in the city under the mountain, but lit by bright lamps, thousands of them. "Cities of light," Kella whispered, awed. One picture showed a square tower soaring high above the others around it, but instead of glass the building appeared to be made of mirrors, each window reflecting the marvelous Oldtime city. Even Pavo admired the sheer beauty of the skyscrapers. It was hard to reconcile the dark, decaying city under Tor, or the rubble above us, with those images.

Jik was the first to find a map, and soon after I came across a section containing books on machines. They meant nothing to me, but Pavo went through them carefully, rejecting this, keeping that.

He waved away the books of half-fish people, saying these derived from a race which had become extinct before men came.

These were fascinating, but we did not have room for such things, he said.

He also decided not to use his valuable space for books about the Oldtime. "The Beforetimers are as extinct as the fish people. We are the future," Pavo said with such unconscious arrogance that I was reminded of something Brydda had said when asked what his allies would make of our abilities.

"I think they might accept for a time, while they helped us to win our war. But in the end, they would come to resent you, and be jealous of your abilities..."

Ranging through the shelves, I began to feel dizzy.

There were hundreds of books on very trivial subjects—books that told how to dress your hair, or make a garment, books on how to set flowers in a jar and even a book showing how to fold paper to make the shapes of animals and flowers. It struck me that the wondrous Oldtimers had possessed a silly trivial side.

There were books on every conceivable—and inconceivable—subject. Books on machines that carried men and women over land, over sea, over water and, even, as Jik had once said, up to the stars. So many books, and the more I read, the more I understood that the old world really had passed away forever. So much had changed and so much knowledge lost that could never be regained. The teknoguilders' fascination with the past suddenly struck me anew as pointless. The future was what really mattered, not the past. And perhaps the past was better lost, if it had led the Beforetimers to the Great White.

"It is such a waste," Pavo lamented, wrapping books in waxed cloth to be carried by Jik to the foot of the stairs. "Now that we have broken the seal, the books will decay quickly. You must tell Garth to send another expedition soon, before they are lost to us." I felt a chill at Pavo's calm acceptance that he would not be there to do the telling.

I was about to turn into another aisle when a title seemed to jump out at me.

Powers of the Mind.

I stared at it as if it had eyes and might stare back. Breathing fast I took it down. I let it fall open where it wanted, then struggled to read the tiny script.

...Every mind possesses innate abilities beyond the five known senses. For most people, these abilities remain hidden and untapped. Sometimes, they are used imperfectly or accidentally, and called hunches, insight, or inspired guesses. Even those who have demonstrated these mental abilities or extrasensory perceptions, are barely touching the edge of the true potential. It would take some immense catalyst to break through the mind's barriers and allow men and women to use and develop that hidden portion of their minds...

I felt hot and faint, for what could it mean but that the Oldtimers had speculated about Misfit abilities? I shivered at the revolutionary idea that the powers we had always imagined to be mutations caused by the Great White might have existed before the holocaust; that they were not mutations, but some natural development of the mind. And as to a catalyst, what was the Great White but a catalyst to end all catalysts?

Excited, I flicked a few more pages and read.

...For time eternal, some men and women have exhibited flashes of future knowledge, and been called fey. But who is to say they are not simply the forerunners of some evolutionary movement, destined to be scapegoats and ridiculed, tormented and even killed for ther strangeness, until the rest of the human race catches up...

My hands were trembling so violently, I could barely read. I bit my lip and read those words again: "*...destined to be scapegoats and ridiculed, tormented and even killed, until the rest of the human race catches up...*"

My eyes flew down the page. Flicking backward and forward feverishly, I found the book mentioned many of the abilities shown by Misfits, and even some I had not encountered, but they made no mention at all of others such as coercing or beastspeaking.

My head ached with the tremendous feeling of having made a discovery that might well change our future. If the Council were to see such a book, they would have to admit Misfits were not mutations. But the Council called such books evil and burned them.

I thought again of Brydda, saying people would come to resent our additional abilities, be jealous of them, uneasy about the advantage they gave us over ordinary unTalented people. And worse, if we and our kind were the future and not some freakish sideline, what were ordinary people but a dying breed?

I shivered and read on more soberly.

> . . . The Reichler Clinic has conducted a progressive and serious examination of mental powers, and has produced infallible proofs that telepathy and precognitive powers are the future for mankind. Reichler's experiments have taken mind powers out of the realms of fantasy and set them firmly in the probable future.

I shivered again, knowing in my deepest heart that the truths contained in the book would not make us more accepted.

"Elspeth?" Jik asked. I started violently, then closed the book with shaking fingers.

"Are you all right?" he asked curiously.

I nodded, slipping the book into my pocket. "What is it?"

"It's Reuvan. Pavo thinks he heard him call out," Jik said.

I bit my lip, cursing the unyielding tainted earth that would not let me reach Avra mentally. Returning to the stairs where Pavo waited, I said, "I'll go up and see what's happening." Climbing up the steps, I poked my head above ground. It was nearly dawn and pink light showed faintly in the east. There was no one in sight, but I sent a query to Avra.

"He has gone," the mare sent perplexedly. "I could not find your mind. The funaga ran away."

"What did he see? What frightened him?" I asked.

"I saw nothing. There was nothing," she sent.

Bewildered, I lifted my torch and climbed out, wondering what could have frightened Reuvan badly enough to have made him desert us.

I opened my mouth to call down the steps, but the words died in my throat. Terror flooded into my mind and the lantern slid from nerveless fingers.

Fear.

My heart pounded and the night was suddenly ice-cold. The air in front of my eyes shimmered and smoked. I came dreamily close to fainting as the smoke coalesced into a face so grotesque and malevolent that some Herder hell must have spawned it.

The spectral face smiled and changed into a creature with smoke spiraling from distended nostrils and an elongated face filled with rows of razor-sharp teeth. The mouth opened.

I felt the hair on my neck and arms stand up.

I screamed then, the footsteps gonging on the metal steps behind me sounding distant. I heard Kella cry out before she fell at my feet in a dead faint. That shook me enough to break my trance, and I called Jik and Pavo. I dashed the books from Pavo's arms and half dragged him out. He stared at the smoky creature in astonished wonder.

"Ghosts ..." Jik moaned.

I slapped him hard and made him help me lift Kella. We had to get out of the city. That was the only object in my mind.

Suddenly, I heard a savage growling from somewhere near. Abruptly and unexpectedly the smoky demon vanished and, with it, my terror.

Then I heard a high-pitched scream.

"What is it?" Pavo asked.

Jik started forward, his face transformed. "That growling. It was Darga."

I thought fear had deranged him, but there was more barking, and this time I recognized Darga. But where had he come from? And who had screamed? And where had the demon ghost gone? Something very odd was happening. I sent out a probe and immediately encountered Darga.

"There you are," he sent imperturbably. "Come to me."

Startled, I told the others to wait and picked my way over the rubble, tracing his probe onto the second story of a building fronting on the alley. Peering through a window, the fluttering torch light lit up a dangerously holed floor. In one corner, a growling Darga held a thin, ragged figure at bay.

I was beside him before I realized it was a girl cowed against the wall, her skin as black as if she had rolled wet in the mud. To my amazement she growled and bared her teeth at the sight of me.

All at once fear assaulted me. Darga growled and the fear vanished.

I stared at the girl in wonder. "*She's* doing it."

"I came looking for you when I could not find the others," Darga sent. "I learnt from a dog that you had been seen leaving the city. I followed your scent here. Then I saw the child-funaga's mind making you see things. I scented her out and frightened her to break hergrip on yourmind. She does not know how to speak to mymind, so she can not make me afraid."

I stared at the filthy urchin. She snarled, pressing herself deeper into the corner.

"She is near wild," Darga sent.

I looked at the girl. "Well," I said aloud in a gentle voice, "if you are wild, then I will have to tame you." I backed away, telling Darga to follow. The girl watched us withdraw suspiciously, then ran forward and slithered down a hole in the floor, swift as a snake.

I reached out, but could find no trace of her mind.

Returning to the others there was a joyous reunion between Jik and Darga. The others were astonished and relieved that the demon we had seen was no more than a vision. Pavo was all for returning to the library, but I decided we had better find Reuvan and Brydda.

"It's been a long night. Plenty of time to go through the books. We'll have to stay until I can tame our wild girl."

We found Reuvan unconscious, having run into a jutting piece of stone in the darkness. Brydda was fascinated to hear about the girl's ability to create fear visions. Though still wary, he had agreed to come into the city. But hearing about my encounter with the girl, he was sceptical about my being able to tame her quickly enough.

"If she really is wild, you won't have enough time," Brydda said. "You might as well give up."

I shook my head wearily. "I can't. I have to win her trust."

"Why?" Brydda asked. "What does it matter?"

I looked at him. "Don't you understand? I have to make contact because *she* is the one I came to find. She's one of us, and I have a feeling she needs us as much as we need her."

XIX

We called her Dragon, after one of the pictures I had seen in the library.

After two days sorting, Pavo had nearly completed his collection.

Brydda had refused to go underground despite the lack of ghosts. "Soon enough for going under the ground when I am dead," he said. He spent the days watching patrols of soldier-guards combing the plains, and making sure there was no interest shown in the ruined city. It was an irony in a way, that Dragon had kept the library safe, guarding it with her powers.

Each night I had set food out on a mound hoping to make her understand I meant no harm. We had set up a comfortable camp inside the roofless shell of a building with a clear view of Aborium. But though the food had been gone each morning, we did not catch sight of her. Sometimes I sensed her watching us, but could not reach her. After a few initial attempts to instill her particular brand of fear into one or another of us, and being fended off by me, she had given up trying to frighten us away.

The third night fell, and I was silent and preoccupied with thoughts of the ragged urchin girl. Kella was trying to force Pavo to set his notes aside and eat. Finally losing her temper, she shouted at him.

"You'll be dead before you have the chance to get your precious books out of their hole in the ground, if you don't eat."

She broke off, looking horrified at herself. Pavo burst out laughing. "Kella, what would I do without you? All right."

We all laughed at the martyred expression he gave the flushed healer. "I wonder what sort of powers could create those visions and the fear?" Pavo said.

I frowned. "Coercing and . . . maybe empathy, though they are an unusual combination."

Kella gave me a quick look. "It's more than coercing. Domick can't make things appear in the air."

I shook my head. "I'm not so sure they did appear. Remember when I told you the second face she made looked like that lizard creature I saw on the edge of the map where it said 'Here be dragons'? The more I think of it the more sure I am that it was exactly the same face. And the first face was nothing more than a distorted human face. I think she read those things out of my mind, and somehow projected them into all our minds, just the way Angina does with Miky."

Brydda yawned. "I saw no patrols today. I think they have moved the search to Port Oran or Morganna. I don't think they'll bother with Murmroth or Rangorn. As soon as you've finished with the books, we can leave."

Pavo nodded absently. "I feel as if I could never be finished, but I'll have as much as we can carry safely by tomorrow."

No one looked at me, but I knew they were thinking of Dragon.

Time was running out, yet I seemed no closer to reaching the girl than when I had begun. I went out to the mound, set down a pot of stew, and sat down to wait, determined to make some sort of contact. Hours passed and I was beginning to drift off to sleep, when I heard a faint sound.

Snapping wide awake, I sensed her trying to drive me off. Frustrated and baffled, she paced outside the light like a hungry wild cat. Her mind was strong but untrained, and under all the dirt and savagery, I suspected she was little more than a child. This last thought prompted me to act.

"Hello?" I called softly. The wind hissed in scorn, but there was no answer. I took up the pot of stew and held it out.

Still no answer, but instinct told me she was watching. I sighed, feeling suddenly defeated.

Then I heard a movement and she was there, the half-moon shedding a wan light on her grubby face. I was careful not to make any sudden movements as she crept forward, never taking her eyes from mine. She reached out abruptly and snatched the pot from my hands, turned, and ran into the night.

I sighed heavily and went back to the campfire. Reuvan had sought to comfort me earlier, saying he thought sheer curiosity would make Dragon follow us when we left. That and our food offerings. I was not so certain, but we had no more time to spare.

~

That night, we left the city after concealing the entrance to the library under rubble. If Dragon did follow, the city would have lost its guardian. Brydda had wanted to burn the remaining books to keep them from falling into the hands of the Herder Faction. We compromised by setting a fire trap that would destroy the library if it were disturbed.

There was no sign of Dragon as we left, but I sensed her eyes watching us from some dark corner of her lonely city.

I sent out a broadspan beckoning call, but there was no response.

We had chosen to leave at night to avoid being spotted by the men in the watchtowers, and to ensure we reached tree cover before daylight. We meant to travel along the same trail we had used coming to Aborium.

"Stopping here so long and then going to Rangorn is the

least likely thing for me to have done, and therefore the safest," Brydda said. "The soldierguards will think I have developed magic powers along with my other infamous talents."

Pavo, Jik, Kella, and I traveled in the cart with the books, and the others rode. Brydda had become adept at communicating with the animals and spent more time conversing with them than with his human companions. Pavo slept, the energy of the last days having deserted him as soon as we left the city. He lay back against his precious books looking gray and exhausted.

We were all tired, but had decided to go as far as we could before night fell.

Huge flies plagued us and the heat of the day made me long for the cool of the mountains. I consoled myself by thinking it was good for my feet, which had begun to heal again.

I felt weary when we stopped at dusk the next day. The others talked and sparred while setting up the camp and nightmeal, but I could not help thinking of Dragon and wondering if she would go on as she had before our departure. I had given up hope of her following us and wondered if Maryon's prediction meant that all aims of the expedition had to be achieved to avoid whatever disaster she foresaw. If so, then everything we had done was for nothing, because I had failed to bring Dragon back.

Remembering how she had cowered back against the wall, I was filled with pity and self-reproach for having failed to reach her. Depressed, I went to bathe in a stream not far from camp. Brydda did not like the idea of me going alone and made me have Darga along.

The air had a misty mauve tone and, in the west, streaks of dusky sunset ran across the horizon.

Darga's mind broke abruptly into my thoughts. "She follows."

My heart leaped, understanding instantly whom he meant. "Where?"

"Behind the trees," he sent.

I forced myself to walk naturally until I got to the stream. Darga sniffed the water and pronounced it clean. Stretching himself out on the bank, he pretended to sleep. I stripped off my clothes and slid into the icy water with a gasp of delight. Rubbing sand against my grubby skin, I reveled in the coolness, but only half of me was enjoying the bath. The other half was searching for the slightest evidence of Dragon's presence. I was forced to concede that without Darga I would not have known she was there.

I took up a handful of sand and rubbed it against my scalp until the tangled mass of my hair felt clean, then I ducked under to wash out the sand. Floating beneath the surface and holding my breath, I opened my eyes and looked up.

To my astonishment, Dragon was leaning over the stream, staring with gape-mouthed terror into the water. Gasping and spluttering I bobbed to the surface. She sprang back and gently I fended off her visions and the waves of fright she was generating. I reached for her mind but again was unable to penetrate her shield.

"It's all right," I said softly, realizing she thought I had been drowning. "I'm Elspeth," I said slowly, extending a dripping hand.

She cringed away, but I was not sure if she feared my touch or the water.

"She fears water," Darga sent. Dragon looked at him uneasily, though he had not stirred. I gathered up my towel and dried slowly.

I looked up to find her looking at my naked limbs with a hint of bafflement. I stood very still as she reached out one blackened finger and touched my pale belly. Her finger left a dirty smear and she stared at it, frowning.

Very slowly, I reached out a wet finger and touched her bare stomach. An anonymous rag twisted around her body exposed most of her skin, but rag and skin were indistinguishable, merged together in uniform gray. She suffered my touch, then looked amazed at the clean mark my finger had made. She gazed from the dirty mark on my stomach to the white mark on her own flesh, as if our skins had rubbed off on one another.

"Elspeth," I said, pointing to myself. I bent down to put my clothes on. My trews were worn to shreds, but Kella had given me an old skirt and underskirt to put on.

I thought Dragon looked wistful as I pulled the skirt on and, impulsively, I held out the blue underskirt. Eyes shining she reached out, then froze, mistrust clouding her expression. I did not move and, finally, she reached out and grasped it, folding it into her arms and stroking it as if it were an animal. I went on dressing, pulling on Kella's darned stockings, my shoes, and a cloak.

"Esspess?" she said suddenly, in a rusty whisper.

I gaped, for I had begun to be certain she was mute. I had even thought this might be why she had been abandoned.

I pointed to myself. "Elspeth," I said distinctly. "Elspeth." Then I pointed to her.

"Elspess," she said obligingly. I grinned, wondering if my name were the only word she would say. I pointed to myself again. "Els-peth." I pointed to her. "Dragon . . . Dra-gon." Later when she could talk, she could choose a more suitable name.

She frowned. "Drang-om."

I nodded. She pointed to me. "Elspess." She pointed to herself. "Drangon."

"Close enough," I said. "Food?" I asked, rising slowly. Alarm flared in her eyes. I mimicked eating, and hunger replaced the fright.

Summoning Darga and warning him to move slowly, we made our way back to the camp. Whenever Dragon stopped, I would mimic eating. I sent a probe to Jik, telling him to warn the others not to do anything to frighten her.

Approaching the light of the fire glimmering through the trees, Dragon hesitated. I had to coax her the last few steps with exaggerated mimicry of how delicious the food would be. When we were close enough to smell Kella's stew, she sniffed at the savory odor like a hungry animal. The others were sitting very still around the fire, fascinated, for this was the first time they had seen her. To my surprise, she barely looked at them. Her eyes darted about hungrily. Kella had set a pot beside the large pot, and I took this up and held it out to Dragon.

The firelight showed her as an emaciated scarecrow with a mop of filthy hair, clutching the blue underskirt to her chest.

Reaching out to take the pot, she squatted unceremoniously and plunged her filthy fingers into the pot, scooping the stew to her mouth with ravenous dexterity.

Kella grimaced and wondered aloud softly, whether she had not already poisoned herself with dirt. I was filled with compassion rather than revolted. I had never imagined that the Talent I had come so far to find would be a half-wild savage who could barely speak. I had imagined a calm discussion ending in an offer of a home.

No one spoke while she ate, with much lip smacking and slurping, and when she was finished she licked out the pot, sighed gustily, and sat back on her haunches.

"Well," Kella said faintly. Dragon's lambent eyes turned to her.

"Meet Dragon, our newest recruit," I said with a broad smile.

For the rest of the night Dragon sat close by my feet, listening to us talk as if to exotic music. She had the disconcerting habit of staring fixedly at first one then another of us, as if she were trying to memorize our faces. She would not allow any of the others to come near her, but eventually fell asleep against my knees.

The next morning we left early hoping to make Rangorn by nightfall. We had expected to be able to move more quickly now that Dragon had joined us, but she refused completely to ride in the cart or on horseback, and loped alongside us, seemingly tireless.

Brydda grew more silent as the day wore on, and seemed increasingly preoccupied. Finally I asked him if anything were wrong.

"I don't know," he said. "I feel uneasy about my parents. And we're moving so slowly." He looked down at Dragon with mingled pity and frustration.

"Why don't you go ahead?" I suggested. "We can't be more than a few hours away at a fast gallop."

Brydda bit his lip and looked thoughtful. "I think I will. Reuvan can come with me." Thinking of his "knack," I wondered what he feared.

The triumphant mood of the day occasioned by Dragon's presence evaporated with Brydda's departure. He told us to wait at the Ford until he returned to tell us the way was clear. He refused to say what he was afraid of, but his elaborate precautions only served to heighten my apprehension.

As if to mirror my thoughts, a heavy, dark bank of cloud looming on the horizon billowed in to veil the sun near the end of the day, and we reached the Ford just as a light rain began to fall.

There was no sign of Brydda or Reuvan, so we decided to make camp behind a copse of trees within sight of the Ford. It proved nearly impossible to light a fire with the damp wood, but finally we managed and sat around it shivering in the chilly wind. No one felt like talking. Pavo was nearly blue with cold, though Kella said this was a symptom of the rotting sickness.

Dragon had reacted to the sight of the Suggredoon with real terror, and it had taken all my strength to reassure her. I was afraid she would run off and be lost. Her reaction to the river and to my submersion seemed to indicate something had happened to her connected with water, but I could not penetrate her mind, and she was unable to explain, only clutching at me in mute plea. In the end, I found myself patting her as I would pet Maruman.

"At least she doesn't stink," Jik said earnestly when we

wondered what might have caused her fear of water. We laughed, but oddly this was true. She smelled like rich, dark dirt after rain.

She had not used her remarkable illusory powers since joining us. I hoped she would not tame to the extent of forgetting them altogether. I was trying to persuade her to drop her shield, when I heard the drumming of hooves in the distance.

We all stood, the underlying fears that had gnawed at us since Brydda's departure showing clearly in our faces.

There was one rider, coming fast. Idris gave a shout of joy, as he recognized Brydda's horse, then he fell silent, seeing the rider was Grufyyd, whose face he did not know. Reining the horse in, Grufyyd looked pale and there were dark shadows in his eyes. After a brief greeting, he urged us to pack up quickly and come with him to the cottage.

The serious note in his voice warned me something was badly wrong.

"Brydda?" Idris began worriedly.

"My son is fine," he said, then once again urged us to make haste.

As we forded the Suggredoon and traveled the road bypassing the village, he said, "The soldierguards have been here. Luck kept you from coming sooner. They only left yesterday. If you had come before, they would have taken us all."

"They were looking for Brydda?" I said. But Grufyyd shook his head.

"They said they were looking for Seditioners. Halfbreed gypsies," he added significantly.

I stared. "But how could anyone know we were gypsies! The disguise was gone before we reached the lowlands. Unless . . . unless somehow the Druid's friend on the Council tipped them off." I chewed my lip. "That means they must think we reached the lowlands. I am certain he believed we were gypsies, so why these elaborate precautions for a few rag-tag halfbreeds?"

"Perhaps they no longer believe that," Gruffyd said. "One

of the soldierguards said the gypsy attire might be a disguise."

Uneasily I remembered the look of anger and frustration on Saul's face. He had not liked Gilaine revealing so much to us. Perhaps he had somehow warned the Druid, who had in turn warned his friend, both wanting us dead for different reasons. If the Druid thought we had lied about being gypsies, then he might also wonder at what I had said of Obernewtyn. Suddenly I was frightened.

Katlyn met us at the door of the cottage with smiles and talk of a hot meal and warm beds. Despite everything it was the happiest gathering I had been to since leaving Obernewtyn, the one sad note being Pavo's obvious deterioration.

Wrapped in a blanket and shivering from a chill no fire could abate, he was clearly in great pain. His neck and arms were covered in bruises, another symptom of tissue degeneration. The slightest bump left a livid mark on his skin. Katlyn had done her best for him, feeding him decoctions to numb the pain, but they were only temporary measures, for Pavo was dying.

This knowledge added an unspoken bittersweet note to the celebration, for it seemed to underline the precarious nature of all our lives and hopes.

"He is content," Darga sent from where he lay on the hearth. "He is not afraid to die."

After we had eaten, Katlyn managed to do what we had failed, and persuaded Dragon to wash.

Jik, Idris, and Reuvan went off with Grufyyd to organize sleeping quarters in the barn, and Kella went to sort out blankets.

I was glad to find myself alone with Brydda, having had no chance to question him about the soldierguards. As if by agreement, nothing more had been said of it.

His first words took my breath away. "I don't suppose you come from Obernewtyn?"

I gaped at him.

He nodded. "It was a thought I had earlier, for I guessed you weren't quite telling the truth when you said you came from the highlands. Then my father said one of the soldierguards had mentioned Obernewtyn, and everything came together. The soldierguards were here looking for Seditioners possibly disguised as gypsies, and they asked about Obernewtyn. I heard the place was burnt out by a firestorm."

"A lie to keep people away," I said, realizing there was no point in further lies. "Do your parents know?"

"I don't think so. My father only spoke of it in passing as a curiosity. But I would not panic just the same. Perhaps the soldierguards were told to mention it to see if there was any reaction. I don't think they knew anything for sure. How could they?"

"They couldn't have managed to connect us and Obernewtyn . . . unless the Druid is mixed up in it."

"You think the Druid has got his friend to send out soldierguards?" Brydda asked. I had told him earlier what had happened in the Druid camp.

I nodded. "I told them I had seen Obernewtyn burned out, but if he has guessed we were not real gypsies, he might question it. I must warn Rushton."

Brydda nodded. "It might be safer for you all to leave Obernewtyn. Especially if an investigation is going to expose the lie about the firestorm. If you ever need refuge, I would be happy to have your people join me."

"Rushton will have to decide that," I said.

Idris opened the door and asked Brydda to help shift the books from the cart into the shed because it had begun to rain again. Left alone except for Pavo, I tried to imagine how it would be to leave Obernewtyn. I could not bear to think of it. I looked at Pavo and felt a pang of sorrow at the thought that he would never see Obernewtyn again.

Seeming to read my mind, his eyes fluttered open. "Don't be sad for me, Elspeth." His voice was barely audible. Even talking exhausted his meager reserves. "I have lived free in a world where freedom is rare. I have pursued work I love. I have learned much and I have had good friends and perilous adventures. What man who lives three times my span can say as much?"

I blinked hard and found I could say nothing without crying. I was glad to see everyone troop back in laughing and talking. Kella called out that she was warming some fement. This prompted Brydda to sing a rollicking song about a drunken seaman. In the midst of uproarious laughter, the door opened and Katlyn entered with a stranger.

The room fell into an astounded silence. The unknown girl was slender as a willow wand with creamy pale skin and a flame-coloured mop of curls. But the most startling thing of all was the girl's extraordinary beauty.

Slowly it dawned on us who we were looking at.

It was Dragon.

"I don't believe it!" Jik gasped.

I was stunned. Who would have suspected what lay under the dirt? Even clad in a rough hessian shift, she was fair. And her hair! I had never seen hair that color—like gold and flames entwined. Later Katlyn told me it had broken her heart to cut it, but it had been so matted and fused with dirt, she had no choice.

Dragon's eyes, blue as the summer sky, flickered round uneasily.

"Don't stare at her. She doesn't understand," I said softly.

Though unable to stop looking, the others sank into more natural poses. Beaming with pleasure, Katlyn ushered Dragon around to my side. Reaching out, I tugged at one springing fiery curl.

Dragon took the strand of her hair and pulled it round to her eyes, then she let it loose and promptly lifted the shift to show the blue underskirt I had given her.

Reuvan burst out laughing. She looked up at him startled,

and bared her teeth. That broke the spell woven by her dramatic transformation. "She may be a girl," Reuvan said, "but she is still dragon-natured and had better keep her name as a warning to anyone who might think otherwise."

Brydda patted his mother's shoulder. "Well, I always knew you were a witch."

Even Pavo smiled at this absurdity.

Over steaming mugs of fement, we talked of ways and means to get to our various destinations. I told Katlyn and Grufyyd the whole story of Obernewtyn, deciding they knew so much already, it was better to take them into our confidence. If Obernewtyn were under investigation, we would have to leave it anyway, and if not, I had an idea that Katlyn and Grufyyd would be a great deal more content in the mountains than in Sutrium. Besides, like Brydda, I felt we would be allies.

Our only chance of reaching the highlands before winter set in was to take the same path as Brydda planned, fording the Suggredoon, round Berryn Mor, to avoid Sutrium and along the main road, since the soldierguards would have returned to their camps. My one concern was our dwindling hope of reaching Obernewtyn before the pass froze. Even without the inevitable delays, it would be a trip of many days.

"If only the Olden pass had not been poisonous," I sighed.

"Poisonous . . . ?" Brydda began.

Suddenly Darga growled and Dragon jumped to her feet.

"What is it?" I said, but Brydda hissed. In the silence we could hear a horse galloping fast toward the house.

A lone rider could not mean soldierguards, but who would come out so late in a cold wet night? There was nothing to do but wait, and there were enough of us to deal with one soldierguard, so we waited calmly, listening to the horse approach and its rider dismount. There were steps on the porch and the door was flung open.

"Domick!" cried Kella starting to her feet. For a moment Domick stared at her, then he strode into the room.

"Thank Lud you're here. You must leave here tonight, all of you," he said.

"What is it?" Brydda asked sharply, rising to tower over the coercer. Domick's face changed as he noticed Idris, Reuvan, and Dragon.

"It's all right, Domick. They're friends," I said quickly. "They know about us and Obernewtyn."

The coercer looked less disapproving than I expected. He glanced at Brydda speculatively. "I guess you are Brydda Llewellyn, better known as the notorious Black Dog. It is good to meet a man whose name I have heard so many times as a force that opposes the Council."

Brydda met this with a curious look. Domick sighed. "It's a long story. Too long for now, but I'll give you the meat of it. Why you have to get away from here tonight, and how I have heard Brydda's name so many times, are part of the same tale, so I'll start at the beginning."

He threw off his dripping oilcoat. "I first heard the name of Brydda Llewellyn here, but I heard it again before I had even crossed on the ferry. Soldierguards were watching the ferry, looking for you. I overheard them saying Brydda Llewellyn's network of Seditioners had been exposed and he was on the run. I wanted to come after you, Elspeth, to warn you, but I knew I would be too late to get to you before you got to Aborium." An expression of such indecision crossed his face that I realized what a struggle it had been for him to go on to Sutrium.

"The first thing I noticed about Sutrium was the number of Herders about. They seemed to outnumber Councilmen, and there was a definite feeling of fear whenever they were around.

"I mingled with people wherever there were crowds. I had the feeling I was safer in that way. I let people understand I was a trading Jack until my cart had been burned in a firestorm. That explained my ignorance about customs lowlanders take for granted. And it let me ask questions. I spent handfuls of silver trying to loosen men's tongues with fement. I knew I had to get close to the Council, but I couldn't think how.

"Then one night in a drink hall, I heard two men talking about a third man who was to take up a job at the Council. They were laughing and warning their friend that his new job was dangerous and risky. The third man was beside himself with fear by the time they left. I got into conversation with him by offering him a mug and learned that he had come from the highlands to work in Sutrium. He had been recommended by a Herder, and though he neither wanted nor liked the idea of going to Sutrium, he dared not refuse. In the end, I managed to persuade him to let me take the job." Domick flicked a look at me which told me what sort of persuasion he had used. "I turned up in his place, and was accepted at once, since they were expecting someone from the high country."

"At first I heard nothing useful. It was a menial job and I began to think I would have been better off applying to be a soldierguard. Then I realized I could not have found a better way to spy on the Councilmen. Once my face was familiar, it was as if I were nothing more than a broom or mop, and they talked quite freely in front of me."

"I heard them talk of a sweeping investigation of the Highlands planned next year to flush out traitors and Seditioners, and I heard enough to make me certain the Council knows the Druid is alive. I heard much talk about the Black Dog and his efforts to undermine authority and plunge the Land back into chaos. They think of you as a terrible threat, Brydda, and hunger to get hold of you. They were expecting news of your capture from Aborium, but I guess it was bad news." He grinned at Brydda.

Domick paused to drink thirstily from a mug Katlyn had given him.

"What about the Druid's friend? Did you see him?" Kella asked.

Domick looked grim. "Almost from the first day, I heard

talk of a special agent who worked for both the Herder Faction and the Council getting information to help expose Seditioners. It was he who masterminded the capture of the man who betrayed your network, Brydda. And he who made him talk when no one else was able. The agent was said to be brilliant and completely ruthless."

"Then you heard no talk of Obernewtyn?" I mused, wondering how the soldierguard had come to mention it. Unless the Council did suspect Rushton of their own accord.

Domick shook his head. "I had heard no mention of Obernewtyn—until two days ago. I overheard a conversation between two Councilmen about this special agent and his certainty that something was going on at Obernewtyn. One Councilman said he didn't think there was anything in it, and the other reminded him that the agent had seldom led them wrong. I became certain then that this special agent and the Druid's friend were the same person."

"The Druid must have decided he wanted Obernewtyn investigated after our escape," I said, regretting mentioning Obernewtyn to the Druid. "It must have made him suspicious."

But Domick frowned. "That's what I thought at first, because what other reason would this agent have for wanting Obernewtyn investigated?" He looked so stern, I felt suddenly frightened of what he was about to say.

"I never saw the agent," he went on slowly. "Though I often heard him spoken of. And I never heard any name mentioned. It made sense for such a man to prefer his face and name to be secret, but I was curious. Someone told me he only came very late at night to make reports, so I managed to get myself put on to night duty. Twice I was able to catch glimpses of him, but he always wore a hooded cloak that concealed his face. I ought to have left once I heard them talk of Obernewtyn, but my curiosity got the better of me."

"One night I heard him talking, and I had the strangest feeling I had heard his voice somewhere before. That made me more determined to see what he looked like. The next night he was to make a report, I hid in a cupboard in the meeting room. I saw him come in through a crack in the door, but he kept his hood on all the while he talked. I could not see his face, but I could hear him clearly."

"He told the Council the man he tortured for information about Brydda had said he thought Brydda had family in Rangorn. A mother and father. Apparently he had overheard that because it was thought Brydda Llewellyn was an escaped orphan. The agent said he had sent soldierguards to the area and their report showed only one couple fitting the description. He wanted Council permission to bring them in for interrogation. This would ensure the capture of the Black Dog."

"The Council voted to send a troop of guards to Rangorn. They are on their way here now."

Brydda's face was pale and tense. "I did not know anyone knew—he must have seen or overheard something. Poor Bom."

I said nothing. There was something in Domick's manner that warned me the story was not finished.

"I nearly died when I heard them talk of coming here. I knew they would catch Katlyn and Grufyyd, and possibly you too. I didn't know Brydda would be here as well."

"I was desperate to get away to warn you, but I had to wait until the room was empty. At last the meeting ended and all the Councilmen left but the main one. Only then did the agent take off his hood, and I saw his face."

"You . . . you recognized him?" Kella breathed.

Domick nodded.

"Ariel," he said. "It was Ariel."

Part III

The Ken

XX

It was too risky to try for Sutrium with the soldierguards on their way, so we headed toward the mountains where we would hide until the danger was past. No one would guess we would deliberately trap ourselves in a cul de sac.

"The soldierguards aren't subtle enough to suspect we would do anything other than the obvious," Brydda said. "When they don't find us here, they'll think we have escaped by going around Berryn Mor because that's what they would do in our place."

Brydda knew of a place where we could make a safe camp at the foot of Tor where a thick copse of trees concealed a narrow valley running into the foot of the hills. From the other side no one would suspect the trees continued for more than a few steps before reaching the steep mountain side. Brydda had played there as a boy and remembered it well despite his long absence.

Jolting through the darkness, and chilled by a damp, blustery wind, I thought bitterly of Domick's news. Obernewtyn was in danger. We were in danger. With Ariel to force the pace, I had no doubt the soldierguards would appear in spring directly after the thaw. Ariel, of all people, would know that Obernewtyn was at its most vulnerable then. If we failed to get back in time to warn Rushton, Obernewtyn would be completely unprepared, defenseless against the soldierguard onslaught.

But it was a matter of days, perhaps a quarter moon, before the pass would be snowed shut. Domick must have known, when he came to us, that he was losing the last chance of warning Obernewtyn. But if he had not delayed and ridden to warn us, the soldierguards would have taken us all.

I could not imagine how Ariel had survived and what course had brought him to the Council. After initial disbelief, we realized he must have found a way through the mountains to the highlands and, there, stumbled on the Druid camp. His beauty would have endeared him to the exiled Herder, with his fanatical desire for perfection, but how had he risen to such heights in Council esteem? And what was his interest in Obernewtyn?

Ariel had hated Rushton when he was the overseer. I tried to imagine his reaction at learning Rushton had legal claim to Obernewtyn. How it must have galled him.

Ariel must have persuaded the old Druid to let him go to Sutrium. To begin with, he might have meant only to get away, but soon enough he would have seen the advantages in such an affiliation, the chance of playing both sides against the middle.

I shivered, as certain as I had ever been of anything in my life, that Ariel wanted revenge; that this was the real motivation behind his laying the seeds of suspicion about Obernewtyn. His quick ascendancy within Council ranks proved he had lost none of his ability to manipulate. Ariel had a way of easing himself irrevocably into advantageous positions and making use of people.

It was Brydda's thought that Ariel would probably have begun by offering information about the Druid to the Council—just enough to whet their appetite and give himself credibility. Not enough to give the Druid away completely. He would have made the same offer to the Herder Faction, and it would have been easy to use information learnt from one group to feed the other, rising in the estimation of both. No matter who won, Ariel would triumph.

The only mystery lay in Ariel's accusation of Sedition at Obernewtyn, and his apparent certainty that the firestorm story was a lie. Domick said he sounded as if he knew Obernewtyn had not been burnt out, but there was no way he could have known that.

"Perhaps he means to plant evidence of Sedition," Idris offered diffidently.

I looked at him. "If Ariel is only guessing, then the irony of it is that everything he claims is true. It's almost too much of a coincidence."

I had the feeling I had overlooked something vital, but was too tired and worried to dwell on it further. We had spent precious time packing Katlyn's invaluable store of dried herbs. Almost everything else had to be left behind and tears coursed down her face as Brydda threw a flaming torch on the roof of the cottage.

"It is only stone and mud and straw I know, but all the memories of happy years are in those walls, and now they burn. Perhaps it is a sign," she sobbed.

It did not take us long to reach Brydda's hiding spot. It was as good as he had led us to believe. We could even see the cottage burning in the distance, while we were invisible behind a thick girdle of Eben trees.

As soon as we arrived, Brydda set Kella and his mother to organize supper to occupy their minds. He asked me to walk with him to find some firewood, leading the way purposefully through the trees. I looked around curiously. The ground sloped up steeply, offering a sweeping view of the area.

"This is a sight I remember well," Brydda said softly. Over the treetops, I could see the dense darkness of the Blacklands in the moonlight like a shadowy stain across the Land.

Pavo had once said the Blacklands would recede in time, but I could not imagine anything growing on the black stinking soil. I shuddered, and for a moment it seemed to me that Ariel and the Blacklands were symptoms of the same evil.

Beyond the hills was the silvery rush of the Suggredoon and the huddled village of Rangorn. I could even see the mists that hung above Glenelg Mor. Behind me was the towering bulk of Aran Craggie and Tor. So many ways to go and none fast enough to get us to Obernewtyn in time.

The wind in the treetops sounded like the whispering ebb and flow of the sea. Brydda stirred as if the same wind had blown through him, ruffling his thoughts like so many leaves. I bent to pick up a stick, but Brydda touched my arm and shook his head.

"I wanted to talk to you alone. I think you should consider coming back to Sutrium with me, all of you," Brydda said seriously. "Domick must go back. Very few people have managed to work their way into such a position on the Council. He will be valuable to both our causes. Pavo is not capable of the trip to the mountains, you know that. He needs Kella with him. I will organize a safe journey for you all to Obernewtyn after winter."

I nodded. "It would be too dangerous to have Jik in Sutrium after what happened in Aborium. Especially if there are as many Herder Priests about as Domick said. And Dragon could not be confronted with a city. I would be grateful if you would take Kella and Pavo for the time. But one of us must try to reach Obernewtyn before the pass freezes to warn them. I will go and take Dragon and Jik with me."

"Why can't you speak to them with your mind?" Brydda asked.

"Impossible," I said. "First, the higher I am above sea level, the more powerful my farseeking range. But even if I were to make it to the highlands, where my range is better, the tainted mountains between the high country and Obernewtyn are a barrier I can't penetrate. There is only one way to warn them. Someone has to go there."

"Is it wise or sensible for you to go, Elspeth? What about your feet?" Brydda protested.

"My feet are well enough, and I am better equipped to deal with trouble than any of the others, even Domick. Even so, I doubt I will be able to get up into the mountains before the pass freezes, but I must try."

To my surprise, Brydda grinned. "I might have a way to shorten your road back to Obernewtyn. Let's get some wood and go back to camp. I have an idea I want to put to you all."

It was after midnight by the time we had eaten and Brydda laid his plan out. Pavo, Kella, and Domick were to go back to Sutrium with Brydda's protection. In exchange for shelter and the setting up of a safe house as Rushton wanted, Domick would share all he learnt with Brydda, unless the coercer believed it would harm Obernewtyn. All the horses would also go to Sutrium for the winter. "Elspeth, Dragon, Darga, and Jik will travel through the mountains to warn Rushton of Ariel's machinations," Brydda said.

"Through . . . the mountains," Domick spluttered. "Impossible!"

"Through the Olden way," Brydda went on.

Kella gaped at him. "But the pass is poisonous."

In answer Brydda pointed to Darga. "Not all. And that is where Darga comes in. I have seen with my own eyes that he can tell poisoned substances from clean ones. Therefore he will be your guide."

"You talk as if you had seen the pass," Domick began with a touch of resentment.

"I have," Brydda said simply. "I told you I roamed these hills as a boy. I know where the pass is. I recognized your description of it. I have been into it from this end, though not right to the top, and I'm not dead. Probably there is only a section tainted near the Druid compound."

"You don't know that," Domick said belligerently.

Brydda nodded. "I know. But it is the only way to reach

Obernewtyn quickly. The rest can travel there in the spring, as soon as you send word that all is well."

I nodded with a rush of hope. "It is the best chance we have to warn Rushton about Ariel."

"Then I'll go," Domick said.

I shook my head. "Kella and Pavo will need you. And Brydda is right about the job you have in the Council. It is too important an advantage to waste. Rushton would want you to stay and find out as much as you can. But you'll have to stay out of Ariel's way. If you remember him, you can be sure he'll remember you."

"What about the Druid?" Kella asked.

I grinned. "I only have to worry about the compound since the settlement is some distance away. The compound is lightly guarded and we'll only need a distraction to slip by. I'll have Dragon with me. She can make her dragon face to distract them."

The others laughed, including Dragon who, though she did not understand, seemed to find laughter itself funny.

"Rushton will never forgive me for letting you go to danger," Domick groaned.

"Tell him that I refused to listen," I said firmly. "But I think he will be more interested in what you can learn. If you can get back to Sutrium before tomorrow night, no one will even know you were away."

It was decided. I would go at first light. Brydda would take us to the start of the Olden way and we would go on alone. He and the others would wait until the soldierguards had gone before going to Sutrium. Brydda gave me careful instructions about how to contact him.

∽

We left in the cold, gray light of the very early morning after saying our farewells. First to Katlyn and Grufyyd, who had been so kind, to Idris, Reuvan, Avra, and the horses, then to Kella and Domick.

I said good-bye last of all to Pavo, knowing it might be the last time I would see him. I could not hug him, because any sort of pressure was unbearable for him. He was delirious most of the time, and he blinked at me in a puzzled way, as if his memory were disintegrating.

"He is content," Brydda said gently, when we had left the camp behind.

"That's what Darga said. But I'm not content. What a world this is in which someone like Pavo has to die so young," I said.

"People will always be dying too young, whether in the Beforetime, or now. That is the way of the world."

It took less than an hour to reach the fall of rocks which Brydda said concealed the opening to the Olden way. My feet were already hurting, though we had traveled at an easy pace. Brydda left us at the foot of the pile of fallen stone which hid the opening to the Olden way.

Before leaving he hugged us all tightly. Jik and Dragon, who both liked the big man, cried unselfconsciously. Darga wagged his tail slowly. Last of all Brydda looked at me seriously. "Be careful, little cousin, your trials are not yet over. But I expect to see you in the spring."

After he had gone I straightened myself, determinedly throwing off a wave of depression. I took a deep breath and started to climb, instructing Jik and Dragon to stay close behind Darga. Once we got to the top of the rockfall, I was disheartened to realize we would have to climb down the other side again before we could begin the ascent to the pass entrance.

It took us a considerable time to get up to the opening, and we were all dirty, grazed, and exhausted before we reached the narrow slit which would barely fit a man through. Avra had wanted to come with us because of Gahltha, but Brydda had convinced us the pass was too steep for a horse. I thought it unlikely she would have fit through the opening to begin with. Thick vines had grown across it like a net, and some sort of spiders had made a web in them. It was years since Brydda had last gone there, and I suspected nothing had passed that way since, for the webs were intricate and many layered, and covered in thick dust.

Dragon would not go through until she was certain none of the cobwebby tendrils would touch her.

It was late in the morning when we finally stood inside the Olden way. Darga sniffed, saying he scented no poisons in the vicinity.

Dry reedy grasses made a papery, whispering noise as we made our way up the incline. It was not as steep as the rock fall, but my feet ached with the strain of digging in for purchase. The trees growing in that early section were stunted, with spiky grayish leaves and stonelike buds, but ahead we could see a dark green belt of trees. On either side of us, the mountains soared straight up, gray, pock-marked walls.

It was a long arduous climb to the treeline and we were all puffing by the time we reached it. I was disappointed to find the ground did not level out. The trees had only given that illusion. It was darker beneath the canopy of entwined branches and leaves, and an eerie silence reigned that reminded me of the Silent Vale, where I had gone to collect whitestick while in the orphan home at Kinraide.

I thought it would be strange if it turned out that Brydda was right, and there was only a narrow region of tainting in the pass. That would mean we might have escaped into the Olden way after getting away from the Druid camp. But how much would have changed if we had? We would not have met Grufyyd or Katlyn or Brydda, and we would not have entered Aborium. Strange how so many events meshed together.

Jik had begun trying to teach Dragon to say his name as they walked. I listened with only half an ear, preoccupied by a sudden feeling of unease. When we came out of the trees, I noticed the sky had darkened. The thought of a storm did not frighten me since it would keep the Druid's armsmen under cover and make an unobtrusive exit from the pass easier.

After a short way, the now sparse trees gave way to a high, thick kind of bramble running before us in a solid barrier. It offered no natural paths and was filled with stinging thorns. That meant we had to use knives to hack our way through. The severed branch ends leaked a defensive odor that made our eyes sting.

It took more than an hour to bypass the brambles. On the other side was a narrow, very deep gorge cutting directly across our path, at the bottom of which ran a tumultuous course of water. The stream and the gorge appeared to run all the way from Aran Craggie to Tor. I thought it quite likely the stream was a tributary of the Suggredoon, escaping through some crack from inside the mountain. It was too wide to jump and the only way to cross was to descend into the trench and swim the stream.

Dragon eyed the water fearfully and shuddered back from the edge in ominous terror. We wasted another hour trying to find a less steep descent, but in the end, returned to the original spot to climb down. The stream itself was overhung with a thick trailing fringe of creepers and vines, but the bank on both sides proved treacherously soft. I stared into the water, glumly wondering how we would manage to get across safely. Up close, the water ran very fast.

"I will swim with a rope in my teeth," Darga said. "On the other side, I will pass the rope around a tree and hold it tight. Jik can cross first since he weighs little, then he can tie it."

I looked at the opposite bank doubtfully. "All right. But I'll tie the rope around you and hold the other end in case you get into trouble, so that I can pull you back."

At first Darga disappeared completely beneath the roaring water. But a moment later he bobbed to the surface and struck out for the other bank. The current was so strong that he had to swim at an angle that made it look as if he were trying to make his way upstream like a salmon. He crept forward, drawing fractionally nearer the opposite bank.

By the time he reached the edge he was clearly tiring badly, but the ordeal was not over. I watched in consternation as he tried to scale the soft edges of the bank. Time and again, the treacherous earth gave way, plunging him back into the raging water.

"Pull him back," Jik cried fearfully. "He's drowning."

"No," Darga sent, his mind an exhausted whisper. The soft banks were deeply gouged before he managed at last to get a firm footing. I could see his body trembling with weariness as he dragged himself over the lip.

"Darga." Jik shouted through his tears. Darga flapped his tail weakly twice, then lay like one dead for a long time.

When he had recovered, Darga walked around a tree, then braced himself, pulling the rope taut. I pulled my own end to test the strength of Brydda's rope, then fastened it to a stout tree trunk.

Jik went across hand over hand. The rope creaked and sagged until he hung waist deep in the water, but it held. He reached the other side safely and gave a triumphant yell before untying the rope from Darga and retying it around a rock. I had thought I might have to knock Dragon out and pull her across from the other side with the rope, but watching Jik seemed to have given her confidence. She was pale but surprisingly calm and, when I saw her cross, I realized it was because she had thought of a way to make sure the water did not touch her. She too went across hand over hand, her legs wrapped around the rope. She had been less frightened of the crossing than of the water.

I went last of all, half sorry I could think of no way to untie the rope. It was the only piece we had and might be needed again if there were more than one stream to cross.

I was disheartened at our lack of progress. Unless the way became easier, we were wasting valuable time negotiating endless obstacles. It had cost us more than two hours to cross an area less than two spans wide. Climbing out of the trench was harder than getting down into it and, at the top, I decided it was time to rest and eat.

Jik lit a small fire and I set a pot of soup to swing over it. While we waited, Jik sang a strange song the Herders had taught him about the Blacklands. He had a remarkably sweet voice and at my request sang songs until the food was hot enough to eat.

Heartened, we went on.

Not far ahead were more trees. The bandages on my feet were filthy and I suspected the scars were bleeding again, but the pain was less intense.

We trudged the remainder of the day without stopping, our legs aching from constantly walking up the steep incline. The trees proved less dense than in the first belt and, gradually, the slope became slighter and walking less arduous. Darga assured me we were still some distance from the poisoned region. I thought we had been fortunate, but Obernewtyn still seemed far away. I could hardly believe that in a few days we would be home.

I looked up through the trees at the dim, bleary afternoon fading into a smoky twilight, and again apprehension swept over me.

The night air was distinctly chilly, and we were all glad of the blankets Brydda had insisted we carry. Winter had begun, and the first falls of snow would already be blanketing the higher mountain valleys. Very soon, snow would fall at Obernewtyn, if it had not already fallen. I shivered and pulled my cloak around my shoulders. The moon had begun to fatten in its cycle and should have lit our way clearly but, though visible, it produced only a wan, strained light, and we were forced to set our torches to flame. Moved by some impulse of urgency, I decided to go on despite Darga's warning that we were on the verge of crossing into the poisoned region.

"Can you find a safe way?" I asked him.

He sniffed. "I can smell clean ground amidst foul earth," he sent. We both knew it would be safer to wait until daylight, but I had the queer feeling the delays were bringing us close to some disaster.

I looked over to where Jik was continuing his lesson with the bemused Dragon during the short break. "Ready?" I asked.

Jik looked across at me unsmilingly, and for an instant he looked suddenly old and frail, as near to death as Pavo. Then he smiled and the impression vanished.

We walked single file from then, Darga leading the way. Entering a stand of giant trees with monstrously gnarled and misshapen trunks and thick dark roots writhing up out of the ground, I thought I had seen such trees beyond the compound wall in Matthew's vision and hoped it meant we were nearing the other end of the pass.

At the same time, the ground beneath our feet became wet and soft. Our feet made sucking noises that echoed in the silence. The torchlight flickered on dark odorous puddles of water that seeped into the slightest depression. There seemed no source for the dampness. The light made a bizarre shadow play on the twisted tree trunks, making them look like the faces of ancient men and women. Dragon eyed them doubtfully as we passed.

After a time the wind rose, and leaves flapped sluggishly, heavy with moisture. We waded through a thick blanket of leaves. At once, the smell of the festering layers of leaves below filled the air with a sweet, rotten scent that made us all gag.

Darga sent a constant dialog of instructions as the way became more fraught with danger, and I began to regret not stopping. He warned against certain plants or creepers, areas of bare ground and even some trees, guiding us through the poisonous labyrinth. Without him, we would have been helpless for there was scant outward sign of the poisons other than the distorted sizes and shapes of the trees and bushes growing all around us.

In the end, it was the dog that called a halt, saying he needed to rest. We went on until he found a patch of ground relatively clean of taint. My feet no longer gave me any trouble, for an ominous numbness had deprived them of all sensation. I felt I could walk over flames without feeling anything. I did not dare undo the bandages, afraid of what the loss of feeling might mean.

We ate the last of our store of perishable foods and sipped at the meager remnant of water. I had wanted to fill the bottles along the way, but Darga had pronounced all water in the pass tainted enough to make a person sick. We would have to ration what was left of the water to make sure it would last us out.

Wearily I made a mental note to tell Jik and Darga the following day.

I was drifting into a light, troubled sleep when a terrible savage growling rent the air around us.

XXI

The growling seemed to vibrate in the air, even after it had ceased. Nothing stirred in the silence that followed except for a faint breeze tugging at our blankets.

"What was that?" Jik whispered.

I set my mind loose, searching, hampered by the static given off by the poisons. I found nothing. "Do you know what that was?" I asked Darga.

"Some kind of animal," he suggested unhelpfully.

"Brydda said there were no big animals here," Jik said, half-accusingly.

"He came here last a long time ago," I said, trying to sound calm. Matthew had talked of the horrendous animal cries he had heard beyond the compound barrier while imprisoned.

Dragon was crouched near the tree, eyes wide and frightened. I opened my mouth to reassure her, but another of the blood-chilling growls cut off my words. My skin puckered into gooseflesh. Whatever could make such a noise had to be enormous.

Again the growl faded, but still there was no sign of the creature that had made it. Neither Jik nor Darga were any more successful at locating the mind pattern of the monster, though I did encounter a number of barely sentient minor patterns. But these were mere flickers of instinct rather than thought.

We gave up and sat around staring uneasily into the darkness around us.

Five more times, the eerie howling shattered the night, before I began to accept that it was not, as we had all feared, a signal for attack or a hunting cry. Even so I could not help thinking that a creature who could make such a noise, and conceal its mind, might be clever enough to hide its intention to attack.

But there was no attack.

Morning found us bleary-eyed and ill-rested, for the cries had seemed to grow nearer and more frequent as the night wore on. In the end we decided there was more than one of the creatures, or one was circling us. Both prospects made for uneasy slumber.

To our further dismay, we had not been walking long the next day before the giant stand of trees gave way abruptly to a seemingly endless mire reminiscent of the blighted Berryn Mor. Here the few trees that managed to grow in the sodden ground were thin and sickly looking, bereft of leaf, and shrouded in a furry gray mold.

The only reassuring thing about the spindly skeletons looming out of the mist was that they told us the water was quite shallow. The ground lay only a few handspans below the surface and, though soft, was firm enough to walk on. Darga went ahead, warning us to step exactly where he did, since there were holes and trenches all through the swamp. He said the water was tainted but only slightly.

So began the worst time since we had entered the Olden way. Tired and thirsty, we plodded doggedly after Darga. There was no possibility of resting until we reached dry ground. Soaking through my boots and stockings, the swamp water was tepid. An evil-smelling reek hung low over the surface of the water and swirled about our feet as we passed.

We walked in silence, concentrating on keeping our footing and moving as quickly as we could. I jumped when Jik ventured a question.

"If I fell in this water, or touched one of those poisoned plants, would I die at once or slowly like Pavo?" he asked gravely.

Repressing a flare of anguish at the thought of Pavo, I said, "I don't know. We're not really sure yet if there are lots of different kinds of poisons in the world, or just the one left behind from the Great White. How quickly you die depends on how potent it is. If it's strong, it could work quickly. But if weak, like in the places we find whitestick, you have to be exposed to it over long periods of time before it does any harm."

He nodded thoughtfully, his brow furrowed. "Sometimes on the island, a Herder died if he touched too much whitestick before it was transformed. What is whitestick anyway?"

I smiled. "Your guess is as good as anyone's. Pavo thinks it is a sort of by-product from the Great White, like ash from a fire. Once transformed, it is used for everything from starting fires to making medicines. But surely you know that much?"

"The Herders make a kind of gas with it that makes your skin burn," Jik said.

I looked at him curiously, "I've never heard of that."

He shrugged. "It's a secret. I saw them experimenting by accident. The man who they tested it on was a half-wit. He went blind from the gas, and then his skin blistered. They told everyone a few days later that he had gone to another cloister, but I think he died."

The thought of whitestick being used for such a purpose disturbed me. It sounded as if the Herders had found a way of using it without bothering to transform it. But what possible use could be made of a gas that burned?

"Why did the Beforetimers make the Great White?" Jik asked. He had not long ago completely believed the Herder doctrine he had been taught. He was insatiably curious about our views on the taboo subjects. "The Herders told us Lud sent the Great White because the Oldtimers were evil."

I smiled. When he was older he would realize we would never know for sure what happened. "I doubt anyone meant to cause the Great White," I said. "I don't know how it came to be, no one does, or what it was for. I like to believe it was a kind of accident. But no one knows for sure. Not even the Herder Faction for all they think they know everything."

"They say they do," Jik protested. "They say there were Herders in the Beforetime, and that their knowledge has been passed down."

That was news to me. "People like them maybe," I said. "People who want power to control other people's lives. There will always be people like that."

"Pavo told me some of the Oldtime weapons and poisons might still be hidden someplace, like the skyscrapers under Tor," Jik said seriously.

I forced myself not to react.

"It's possible," I said slowly.

"What would happen if someone found it? Someone like Ariel or the Druid. There might be another accident..." His voice trailed off.

"This is a bad place for such talk," I said.

I noticed a greenish vapor bubbling out of the water nearby. Trying not to panic, I pointed it out to Darga. He told me it was a poisonous gas but too weak to harm us. Gradually the water began to bubble all around us, issuing clouds of colored gas. One virulent yellow gas was dangerous enough for Darga to give a wide margin, while a sickly blue shade made him backtrack hastily.

The region of gases was narrow, but seemed to take hours to negotiate. My nerves felt ragged by the time we left the mists behind. Suddenly, right in front of us, a bluish gas coalesced. Jik almost fell over in his effort to back away from it. I sent a quick command and he steadied himself. "It's Dragon," I said. "She's copying the gases." Jik nodded, staring at the apparition unhappily. Noticing his expression, Dragon's triumphant smile faded and the mist vanished.

"Bad?" she asked contritely.

"Good," I said firmly. "Very good."

"More?" Dragon asked eagerly, waving her hands to indicate that she would make something huge and mysterious and complex.

"Uh . . . Maybe later," Jik said sheepishly.

The gold tint in the sky intensified, transforming the surface of the water into a dull molten gold. I wondered if the entire swamp were somehow distorting our vision to produce the odd color.

As soon as the sun set, the dim day gave way to a starless night and the air resounded again with the mysterious growling noises that had disturbed us the previous night. They sounded much closer, and I could not get over the feeling that we were being stalked, despite a second fruitless mind search.

We were all relieved to stand on solid ground, though the darkness kept us from seeing what sort of land lay ahead. I decided we needed a break, having been unable to stop during the crossing of the swamp. We drank the last of our water with a feeling of recklessness. Already lightheaded from lack of food, I prayed we were close to the compound. The ground had flattened out entirely now, and the increase in my farseeking range told me we had reached highland level. It had also become much colder.

Lying with my back against a tree, I could hear Darga beside me sniffing delicately, tasting the various scents of the night. I could smell nothing but the noxious swamp gases and my own filth, but Darga's nose was incredibly sensitive. The dog was proving an invaluable member of our company. I wondered if his presence was the real truth that lay behind the vague futuretelling of Jik's importance.

A slight breeze ruffled my hair and Darga lifted his head. "A storm comes," he sent.

I nodded impatiently. "But the compound, can you smell it yet?"

"Not far," Darga sent.

That night, I slept heavily and dreamlessly. I woke only once to the sound of Jik's laughter echoing in the darkness.

He had been walking around trying to keep himself warm and alert on his watch turn, when he had accidentally trodden on a small, lumpy-skinned swamp dweller with bulging eyes. Immediately, the frightened creature's neck had blown up to three times its diminutive size, and it had let out the incredible growling rumble that had so mystified us. We had seen dozens of the creatures since leaving the area of bubbling mists, sitting on logs and blinking sleepily at us, but had not connected the giant noises with such insignificant life forms.

Jik's suggestion that the dreadful calling was a kind of love song made me laugh until my stomach ached. I lay back to sleep finally, with a smile on my face. It was good to laugh. I had been doubly amused to find Darga took Jik's suggestion quite seriously. Beasts lacked only one funaga virtue that I regretted and that was a sense of humor.

"You may call it a lack," Darga broke into my thoughts. "So might I lack a pain in my head." That made me laugh again.

I had intended to stand last watch, but Jik had not woken me, saying he had felt wide awake and thought I might as well sleep while I could.

I stretched, feeling oddly lethargic. I threw the blanket away from me, realizing it was hot. At once, my feet began to ache with a new pain, and my head and neck felt damp. I looked down at my feet uneasily. Standing carefully, I could not stifle a gasp of pain at the hot fire shooting up my legs.

"What is it?" Jik asked, catching my pain and fear.

"Nothing," I lied. "My feet have gone to sleep." It was not easy to lie to an empath, but Jik was young and untrained. I turned away from him to hide the fear in my eyes. The numbness that had enabled me to climb the Olden way had been too good to be true. I forced myself to face something that I had known for a while. My feet had become infected. Fighting off a dull drowsiness, I bestirred the others, deliberately isolating the awareness of the pain.

This was a dangerous thing to do and Roland forbade it in all but the most extreme need. Pain suppressed was pain in waiting. Eventually, it had to be endured, and the longer it was allowed to accumulate, the more devastating its final effect. It was possible to suppress minor pain for so long that the accumulation, when released, could stop a strong man's heart. I would pay dearly for my suppression, but I had to get to Obernewtyn. If I could suppress until I arrived, Roland would be able to have the healers siphon off some of the pain.

Resolutely I went on, refusing to allow myself to think about the consequences if I failed to reach Obernewtyn before the pass was closed.

We had been walking less than an hour when Darga stopped abruptly, his fur bristling. "Funaga. Just ahead," he sent.

I told the others to wait and limped through the trees. Catching sight of the compound wall, I had to fight back tears of relief. The compound was the last obstacle between us and Obernewtyn.

I peered over the wall warily.

Three or four men stood near the diggings talking. The yellow sky cast an ivory light on their faces making their flesh a sickly sallow hue.

On the other side of the clearing nearest the fence, an armsman was deep in an argument with a white-robed acolyte. The acolyte looked angry. A few steps away stood another armsman, leaning on his spear and yawning. There was a lot more open space than I remembered from Matthew's vision, and no way of passing over it unnoticed without a diversion, unless we waited for nightfall. But the moon would be brighter then, and we could not afford to waste a whole day. Jik brought Dragon up to the fence. It was difficult to make her understand what was needed, and even then I was unsure I had made my meaning clear. But she nodded, her pupils enormous with excitement.

A low rumble of thunder sounded in the distance. Dragon shuddered from head to toe and half started up in agitation. I wrenched her down beside me, hissing angrily at Jik to keep her down. The last thing we wanted was to be seen and pursued. Dragon pointed at the sky and gibbered fearfully. I patted her arm, realizing she was afraid of the storm. That was all we needed.

I turned to Darga, who was looking up and sniffing the wind.

"We'll have to go straightaway. Dragon's frightened of the storm and she might not be able to make a vision if she gets any worse."

As if to underline my words, lightning flashed directly overhead, and Dragon cowered to the ground, hands over her ears. I had a sudden impression that time was folding back on itself. My apprehension had increased to the point where it bordered on premonition, but I knew the suppression of pain could confuse the other senses. And Dragon's growing agitation made it imperative we moved at once.

I pulled her round to face me, and was astonished to see she was as white as bone. I stroked her face gently and slowly she relaxed.

I turned to look over the wall and premonition struck at me so violently that I felt my knees buckle under me. I grabbed at the fence, fighting a wave of formless terror. I forced myself to be calm and looked searchingly at Dragon. She nodded seeming to understand.

Lightning flashed as she rose, and she flinched. A moment later the man leaning on his spear gave a muffled shout and another man actually screamed with such terror that my hair stood on end. Then chaos broke in the compound. For a moment there was a hail of cries and panicked shouts. Peering through a crack in the fence, I could see nothing and wondered what Dragon had conjured up. I watched until I could see the clearing was deserted, then hissed at the others to run.

Lightning flashed as we thrust aside the barrier of stakes, but no one cried out. I saw a lone man running frantically for the huts, and wondered how Dragon had managed to get them all to go inside the huts, whose doors faced away from the clearing.

Another deafening burst of thunder rent the air and a vivid flash of lightning told me the storm was almost on us. We were on our way home, I thought incredulously. Distantly, I sensed that running had pushed the suppressed pain to dangerous levels.

Lightning flashed with lurid brilliance and, for a second, our shadows ran before us elongated and sharp-edged, merging with the treeline just before us.

We had reached the White Valley!

Thunder crashed again and this time the air vibrated with its force.

As soon as we reached the trees, I urged the others to run ahead, and slowed to a limping walk. There was no more need to run, and I did not want to aggravate the suppression any further. Preoccupied, I did not notice a rock in the grass and tripped, sprawling headlong. Hearing my involuntary cry, Dragon turned to help me to my feet. Then she froze.

I looked up at her, puzzled, and my heart jerked with sickening force. Her face was a grotesque mask of terror, her lips stretched wide in a silent scream. I tried to pull her down beside me, but she fought me silently, eyes wide and unfocused. I thought she was having some sort of fit.

Again thunder rumbled, and the ground seemed to vibrate. Without warning Dragon began to shriek hysterically. I drew back a hand to slap her and at the same time looked over my shoulder to see what she had seen.

My legs seemed to liquefy with terror.

Less than fifty spans away ran a wall of fire and there was

no mistaking the greenish tint of the flames or the blue crackle in the air. I had seen it before—the miscolored sky, the dull bleared light—but I had not recognized it.

A firestorm, and we were out in the open!

XXII

"Get up and run, girl, unless you want to die!" cried a voice.

Wrenched violently to my feet, I found myself half dragged, half carried along by a tall, brown-faced youth. Dragon ran before us, her eyes wild with terror.

"That way. There are caves," he shouted, pointing. Dragon swerved the way he indicated, disappearing into the trees. The acrid stench of smoke billowed around us and, dimly, I heard the muffled crash of thunder in the distance. A wave of heat flowed over us, and the air burned. I dared not glance over my shoulder to see how near the flames were. All I could think of was the burning of my mother and father. The screams and the dreadful smell.

"Thank Lud!" the youth said harshly, as the trees parted to reveal a rough hill of granite knolls.

"Inside, there," he said, thrusting me unceremoniously into a shallow cave in the side of a steep stony hillock. "This is not deep enough, but there's no time to search further. Pray the wind changes or we'll fry," he shouted, over the roar of the flames bearing down on us.

I turned to watch the flames racing across the countryside. Black smoke rose above the trees, blotting out the sun. The youth pressed me into a depression in the deepest section of the cave and forced himself in beside me. Our breathing sounded unnaturally loud.

The flame wall came to less than a span from the hill, before sweeping to the left and away. I found myself trembling from head to foot at the thought of how close I had come to following my parents into the purifying flame.

"That was hellish close," the youth said shakily, wiping sweat from his face. Though we were no longer in immediate danger, the heat was intense, since the firestorm still raged all around us. "If we'd been caught in that we'd be charcoal now."

"Dragon!" I gasped, starting at the entrance. "Jik and Darga!" My rescuer dragged me back into the cave.

"Are you mad? The girl who was with you came this way. There are many caves she might have taken refuge in," he said.

"You don't understand. There were others—a boy and a dog," I cried.

He shook his head. "Either they found shelter, and are safe. Or . . ." He looked at the fierce orange glow of the flames, still uncomfortably close.

I sank to my knees, realizing there was nothing I could do until the firestorm ended. Abruptly, the youth leaned down and twisted my face to the firelight.

"You are not from the camp. Who are you?" he demanded in a queer tone. Through a haze of smoke, brown eyes surveyed me from a craggy, tan face. His hair was brown too, and longer than lowland fashion dictated. He was about Rushton's age and wore the unmistakable garb of a Druid armsman.

Recapture by the Druid meant trouble. But that was overshadowed by my fear for Jik, Dragon, and Darga. Only the thought that they might live prevented me from releasing the suppressing barrier. I tried to farseek them but the air was filled with static generated by the firestorm.

The young armsman dropped to his knees beside me. "Look at me!" he commanded. "Don't you know me, Elspeth?"

I looked at him properly, for the first time, and incredibly, realized I did know his face.

"Daffyd?" I whispered, unable to believe my eyes.

He sat back on his heels. "Lud save us, it is you, grown into near womanhood. I met you only that once, yet I never forgot your face."

I sat up too quickly, and the world tilted crazily out of focus. I leaned forward and vomited on the ground, heaving until my stomach ached. Gently, Daffyd wiped my mouth with a piece of cloth. I felt no pain, and the nausea was swallowed up immediately by the suppression, but I stared down at my legs, frightened. I sensed pain radiating out from them in a fiery arc and being absorbed by the barrier.

"I think you'd better stay still," Daffyd said. "You must have breathed in too much smoke. You're lucky I came along when I did."

I looked at Daffyd searchingly. "You may call it luck. I call it fortunate chance ... unless you mean to turn us over to the Druid."

He smiled. "Gilaine spoke to me of you and your friends. This is one Druid armsman you need not fear. I was surprised when she called you a gypsy, then I realized you must have escaped during the fuss over the Seditioners at Obernewtyn and somehow ended up traveling with gypsies."

Daffyd screwed up his eyes and I was astonished to feel a clumsy probe seeking entrance to my mind. The weakest shield would have held him off. It was like watching a baby trying to walk. He sighed. "I'm not very good at it. Gilaine showed me how to think outside Lidgebaby's net, the way you showed her. It is odd to think we were both Misfits when we met in the Councilcourt that day, though I did not know it then."

He coughed, as a thick cloud of smoke blew directly into the cave. "We thought you were dead. The Druid had everyone out searching for you when I arrived. He was convinced it was

a trick, even though Gilbert saw the raft go into the mountain."
He frowned. "Was it a trick then? Have you been hidden in
the valley all this while?"

"The raft carried us through the mountain and down to
the lowlands safely, though I would not want to take such a
passage again. I came back through the Olden way," I said. "It's
less poisonous than the Druid thinks. We were trying to get
through the compound when the storm struck..."

I looked at the cave opening worriedly. "I hope the others
are safe. I pray this firestorm ends quickly." I made to rise, but
all the suppression in the world could not make useless limbs
work.

Daffyd laid a gentle hand on my arm. "Be patient. Even
when the storm front passes, there is the rain. We can't brave
that and live." He looked at my legs speculatively.

As if his words were a signal, it began suddenly to rain
with great force. For a moment we both looked outside watching steam hiss and billow from the dying fires. I bit my lip and
hoped Dragon understood the danger of being out in the stinging rains. It was clear she had known what a firestorm was and
had recognized the signs.

The cave we were in was no more than a shallow scoop
of erosion and if the rain had been slanting from the opposite
direction, it would have filled the cave. As to the fire, the blackened ground showed that it had come to within a single span
of the rocks. I shuddered. The area visible from the cave was
devastated and some of the trees were still aflame with their
eerie blue halo. The beat of falling rain was curiously soothing
amid the sight and smell of destruction and my eyes drooped.
The suppression was draining my reserves.

"Elspeth, Gilaine said you were trying to reach the coast.
If you did get through the mountain, why did you come back?"
Daffyd asked.

Forcing myself to full awareness, I looked at Daffyd
squarely. There was a time to be silent, and a time to speak. I

had always found it hard to trust people, but this time I did not hesitate. My infected feet rendered me useless as a messenger, yet someone had to carry my knowledge to Obernewtyn before the pass closed. No matter what had become of Dragon and the others, that was my first priority. Providence had brought Daffyd to me.

"The Druid's friend on the Council," I said. "What do you know of him?"

Daffyd looked at me closely as if trying to judge if I were delirious. Then he glanced out at the teeming rain and shrugged. "A couple of years back, a boy stumbled into the camp more dead than alive. The Druid had him looked after, in the hope of some useful information. When he regained consciousness, he claimed to have lost his memory. Eventually, the Druid decided to let him join us. Though fair-faced, he was not well liked, yet he had a charm, when he chose to use it. The old man grew fond of him, began to think of him as a son. In the end, he was privy to the armsmen Councils. Then he came up with a daring plan to infiltrate the Council and feed information back to us. It was a dangerous proposition, but he is an insidious sort of fellow. If anyone could carry out such an audacious plan, it was he. So he went off to Sutrium." Daffyd shrugged. "A lot of us thought he would disappear as soon as he was out of the Druid's sight, maybe even betray us, but he did as he had promised, supplying us with luxuries and information, working for the day the Druid comes out of hiding to challenge the powers that be."

"Ariel..." I murmured, not believing for a minute he had lost his memory, or that he worked for the Druid.

"It's strange to hear him named openly," Daffyd said. "The Druid has forbidden us to speak of him by name. How did you come to hear it?"

"We met before he came to the Druid," I said bleakly. "He is a mutant, from Obernewtyn. You have heard of the Seditioners, Alexi and Madam Vega? He was their creature. I did not leave Obernewtyn to join the gypsies. I had to let Gilaine believe that to protect Obernewtyn. The new Master of Obernewtyn has made it a secret haven for our kind of Misfit. We were on a mission when your Druid got hold of us."

"Then Obernewtyn was not ruined by a firestorm?" Daffyd said.

"No. It is quite safe—so far."

"But, why are you telling me all this now, if you would not speak of it to Gilaine?" Daffyd asked.

I sighed. "Because I need you to warn Obernewtyn that Ariel is behind the investigations of Obernewtyn, before the pass is snowed closed."

"It will open again when the wintertime ends," Daffyd said.

"By then it will be too late. The soldierguards will be waiting to ride into the mountains at Ariel's instigation. They will find no firestorm-racked ruins."

Daffyd looked pensive. "Ariel always seemed fanatical about Obernewtyn, now that I think of it. He convinced the old man that it was a threat to us. Does he know about you?"

"He thinks I'm dead. And as far as Sedition at Obernewtyn goes, he's guessing. He can't know the truth, but once the soldierguards get up there, it won't make any difference."

"You know, we heard stories about a place where Misfits would be safe...but Obernewtyn."

"Daffyd, you must help me. Everything we have worked for is in danger unless I can get to Obernewtyn before the pass freezes. Maybe they'll evacuate, go higher into the mountains. Maybe they'll decide to fight, defend the pass. But if I don't get word to Rushton, they'll be defenceless. Ariel will have won."

"I still don't understand what Ariel has to gain out of destroying Obernewtyn."

"Revenge," I said bitterly. "He and his Seditious masters were routed by Rushton, the true Master of Obernewtyn. Ariel escaped. We thought he had died. He knows Rushton can expose him to the Druid, or to the Council, as a mutant and a Seditioner."

Daffyd's eyes narrowed. "You're lucky I found you and not one of the others. Ariel came up here not long after you had gone. He was very interested in you and your friends. He cursed when there was no trace of your bodies, and swore you had not died."

"I'm not sure if luck is the right word for it. Daffyd, will you help me?" I asked, too weak for pretence. "Will you go to Obernewtyn?"

Daffyd's eyes flicked to my legs. I nodded. "They're badly infected. So far I've been able to block the pain so it wouldn't slow me—one of my more useful Talents. But stopping the pain can't make these legs carry me any further. Help me warn Obernewtyn and join us, you and the others."

"What about you?" Daffyd asked, after a long pause.

"I'll be fine. I'll wait for Dragon and Jik, and Rushton can send help for us. The storm is interfering with my farsensing, but once it's over, I will call them to me."

I looked out of the cave. There were no more flames and a gray curtain of firestorm rain obscured the outside world. Carefully, I related to an astonished Daffyd all that had befallen us in the lowlands. When at last the rain ceased, I urged him to leave at once.

"You must go now . . ." I began, when an anguished cry shattered the stillness.

It took a moment for me to understand that it was Dragon screaming, the grief in her voice tangible and terrifying. Daffyd gave me one startled look, then plunged out into the open.

Long moments later, he returned carrying the prostrate form of Dragon.

"She's not . . ." I began, but he shook his head.

"Fainted," he said stiffly as if his lips were frozen. His face was very pale as he laid her on the ground inside the cave and wiped the wetness from her bare skin.

"What is it?" I asked, sensing disaster.

He looked up bleakly. "She had found a body. Burned beyond recognition. It might be one of the people from the compound," he added unconvincingly.

He reached into a pocket. "I found this in her hand." He held out a hand and something glinted dully in his palm. It was a small empath novice token.

I felt the suppressing barrier weaken with shock and revulsion.

Jik. It was Jik.

I was filled with a guilt deeper than anything I had ever imagined possible. I was responsible for his terrible death. I might as well have killed him with my own hands. If only I had left him with Brydda. If we had not brought him away from Obernewtyn, had not brought him out of the cloister. My teeth chattered and I felt dizzy with horror.

Daffyd knelt beside me and made me drink water from a tin jar. My teeth clattered against the rim. "It's not your fault," he said. I held up my hand to stop him offering excuses, trying to make myself cold. But his eyes, filled with honest pity and compassion, were my undoing. I wept then, great choking tears that seemed to take pieces of my soul, because I knew in my heart that Jik's death was no one's fault.

Yet his face rose in my mind's eye, sweet and grave, with eyes always a little too old for his years. He had hardly joined us before we had set him on a path to this horrible death. And what had bringing him achieved? Maryon had said he must come, or the expedition, and ultimately Obernewtyn, would fail. I was now certain Jik's presence had been necessary on the expedition only because it ensured Darga's. Maryon had admitted her prediction was unfocused. I could not recall any vital action of Jik's, but without Darga, we would never have found Dragon, or completed our survey of the library, could not have come through the Olden way. But even if Obernewtyn were warned in time, was even that enough to justify Jik's death?

"There was no sign of the dog," Daffyd said quietly. "It might have escaped." I shook my head, knowing Darga would never leave Jik in danger by choice.

I wept myself empty of tears.

Daffyd went to bury what remained of Jik's body, and returned looking pale and weary.

"Daffyd," I said. "You have to go now, if you mean to go, or it will be too late. Take Dragon."

"I'll carry you," he said. I shook my head. I would slow them to no purpose. Not even Roland could help me now. Too much pain had accumulated.

Dragon was less easy to convince when she woke, since she could not be coerced. She only agreed when I told her Daffyd's friends would be coming to help me. I told her he needed her help. Jik had told her about Obernewtyn and she had built it up in her mind to be a place of endless happiness where everyone was always safe. Her horror at the manner of Jik's death made her vulnerable, and I exploited this shamelessly.

I made them go immediately, maintaining a calm façade for Dragon's sake. I shook Daffyd's hand, pressing my armband into his hand. "This will make them believe you," I said softly.

"Is there anything... anyone..." Daffyd hesitated.

I thought of Rushton as I had last seen him, his hand raised to me through the driving rain. There had always been a strange prickly affection between us, a bond of sorts. It was hard to believe I would not see him again.

I smiled. "Tell him... Tell them, good-bye..." I said.

When they had gone, I sank gratefully into a black feverish sleep filled with dreams, but I did not release the suppression. At the end, life and sanity were too sweet to give up involuntarily. I knew it would not be long before the barrier gave way of its own volition.

I dreamed a horse with wings came and carried me to the

mountain tops. I dreamed Darga was there, and singing to me in Jik's high, sweet voice. I dreamed of Maruman, his fur ruffled by the winds. I dreamed of a voice inside my mind calling and calling.

I dreamed . . . of birds.

XXIII

The sound of a breaking branch in the utter silence of the devastated valley dragged me from my feverish drowsing. I had imagined myself beyond fear, but the notion came to me that the sound had been made by a predator seeking easy prey in the aftermath of the firestorm.

I stared out of the cave craning my neck as far as I could to keep from hurting my legs. I dared not overload my mind with any more pain. Miraculously, the suppression was still intact, although my vision and hearing seemed distorted.

I could see nothing outside but blackened trees and earth, and a drifting haze of smoke. There was no sign of life anywhere, but I felt I was being watched. My scalp prickled and I groped for a rock to use as a weapon, when I heard a distinct rustling noise outside.

"Who's there?" I called, my voice sounding slurred and groggy, a dry, frightened croak.

Letting my mind loose in desperation, I was astounded to find myself listening to a mental dialogue.

"What do you think it is?" one mind asked, sounding perplexed.

"A funaga, of course, what else makes such ugly noises?" came the fastidious response.

Astonished at the strength of minds which were clearly nonhuman, I projected, farsending my own thoughts, "Who/ where are you?"

"It spoke!" came a third mental voice. Younger than the others, and less controlled, I thought. There were quick shushing thoughts from the other two, who recognized the significance of my mental questions.

I gathered myself, trying to decide if I was dreaming.

Forcing down a mad urge to giggle hysterically, I made an effort to sound normal. "I know you're out there. There are three of you and I can hear your thoughts!" Nothing. "Answer me!"

I heard a faint movement and craned my neck, trying to work out which direction it came from.

A shudder of branches caught my eye. Squinting, I realized there were birds in the tree. I let my eyes follow the trunk to the ground, thinking the three Talents might well have disturbed them.

No one.

The branches rustled again and I looked up, wondering what had brought the birds to such a place. Animals generally avoided firestorm-devastated areas for months after, sometimes years. There was no small prey, no insects and no plant life. No reason—yet there they were, just sitting and staring.

One of the birds extended its wings and I drew in a sharp breath at the flash of red on its plumage. Guanette birds. I had seen one up close only once, a stuffed trophy. Even dead, the bird had possessed a quality that had enthralled me, a wild sort of nobility.

I shivered at the memory, for Ariel had slain the bird.

Looking more carefully, I could tell one of the three was a male with the straighter beak and smaller body. The two larger, with curved beaks, were female.

Impulsively, I sent a questing probe to the birds. After a moment, the smaller began to fidget, shifting weight from one claw to the other like a sheepish child. I sent a more aggressive inquiry. The male flexed his wings and gave a faint chirrup.

"Will you answer?" I sent directly to him.

There was no response, and I was unsure I had reached the bird. Its mind was oddly opaque and I felt light-headed and weak. Then I felt a probe in my mind. It had entered with such precise delicacy I had not even been aware of being broached. The finest shield I could create would not bar entrance to such a fine-tuned probe.

"Greetings, funaga," came the thought, shyly, but with undeniable ability.

"I am ElspethInnle," I sent. "What name/shape may I call to you?"

"Do not speak to it!" came a sharp intrusive probe, no less delicate than the first. I wondered if the infection were somehow weakening my natural defences.

The first hesitated, then spoke again, its presence the merest cobweb in my thoughts.

"My name is Astyanax," he sent. I heard a brief aside directed to the other mind. "And it is a She."

The two females, still side by side on the topmost branch, exchanged a doubtful look and the effect was so like two old women conferring that I laughed in spite of everything.

All three looked up at the sound of laughter. One of the others addressed me. "Funaga, we of the Agyllians do not give our names lightly. But answer this: are you a male or a female of your kind? It is not easy to tell your sort of creature apart. You all look so much alike, plucked and naked as an eggling."

"I am female," I sent, wondering why the strange word sounded familiar. "What are Agyllians?"

No one seemed ready to answer, and the two females looked at one another for so long, I sensed they were communicating on some unknown level.

Without warning, the silent communion ended and the largest of the three birds dropped from the tree and glided to land near the cave entrance. The bird was much bigger up close, standing higher than a tall man. I drew back nervously, wondering if Guanette birds were carnivorous. For a time after the Great White, many creatures who had before eaten grasses and leaves turned to meat to survive. It was whispered that men had eaten manflesh at the height of the Chaos, but most creatures had reverted to their natural eating habits. Very little was known of the Guanette bird. Pavo once said he believed the bird to be a new species of creature.

"Is it the one?" the bird sent, apparently thinking aloud. It eyed me intently with beady black eyes.

"I wouldn't taste very good," I sent uneasily. "My wounds are poisoned."

"Wounds! Did you hear what it said?" sent the other female. I was beginning to be able to tell them apart.

"She is the one," Astyanax sent with sudden certainty. Both females looked at him pointedly, then the first returned to its inspection of my limbs.

"It is dark. . . . Hard to tell," murmured the bird on the ground. It came closer in a curious drunken gait. My fingers closed around a rock.

"Funaga," it sent. "I am Ruatha of the Agyllians and my companions are Illyx and Astyanax. Do you truthtell about these injuries?"

Bewildered, I nodded. "I was burned a long time ago. The scars have become infected. I'm sure I would taste horrible. I might even be poisonous," I added earnestly.

The bird made a dry croaking noise. "We do not wish to eat you, funaga. Agyllians are not eaters of flesh."

I relaxed slightly but not too much. The bird hopped lopsidedly closer. "Injuries are common after the flamestorms. You do not look very important," it added thoughtfully. "But perhaps Astyanax is right, and you are the one we seek."

My involuntary withdrawal had jarred my legs, and I heard this through a red mist of pain. I fought against faintness.

"Are you Innle?" the bird asked.

The mist cleared for a moment in shock at hearing Maruman's old title for me. And hadn't I heard it more recently? The effort of sustaining the suppressing stopped me thinking clearly.

I felt dizzy, dissolving in a bloody, painful mist. I concentrated, shoring up the barrier and, slowly, the tides of pain ebbed.

The bird had not moved, but the other two had flown to the ground and hovered some way back.

"Why do you call me that?" I asked.

"The eldar sent us to find the Seeker who lay mortally injured in this valley. Many are injured nearby, but the eldar told that you would be alone, waiting to die. It is hard to know if you are the one. The eldar said there was no time for a mistake."

"What is an eldar?" I asked, fear giving way to puzzlement.

This time Astyanax answered. "Eldar is the name of the high council of the Agyllians. Eldar are the wisest of our kind, and the wisest of the wise is the leader of the Council—the Elder."

Now I was sure I was dreaming, or pain had made me see things. Who ever heard of a Council of birds? Even the dogs and horses who were organized had not gone that far.

"What is this Seeker?"

"One who seeks and either you are or you are not. I say not, or you would not ask such questions," Illyx sent with waspish exasperation.

"Peace," Ruatha sent gently. "We will take her."

I blinked, forcing back a wave of nausea. "What do you mean? I thought you said . . ."

The bird ignored me, hopping up to the cave. One last searching look from ice-colored eyes, then she thrust her head beneath one wing and appeared to be trying to pick out the feathers there. I watched this with some horror. She withdrew a pouch in her sharp beak, dropped it on the ground, and pecked at it until the woven edges parted. Inside was a net.

"No!" I struggled to maintain the suppression.

"The Elder can not leave the ken, so you must come there," Ruatha sent calmly, reaching for my leg with one strong claw.

Pain.

More pain.

Darkness.

I fought against consciousness, frightened of what I would find.

"You will not die...." sent a voice, soft in my mind as a falling leaf.

Slowly, I let myself be drawn, opening my eyes to a sky so pale and clear it was more white than blue. The wind fanned my cheeks with icy fingers, and puffs of cloud burst from my lips and dissolved with each breath exhaled.

"Dreaming..." I thought vaguely, watching another puff of cloud float away. "All a dream... but so real." I turned my head slowly to follow it and froze.

I was having one of those horrible dreams where I seemed to be right on the edge of the highest cliff in the world. Below, visible through a veil of drifting cloud, was a vague grayness that might have been sea or green land.

Piercing the cloud rose numerous stone columns. First there had been winged horses, then giant birds that thought more clearly than any human, and now I had been transported to the top of the world. I wondered dizzily if these were the dreams that came to the endless sleep called death.

I turned my head the other way, wondering what else I would find. I seemed to be lying atop one of the immense pillars. A few steps away from me was a cairn of stones. Guanette birds wheeled and flew and skimmed all about the column in an intricate airborne dance. It was one of the loveliest sights I had ever seen.

I heard the rustle of wings and turned to see one of the birds come to ground. It was a male.

"You have woken, funaga. Welcome to the ken. I am of the eldar. My name is Nerat. Among your kind, I would be called a healer." It sent these thoughts past my shield without effort, with the same scything ability the other birds had demonstrated.

He moved closer but slowly, as if his bones were stiff. I looked at his beak with faint apprehension. Even in a dream it might hurt to be eaten alive. Just as Ruatha had done, the bird reached under a wing withdrawing a pouch. Balancing precariously on one foot it took the pouch from its beak, plucking it open with delicate pecking motions. A few grains of yellowish dust drifted on the wind.

"There will be pain, but not much. The infection in your body is bad but not so bad that Nerat cannot draw it. The real difficulty will be in finding a way to drain off the pain you have allowed to build up behind a mental block. Open your mind to me," he commanded suddenly.

I flinched at the hint of strength, for here was a mind easily as powerful as my own.

The bird tilted its head quizzically. "You find that hard? Dying would be harder. Understand that there is only so much we can do from without. Your body must be taught to repair itself and build its immunities. That is a simple matter of teaching and can be done even as I drain the mental poisons. But you must open willingly to me. If you resist, the block will crumble. You will die. Open your mind and sleep. Trust me."

I swallowed dryly, wondering why even in the midst of a dream, I could not bear the thought of opening my mind completely.

"That is a question you will answer for yourself in time," Nerat sent. "Now, open, before the poison flows too deep. I can do many things, but I cannot bring back the dead to life.

You must not die with so much left undone," he added cryptically.

I saw a sudden vision of Rushton's brooding face and felt the curious ache his memory always evoked.

"He thinks of you too," Nerat said absently, then he made a choking sound and regurgitated a grayish lump of paste onto the stone.

"This comes from the substance the funaga call whitestick," Nerat sent. "I have mixed it with various salivas and acids I have generated to fight the poisons. We call this substance narma, because it rose from the ashes of the Great White and is ever a reminder that the poisons in the earth fade. Next time, there will be no narma."

I shivered, imagining all the world fused smooth as glass and black.

"That is how it will be, the next time," Nerat sent. It stared into my eyes. "Open to me, ElspethInnle, for it is not only your life that hangs in the balance. Leave the block in place until I command you to release it."

Slowly, I let my head fall back onto the stone, trying to make my mind a passive vessel.

Nerat was inside my mind then, swift as a snake, smooth as a single strand of silk. "Relax," he sent. "Dream and I will do my work. I am not interested in the longings and secret thoughts of a funaga."

"Release the pain now," Nerat commanded.

And again I drifted between excruciating pain and numbness, burning heat and freezing cold.

And the pain in my legs. The pain. The pain.

For a time I forgot who I was, and it seemed all my life had been spent in a dream of pain on the top of a mountain.

Occasionally I was aware of Nerat's mind weaving a pattern in my thoughts as complex and intangible as smoke in the wind. Sometimes I smelled flowers and herbs and, sometimes, acrid choking smoke.

And then I floated for a very long time.

"She wakes," came a thought bound with weariness and satisfaction.

I opened my eyes and found myself looking into pale avian eyes. The bird was so close I could see the fine crack in his beak, thin as a hair. I felt his mind like tenebrous fingers at the edge of my thoughts, then he gave a strangely human bob of his head and hopped away.

I did not move for a long while, waiting to see where the dream would take me next. Idly, I wondered if I would feel myself plunge into the mindstream when I died. I thought I would like to hear that glorious siren song once more.

Astyanax appeared. "You are well, ElspethInnle. You can get up now, or do you wish to lie there longer?" he sent with all the politeness of a host not wanting to upset a guest. Urged on by the eager expression in his eyes, I lifted my head carefully.

It is a dream, I told myself. That is why there is no pain.

Slowly, I sat upright. There was no pain in my feet or legs. I made myself look, prepared to see ruined evil-smelling flesh and black infection. My legs seemed to rise at me from a dark mist.

Below the skirt they lay before me, pale as cream and utterly without blemish. Even the old childhood scars of skinned knees had vanished.

My heart sounded like a drum beat as I reached for the laces of my boots. They were stiff with congealed blood, but I felt no pain. The socks were the same, but when I pulled them down, they came away from the skin easily. The flesh beneath was as flawless as that on my calves. Unable to believe my eyes, I reached one hand out slowly, convinced I was delirious or mad. Nothing could heal so completely.

The skin felt smooth and flawless beneath my questing fingers. I wriggled my toes experimentally, watching the movement as if it were an exquisite dance.

I laughed, and my laughter seemed to reverberate off the

mountains. No one could heal that fast, and I knew enough of healing to know it was impossible to heal poisoned flesh or banish old, deep scarring.

"Well, met," Astyanax sent pertly. "You are now to sup with Atthis—Elder of the eldar."

I climbed warily to my feet and let myself be led across to the cairn of stones and around to face an opening in the other side. I looked forward to the next development of my dream.

"Greetings, funaga," came a thought from within the cairn so clear and gentle it was like a song in my mind. There was the sound of shuffling movement and, slowly, a very old female Guanette bird emerged, its feathers less red than dusty brown alternating with bald pink patches. The end of its beak was broken right off, but strangest of all were its eyes. There were no pupils and they were white and milky opaque.

It was blind.

Looking at the ancient bird, a mist of terror crept through my veins with the sudden certainty that I was not dreaming.

The old bird stopped, eyes turned unerringly toward me. The movement reminded me of Dameon's blind grace. "So, now you are come, just as was foreseen. You may call me Atthis, and I will call you ElspethInnle, as does the yelloweyes."

I blinked, startled. Did she mean Maruman? Then something else struck me.

I knew that voice!

It was the voice that had called to me in the old cat's mind.

But I'm dreaming, I thought dazedly. That explains everything.

The old bird stepped closer and a suffocating odor of dust seemed to surround me.

"Why do you pretend? You know this is no dream."

I felt as if someone had kicked me in the stomach, sick and breathless all at once.

"You made Maruman sick!" I said indignantly.

"It could not be helped," Atthis sent gently. "We could not reach you otherwise, at such a distance."

Something else occurred to me. "You told me I had to go on a journey. Is that why I'm here?" A dark journey, she had said.

The bird sent nothing for a long moment, but I had the uncanny feeling she could see from those white orbs.

"I did not know, when first I called to you in my dream-travels through the yelloweyes' mind, that we would meet so soon. I did not foresee then that the Agyllians would have some other part to play. Even the wise are sometimes pawns."

The old bird came closer, its tattered wing brushing one of my feet. I looked into its blind eyes with faint horror.

"You do not like the look of my sightless eyes? Well, sight is a facile thing," Atthis sent.

It was nearing dusk, and a fleeting final sunbeam bathed the old bird in crimson for a moment. Beyond the cairn, lay the rim of the world. On one side the sky was night dark and, on the other, the sun shone its final rays. In the west, the moon was rising flat and bright. I looked back to see that the avian face had not looked away from mine.

"ElspethInnle . . . The Seeker," the old bird sent.

"I don't know why you call me that name. It's just a name Maruman made up. I don't call myself by it," I sent.

"Not all names are chosen," Atthis sent. "Some names are bestowed."

"What is this all about?" I said briskly.

"You know," the bird sent, unperturbed. "Have you not wondered at the coincidences and chances in your life? Have you not felt that there were great forces at work about you—forces for good and for great ill? Have you not felt the purpose in your life burning?"

Unwished, a vision came to me of the black chasm I had glimpsed while being tortured by the Zebkrahn. I thought of

Jik asking if it were possible for it to happen again, and of the Druid and his insane search for Beforetime weaponmachines, his greed for power and revenge blinding him to all else.

"You know," sent Atthis. "You have always known."

"Who are you?" I whispered.

"You may call me a chronicler and . . . what do your people call it—futureteller. Long ago I foresaw that the machines which made the great destructions had not been destroyed. I saw that a second and greater destruction would come to the world, if these machines were used. And despite all the funaga did to bury the past, it was inevitable they would be discovered, unless they were destroyed. That will be no easy matter, for the machines have a kind of intelligence, and will protect themselves. Then I dreamed one would be born among the funaga, a seeker to cross the black wastes in search of the death-machines, one who possessed the power to destroy them.

"Then, I foresaw a faltering in that life—a moment when you might easily die. I saw that you would be near to death with such mental and physical injuries that only the Agyllians might heal you. And so I sent out my egglings to find you."

"If these machines are so far away, might they not be useless by the time anyone found them?" I asked.

"The machines have slept without harm for hundreds of lifetimes. The danger of their discovery alone would not be enough to make me act. But I have foreseen that there is another funaga whose destiny is to discover and resurrect the machines. Your paths intersect. If you do not get there first, he will succeed. You are the Seeker, the other is the Destroyer. If you do not find the machines first . . ."

I felt sick. I wanted to tell myself that it was too ridiculous, that I must be dreaming, that prophecies belonged to stories, but too much had happened. I had seen and felt too much, and in my heart, just as the bird said, I had known for a long time that I would find that chasm. The burning of the doors had only been the beginning.

"Why does it have to be me?" I asked. "Don't I have any choice?"

"There are always choices."

I shook my head, feeling suddenly bitter. "If what you say is true, then the future is set out and I have no real choice."

"The future is a river whose course is long designed, but which a flood or time of no rain might easily alter. Whatever choice you make will have its own consequences. If I had not chosen to interfere, and have you healed, your death would have been a kind of choice."

The sun sank and suddenly it was night, the old bird no more than a dust-scented shadow.

"What do I have to do?" I whispered.

"For now, only live," Atthis sent. "What else comes will come."

"You . . . you brought me here for that?" I asked, incredulous.

The old bird seemed to sigh. "The time is not yet right for the journey to the machines. You were brought here to be healed, and so you are healed."

"I'm afraid," I said.

"That is wise," Atthis sent gently. "Yet put aside fear for now. There is nothing here to harm you. Return to your home and friends. Help them in their struggle, for it is worthy and they have need of you. But do not forget that your true path lies away from them and their quests. They will be glad to see you, for now they think you have passed into the great stream of life and mourn you."

"Have you . . . foreseen that I will destroy the machines if I go on this journey?"

Atthis shifted slightly and dust filled the air. "That I have not foreseen."

A wave of weariness flowed through me, and a kind of hopelessness. I sensed compassion in the mind of the old bird. "One day, you will learn that it is not always safest to be alone.

Until then, happiness will elude you. But perhaps it is best for you to be alone until this quest is ended."

"I don't understand," I sent.

"I know. You are tired. Sleep and while you sleep, my egglings will transport you to a place where one waits to carry you back to the mountain valley of Obernewtyn."

The old bird's eyes stared into mine, and I felt myself falling into them, sinking into the soft whiteness as if it were a feather bed.

XXIV

The cold woke me.

I was freezing and I wondered if it had snowed in the night. I felt a sharp stab of grief and was puzzled by it.

Then I remembered Jik.

I opened my eyes.

I frowned wondering at the icy coldness of the air. Perhaps I had slept longer than I guessed, or winter had come early to the White Valley. Even so, it felt too cold for the highlands. I doubted it had ever been so chilled even at Obernewtyn in the dead of winter.

With a shock, I realized something else. The suppressing barrier was gone from my mind, and so was the pain!

The only answer seemed to be that I had slept off the pain somehow, but if that were the case, the infection in my feet would have worsened, being untended. The pain would be dreadful. Better lie still.

And wait.

I frowned, wondering what I was waiting for. I shivered and again puzzled at the chill in the air.

Why was it so cold?

Curiosity overcame my fear of pain. Very carefully I rolled away from the wall, meaning to look out of the cave entrance to find out if it really had begun to snow. I was surprised to feel no pain and guessed the numbness had returned.

Something warm and moist touched my face and I gasped in fright staring wildly into the darkness. Gazing down at me with dark, troubled eyes, was a black horse—unmistakably Gahltha.

"It is I, funaga," Gahltha sent in answer to my thought that I was still dreaming. "I am Galta who was once Gahltha."

"Galta?" I echoed stupidly. My eyes drifted past the horse, and questions about his self-imposed change of name were swept aside in an even greater shock.

I was no longer in the cave in the White Valley, with its pervasive reek of smoke and the blackened skeletons of trees standing outside like silent sentinels.

I was lying on a flat narrow stone ledge jutting out from what seemed to be a cliff face. I had woken facing the cliff, but there were no walls around me, and no roof. I was out in the open. Spread on all sides beyond the gray-pitted cliff face was a vast, flat plain covered in snow. The moon shone a cold bluish light on the glittering snowy plain. In the distance, I could see darkly defined the shape of mountain spurs and outcrops of cracked stone. There was not a single tree or bush in sight.

The ice and snow, the lack of trees, and the incredible brightness of the stars told me I was in the mountains.

Except that it was impossible.

I thought fleetingly that the suppressing had shattered and the accumulated pain had destroyed my mind. Madness seemed the only rational answer. I giggled at the paradox and shivered when the sound echoed.

Gahltha watched me patiently, his dark coat almost blending with the pelt of the night.

I opened my mouth to speak, then closed it with an audible snap, thinking of the queer dream I had fallen into after Daffyd had gone. If it had been a dream. The dream answered all the questions clamoring in me—how I had come to the high mountains, why and when.

The old bird had said I would be delivered to one who would carry me back to Obernewtyn. But how could it be Gahltha? I clutched at this flaw with a rush of relief, since it must mean the dream was just a dream. If it were real, then all the rest must be real too, the prophecy, and the Beforetime machines. And the healing.

Carefully, I levered myself into a sitting position. There was no pain in my feet or legs. I looked down.

My legs were bare and unscarred. I touched them reverently, remembering I had done that in the dream. Only it had not been a dream. Thin legs with knobbled knees and rather long feet, but at that moment the most perfect legs in the world.

"Where are we?" I asked my feet.

"In the mountains," Gahltha answered gently. I looked up to find him staring across the frozen wasteland. "When I came here, there was a lake. Now it has frozen over. I have found a place where we will be warm. We must go there before the storm comes."

"Storm?" I said vaguely.

Gahltha looked down at me with grave serenity, and I wondered at the change in him. The last time I had seen him on the banks of the Suggredoon, he had been almost insane with terror and frustration. The violent impatience and scorching bitterness that had characterized his behavior had disappeared as completely as my own wounds.

"Come," he sent. "If you are too weak to walk, I will carry you. Soon the storm will come and it must not find us in the open."

I looked up at the cloudless sky, wondering why he thought there was going to be a storm. But I left my doubt unspoken. So much had happened that was impossible to explain, that a clear sky might easily hide a storm. I pulled my

socks and shoes back on and slid from the ledge, tensing myself
for the pain that had been part of my life for so long.

There was a faint jarring, but no pain. I stared down at
my feet in fresh wonder.

"Come," Gahltha sent. "There is wood. You will light a
fire for us and perhaps we will live. It will be a bad storm."

I looked up, startled, and realized with a faint shiver that
he was quite serious.

I stepped forward, sinking up to my knees in powdery
snow. Gahltha went ahead, forging a wide track. I followed in
his wake, marveling at the pleasure of walking without pain. It
was ironic—for two years I had longed to be free of the pain
and crippling scars on my feet, and just when I had finally begun
to accept that I would have to live with it forever, it was gone.

The wind whipped my hair and skirt around, now that we
were away from the buffer of the cliffs, and the cold stole into
my bones long before we reached Gahltha's shelter. It turned
out to be a cave at the end of a narrow cleft. I sighed, thinking
I was in danger of becoming accustomed to living in caves, I
had seen the inside of so many. This one was dry and surprisingly warm, being cut off from the wind by its awkward position
in the wedge-shaped cleft. Outside, the wind had begun to whine
sullenly.

"We must block the mouth or the coldwhite will come
in," Gahltha sent.

Under his direction, I labored for more than an hour,
shivering in the light dress and coat, to pile stones in a cairn
round the mouth of the cave. When I had finished, there was
nothing but a narrow slit I could barely squeeze through.

Impulsively, I went outside the cleft, braving a scything
wind. The ledge I had woken on was barely visible, dwarfed by
the immensity of the cliff from which it extended. But it was
there. It was too dark to see the top of the cliff, but I had the
feeling I would not be able to do that, even in the full daylight.

"Now the fire," Gahltha instructed, when I came back inside. Fortunately I still had my hand flint, and Gahltha led me in the darkness to a pile of wood and twigs. I managed to burn myself twice before setting them to flame. The cave was quite big and nearly round. I crouched over the flames trying to warm my fingers, and smoke curled up in a shower of cinders to the roof of the cave. Outside, the wind had reached a shrieking intensity, and snow fell in dense flurries.

I looked at Gahltha searchingly. "I must have gone mad," I said, more to myself than him.

He only stared into the flames as if mesmerized.

"How long do you think the storm will last?" I asked humbly.

He answered simply that he did not know.

I bit my lip. "How did you get here?" Never mind about me, I thought.

Gahltha looked up. "The funaga must know everything," he sent, but without his old contempt. He looked into the fire as if it were a window, and miniature flames leaped in his eyes.

"I spent many days in the place where the mountain ate you. I wished I had died there, for I thought I did not care what happened to me, but when the funaga tried to trap me with their nets, I fought them and ran away up to the mountains. I did not go to Obernewtyn, but higher, to the fields where I ran with Avra. But I could not stay there. I went on and on to the high places where the old equines go to die. I meant to abase myself before their spirits. I hoped I would die myself, that they would demand it of me.

"I did not eat or drink, as is the custom among equines seeking a vision. I waited and, day after day, there was no answer. I thought the old ones were deaf to me and had cast me out. I called myself Galta—nothing.

"Then one night I slept, and in my dream I saw a vision of a high mountain valley, where a lake lay yet unfrozen in the midst of ice and snow. A voice told me to find that place. It promised that I would find absolution there. And when I woke, I remembered, and began to search.

"It was hard and many times I despaired and thought of giving up, but every night in my sleep, the voice came, reassuring me, urging me higher, promising an answer to the pain in my heart and a purpose for my life. It told me many things for my ears alone, and a blackness, which had been inside me all my life, began to melt as easily as coldwhite before the sun. I could have gone back to Obernewtyn then, for I understood that pride and arrogance, rather than true grief, had kept me away. But the voice urged me always to go on.

"At last, I found this valley. Then the voice came again, telling me I had been drawn to the mountains to take part in a quest whose end would concern all living creatures, not only equine and funaga. This was to be my life's most important work, above any other glory I had imagined." Gahltha's thought was faintly awed.

"The voice told me a funaga would be brought here whom I must keep safe. One day, this funaga would fight a great and perilous battle whose outcome was unknown even to the wisest of the wise, but which might mean the destruction of all life on the earth for ever. I must carry this funaga wherever it wishes to go, and protect it with my own life if it were needed.

"It was strange and ironic that I, who had so despised the funaga, should find myself bound to such a task. There was a time when I would have refused, believing funaga to be a blight on the world. But the voice had made me see that no life form is greater than another, and that all are bound up in an intricate and delicately balanced pattern of coexistence.

"In the daylight, I found this cave. And then I waited. Many weeks passed, yet always the voice told me to wait. So I waited. Two moons passed, and still I waited, wondering if it were my punishment to wait for ever in these cold lands for one who would never come," he sent bleakly.

"Two moons?" I whispered incredulously. I remembered how I had imagined time passing in my sleep. If Gahltha were right, winter was near ended. I felt a stab of despair at the thought that Obernewtyn was yet unwarned, unless Daffyd had got there in time.

"Then I found you, lying on the ledge. At first I could not believe you were the funaga the voice had spoken of. But why else would you be there? And how could you have come there—there was not a single footprint in all the untouched snow? Then I thought you were dead, for your skin was like ice, but your heart was beating. So I waited for you to wake."

There was a long silence in the wake of his strange tale. Outside the storm winds howled derisively, and tiny whirlwinds of snow blew through the cave opening, falling in a white drift against the stones. The fire crackled and orange firelight danced silently along the walls of the cave.

"Only someone insane could believe your story. Or mine," I said softly, but my words sounded hollow. I had fallen asleep, half dead, in the highlands, and woken completely healed, sixty days and more than a thousand spans distant, on the highest, loneliest mountain peaks.

I felt a ghostly echo of the dangerous weight of pain pressing against the feebly erected barrier in my mind and shuddered.

The fire cracked and I turned my face to the glowing embers, drinking in the warmth.

"When this storm is over, we will go back to Obernewtyn," I said.

But outside, the storm winds shrieked.

XXV

Hoping the sudden silence was not merely a lull, I used a stick to clear the snow and rocks from the entrance of the cave. We had lost count of time and the firewood was nearly exhausted.

Coming out of the narrow crevice, I was cold and hungry, but I forgot physical discomfort in the dazzling sight that met my eyes. The world was blanketed in pristine white, reflecting the sunshine with painful intensity.

Unaccountably, I remembered sitting at the Kinraide orphan home with Maruman, dreaming of the fabled world of the Snow Queen, a forbidden Oldtime tale my mother had told us. A delicate lace of icicles hung from the ledge where Gahltha had found me.

"It is a hard trek to Obernewtyn," Gahltha warned. "It will not be safe to go too quickly. The whitecold will hide crevices and rocks. We will have to put our feet down carefully."

"Life has always been a matter of putting your feet down carefully," I said, but even the prospect of a long hard trek through frost-bitten country with an empty belly and scant clothes could not quell my joy.

We left at once for there were no preparations to be made. Gahltha led, forging a path; even so, my shoes and legs were quickly soaked. I was glad to walk since the exertion and the sun reflected blindingly from the snow kept me warm.

Gahltha warned me to shade my eyes with a piece of cloth to avoid being snow-blinded.

I looked back once before we began at the mountain in whose skirts we had sheltered. It sloped backwards, outjutting rocks and drifts of snow adhering to the flat surfaces, making it look like the stern face of a very old man. The slant made it impossible to see the top, and I wondered if that were where the Ken of the Agyllians lay.

The more time that passed between the meeting with the strange birds in their lofty eyrie, the more fantastic and unbelievable the whole matter seemed, the more dreamlike. Only the healed scars on my legs and feet reminded me that it had really happened. And how would I explain them?

We traveled across the ice lake and the land beyond seemed to go right to the horizon. This puzzled me until Gahltha said the distance was an illusion. We were on a large flat plateau and would shortly reach its edge.

The wind which had howled for days and nights seemed to have exhausted itself, and the air was clear and still. The only sound to break the silence was that of our footsteps and breathing. We might be the only people alive in all the Land. Hunger increased the heady feeling. I felt as if the air were a kind of fement that one might become drunk on. At the same time, I felt I could understand anything and everything very easily there on the roof of the world.

It was nearing dusk when we reached the edge of the plateau. I was within a single handspan of the edge before I realized. Only a sharp warning from Gahltha stopped me walking off the edge. I looked over and a cold freshening gust of air blew up into my face. What I saw below took my breath away.

Clouds were strung out across the sky like skeins of wool—below my feet!

Glimpsed through a woolly curtain, the Land was barely visible. Seen from above, the clouds were fluffy mounds of cream or sea foam shot with glorious sunset colors—a fairy realm. And between the Land and the plateau there were rank upon rank of mountains, jagged as upturned teeth, streaked with snow and lacking the slightest touch of color or softness.

Some of the mountains were dense and dark, unmistakably Blacklands. Few dared travel through mountainous terrain because a snowfall could hide a lethal plain and much of the poisoned badlands was difficult to tell apart from untainted ground. Yet Gahltha seemed unperturbed, saying only that the voices had told him where to walk safely.

I had often gazed at the distant mountains, but I had never had any real idea of the sheer size and barrenness of them. Gahltha's lone trek to the heights had been an incredible act of faith.

Something glistened on the far horizon.

Squinting, I realized I was looking at the great sea. For a moment I seemed to smell the salty wetness of waves on the shore. All the world lay spread at my feet. The one thing I could not see was a way down. The plateau stood apart from the other plains and mountains. I looked at the black horse and found him watching me inscrutably.

"I brought you here to see the world, funaga. I wondered if it would move you as it once moved a proud and bitter equine. Before this, I saw my own smallness, and understood how stupid and arrogant I had let pride and hatred make me," he sent.

"Not many could see this and be unchanged," I sent gently. "But you haven't said how we can get down."

"Patience," Gahltha sent.

He cast one final look from the heights and turned with a sigh. I followed, wondering what the Elder had said to him.

He made for the opposite side of the plateau and there I looked out, aghast.

Again the plateau was high, but there were no clouds to hide the dreadful vision from us.

Stretched out like a black skin were hundreds of spans of

Blacklands, lifeless and still. I had thought the snowy slopes barren, but this was a terrible dead stretch of obsidian flecked here and there with dark gleaming pools reflecting a tarnished sky. An arm of mountains, breaking away from the main mass, ran across the nightmarish terrain and out of sight. It was the Land, dead and without hope of life. Looking at that it was impossible to believe Pavo's assurance that the Blacklands would not last forever.

Even as I watched, night crept like a dark shadow across the bleak plains, and though the heights were still bathed in sunlight, I felt strangely cold.

"Next time, there will be nothing left . . ." Atthis had warned.

I shivered, chilled to the bone. I had wondered why the Agyllians left me in the mountains when it would have been so easy for them to carry me down to Obernewtyn. Now, I thought I understood. They had known Gahltha would bring me there. They had wanted me to see it.

"I did not know it went on so far. So much land poisoned . . ." I whispered.

"Perhaps, there are many lessons to be learnt in the mountains," Gahltha sent gravely.

I could not take my eyes away.

I thought of the Oldtimers, and wondered whether they would have built their weaponmachines if they could have foreseen what would come to pass. And why create machines that would outlast a hundred lives? Had they been so enamored of war and destruction that they must make it immortal?

No wonder equines despised the funaga. Perhaps it was fitting that the solution lay in human hands.

For the first time, I felt I could understand the original Councilmen and their tyrannous rule. Farmers and children of the Oldtimers, they had understood the will to destroy and the hunger for power that knew no boundaries. Perhaps they had even known the deathmachines existed and had hoped to insure no one would ever use them again. No wonder they had forbidden delving into the past.

They had been afraid.

Unfortunately, the repressive philosophies had become a different sort of threat. I doubted the present Council understood the real dangers any better than those who had made the weaponmachines. I had only to think of Henry Druid and Alexi to know there would always be men and women prepared to pay any price for power. Even our own Teknoguild would risk agonizing death to revive the knowledge of a lost age.

The Elder was right. It was inevitable the machines would someday be unearthed and used. Atthis said I was the only one who would be in the right place at the right time, the only one with any chance of destroying them. So that made me the Seeker. But even she had not been able to say if I would succeed.

I wondered who was destined to revive the machines. The Destroyer, Atthis had named him, even as I was called the Seeker.

Resolutely, I thrust the machines and the Agyllians from my mind, and looked at Gahltha. "I will be glad to go from this place and its foreboding lessons."

He blew air from distended nostrils. "I did not bring you here for lessons. See, there is where we will go down."

I followed his gaze and saw a natural stone path leading unevenly to the next plateau, cleaving to the edge of the slope. The path began not far from where we stood, moving this way, then that, ever lower, across the face of the cliff.

Gahltha looked at me. "You are weak still. Ride on my back and we will travel more quickly." I looked at him curiously.

"You want me to ride?" I asked.

"One warrior will carry another, if the strength of one proves greater. Each has his own strength, but also his own weakness." He spoke with the air of repeating a well-learned lesson.

"Wise words," I said simply. "I am glad to ride on your

back if it will bring us more quickly to the barud." Barud was
the equine word symbol for homeplace.

And so began the last stage of my long journey back to
Obernewtyn.

We traveled that day and the next through the monotonous snow-bound terrain of the high mountains, and on the
third day we came upon a few scant green shoots, thrusting
their tips through the snow. "It will be more dangerous now
that the thaw has begun," Gahltha said. "But I think tomorrow
we will reach the valley of the barud."

The afternoon darkened as snow clouds gathered overhead,
and I shivered in the cold. With the bleak afternoon came unexpected doubts. I began to fear Obernewtyn had changed, and
that I would find there was no longer a place for me there. My
whole life had been spent as an outsider and, even at Obernewtyn, I had felt misplaced, until the journey to the coast. Ironic
if I discovered too late where my own barud lay.

Just on dusk, for the first time, we encountered another
creature. A wolf.

The wolves which frequented the mountains were savage,
pale-eyed wraiths with coats the color of mist and snow. They
were nearly impossible to spot deliberately, and it was sheer luck
that I saw this one. I had been plodding along, shivering and
staring aimlessly into the distance when the landscape appeared
to shift fractionally. I realized I had been staring right at one
of the white wolves without seeing it. It had been watching us,
but now it turned, melting into the white landscape.

Later I heard several desolate calls in the distance. I fancied
the howls were messages concerning the traveling funaga and
equine. I was tempted to try communicating, but the wild keen-
ing calls across the frozen wastes made a desolate song of the
night and did not invite a response.

The calls went on for hours, then abruptly ceased.

I was glad of the respite, but Gahltha seemed more disturbed by the silence than by the bloodcurdling howls. I was too tired to worry and slept leaning against his warm flank. Gradually I felt him relax too. Exhausted and half-starved as we were, we needed sleep. Initial hunger pains had long since given way to an empty ache that was easier to bear. If sleep were all that remained, then that would have to be enough to get us home.

Suddenly, Gahltha stiffened and I was jerked awake. I looked around in the pitch darkness fearfully. Dense clouds obscured the moon.

"What is it?" I sent.

"The Brildane ..." Gahltha responded.

I laid a gentle hand across his back, wondering why he stayed so still, if there were danger.

"What or who are Brildane?" I asked.

"I do not know what name is given them by the funaga, but Brildane is the name they call themselves. We name them gehdra because they are invisible. They have no time for any creature but their own kind. But they hate the funaga because your kind trap and slay their young."

"Are they hungry?" I asked, trying to understand what sort of animal it could be.

"If they were, we would already be dead," Gahltha sent. "They called in the night to gather their brethren. The mountain equines know a little of their strange speech. Their calls concerned us. They wonder what we are doing here. The gehdra claim the high mountains as their own world. Here we are intruders."

"Wolves! The Brildane are wolves!" I cried, suddenly understanding. I looked at Gahltha. "Are you telling me they're just curious?" I asked.

"The curiosity of the gehdra is as savage as its hunger," Gahltha sent quellingly.

I looked around uneasily, wondering how he had known

of their presence. Even now, I could sense no minds but ours. The wolves must have some ability to cloak their minds. And I had not heard a sound.

"Would it help if I sent a greeting?" I suggested.

"No!" Gahltha sent urgently, as if he expected me to leap up and rush into the night with a cry of greeting on my lips. "The gehdra do not think like any other kind of beast. It is impossible to predict what they will do. Speaking to them would not stop them eating us, if that were their desire. If they wanted to confront us, they would do it. But I think they came to look, not to feed or speak. Better to do nothing. With the gehdra, it is always safest."

Gahltha's warnings were underlined by his own tangible fear. I found myself too frightened to move in case it was taken by the wolves as a threat. Bleakly I realized these were the very wolves Ariel had hunted and trapped. Some he had killed. Others he had driven mad and used to hunt their own kind. The wolves were the same kind as the maddened beasts who had torn Sharna apart. I dared not stir a limb until Gahltha reported that they had gone, melting back into the night as mysteriously as they had appeared.

"Are you sure you didn't imagine them?" I asked.

"In the morning you will see," was all he would say.

It was hard to go back to sleep, but eventually I fell into a light, troubled slumber. The night grew steadily colder, and even Gahltha's considerable body heat could not keep me warm. Towards morning, I gave up trying and lay waiting for the horse to wake.

During the night, I had dreamed of Ariel as he had been, a boy with almost unearthly beauty and a sadistic turn of mind that had delighted in causing pain.

Ironic that we had let him escape, so certain he could not survive the winter and the wolves. And how had he survived? That was a mystery in itself. Of us all, Matthew, grief-stricken over Cameo's death, had wanted to make sure Ariel had perished. He, alone, had believed Ariel might have survived. There had been talk of a search, but there had been so many things to do before the pass thawed that it had been forgotten.

Of Alexi, Madam Vega, and Ariel, I had disliked Ariel most. Alexi had been insane and dangerous, and Madam Vega power hungry, but I had never known what motivated Ariel. He had a perverted delight in tormenting anyone weaker than himself.

I felt Gahltha stir with relief. It was barely light before we were off, but light enough to see that Gahltha had been right the night before. The snow all around us was covered in paw prints, some a mere handspan from where my feet had lain.

The Brildane.

I shivered, and suddenly it began to snow. Just a few flakes at first, but blown with stinging force into our faces by a hard, icy wind. The snow was already thick underfoot and made walking tiring. Gahltha offered to carry me, but he could only walk a little faster than I, and was easily as tired, so I refused. I knew neither of us could go much further without proper rest and food.

Near to dropping, I was trying to remember how long since I had eaten when Gahltha neighed loudly. Squinting against the wind and flying snow, I realized he had rounded a spur of rock and was out of sight. Forcing weary limbs to hurry, I caught up.

"What is it?" I sent, wondering if I had strength enough left to deal with another obstacle.

"We have reached the valley of the barud."

I blinked stupidly. Barud? "Obernewtyn!"

All weariness fell away from me then, but alongside joy was the nagging fear that something had gone wrong. I was close enough to have sent a questing probe, but something kept me from it, a desire to have my first glimpse of Obernewtyn unhampered by greetings and explanations.

I had just begun to recognize some of the hills and stone

hummocks when the wind fell away and the snow stopped making our first glimpse of Obernewtyn clear and unmistakable.

A cry of happiness died in my throat, stillborn. I stumbled to a halt, unable to believe my eyes.

All that remained of Obernewtyn was a charred ruin.

XXVI

Only a firestorm could have done so much damage. Little remained of Obernewtyn but rubble. Walls and buildings were no more than jagged, blackened stumps of stone. The wind-blown snow adhered to the crevices and a rambling kind of thorn-brush thrust its roots deep into the cracked stone.

It looked like a ruin of years rather than moons. How had it degenerated so quickly? I blinked, for when I stared hard, I seemed to see the ghostly shape of Obernewtyn as it had been.

Tears blurred my vision, and the wind froze them before they could fall. It was bitter cold on the hillside, but I scarcely felt the chill. To have traveled so long and far, and find Obernewtyn a ruin was beyond a nightmare.

"Come," Gahltha sent.

I stared at him incredulously.

He asked doubtfully, "Do you not want to go to the barud? I am sworn to take you wherever you will."

I shook my head, disturbed by his lack of emotion. Perhaps he had changed less than I realized, and welcomed the downfall of any funaga institution. I looked back at the wreckage and wondered whether any had escaped the firestorm.

Stumbling forward, I prayed I would find some clue as to where everyone had gone. The ground was sodden from the melting snow, and fresh flakes fell like salt on the dark wet earth. What a tragic irony for the lie that had protected us for so long, to come so horribly true.

Abruptly I stopped and stared, squinting against the cold wind blustering across the valley. I thought I had seen a smudge of smoke.

It had come from somewhere on the far side of the valley, near the pass to the highlands. My heart beat faster as I made out a number of dark shapes that might be buildings. It seemed to me I was looking at a small settlement.

Gahltha offered to carry me, though he seemed puzzled at my instruction not to pass too close to Obernewtyn. It occurred to me that equines might not know that a poisonous residue was left behind by a firestorm.

Coming closer to the settlement, I saw a movement that warned it was not deserted. Some obscure instinct of caution stopped me riding directly into the camp. I asked Gahltha to take us into a clump of trees a short distance away. With the mountains behind and on one side, and the ruins of Obernewtyn on the other, we were safe from detection.

Peering through the greenery, I could see several roughly constructed stone-and-thatch huts, set in a circle, and surrounded by a wall of stripling branches. Even at a distance, it was clearly a poor settlement and an air of hopeless dilapidation hung over it.

Two men emerged from one of the hovels. I bit my lip.

Soldierguards! There was no mistaking the yellow cloaks they wore as a badge of office.

They could only have come through the pass. That meant the thaw had opened the way. Bleakly I reflected that the Council would have no more cause to doubt Rushton's word, if he had survived the firestorm. A strange feeling of despair filled me at the realization that he might be dead.

I felt Gahltha's restive movements and looked at him.

"Perhaps we should go to Obernewtyn to find out what has passed here," he suggested.

I shook my head impatiently. "What good will that do? Besides it would be dangerous to go there now. I want to get a better look at that camp. The soldierguards can't have built those huts. I want to know who did. We'll go back the way we came, and right around to the other side. There are trees close to the settlement there and we can get much closer without being seen. Whatever happens, we will be able to shelter in the teknoguild cave network. Who knows, perhaps we will find someone there."

Gahltha made no response. Puzzled by his peculiar behavior, I stood to mount when he neighed softly and sent a warning that someone approached.

I prayed whoever it was would not walk right into the trees.

To my horror, it was three soldierguards. Fortunately, they stopped in a clearing a span from where we were hidden. Grumbling about the cold, they sat on logs, rubbing their hands and faces.

"I tell you I am weary of this hellish place," said one man resentfully. " 'Get wood,' the captain orders, but what is the use of it? Quick as the fire warms you, the wind chills you to the bone."

"That fellow Rushton does nowt seem to feel th' cold. It whistles through t' holes in his clothes an' he nary shows a shiver. His blood must be as cold as th' snow," said a big burly man with a highland accent.

"No sense, no feeling, they say," said the first. "No sane man would want to stay up here, yet that fool claims he will rebuild Obernewtyn once the taint is faded."

The big man nodded. "I heard he were offered a billet in th' lowlands, but chose to come back here. Is that th' act of a sane man?"

"He is proud enough to want his inheritance rebuilt. But I think pride is a kind of madness in him. They say he fought off Seditioners to make his claim on Obernewtyn. If that's so, why would he then become a Seditioner and risk it all? It makes no sense. I swear this is a fool's errand," said the first speaker, rising and stamping his feet.

"Three suns have risen on this barren valley since we came here. And why?" he went on.

"Why indeed?" asked the third man who had not spoken yet. He had an unpleasant hissing sort of voice and quick, sly eyes. "The story is that we are to find out if Obernewtyn is truly burnt, and if there is truth in rumor of Sedition here."

"One look answered those questions," said the first man.

"Did it?" asked the third in an insinuating tone.

His two companions eyed him curiously.

"Do ye say there is Sedition here? I have seen no sign of it," said the big highlander at length.

"I say neither yes nor no to it. But the captain is no fool. He would not stay here for pleasure. Perhaps he knows something we do not."

"What do ye mean?" asked the highlander.

"Just this: Captains, as a rule, know more than rank and file soldierguards. I heard he had his orders direct from the Council's agent. Who knows what was told him," said the hissing man.

"There is somethin' strange about these mountain folk," opined the highlander after a moment of thought. "I dinna know what it is, but when I am among them, my skin creeps."

"Mine too," said the first man. "Ariel spoke certain of Sedition, and he's seldom wrong."

"Call him not by name!" snarled the third man, glancing about as if he feared immediate reprisal.

"His name is not so secret," sneered the first.

"Well then, call him by it when next you see him, fool.

There is one to make a man's skin crawl," offered the third man.

"I say we mun just as soon kill them all, miserable creatures," the big highlander pronounced. "Then we need not trouble ourselves with findin' out if they be Seditioners."

"Usually, we are told to bring back prisoners alive. But I have heard it whispered the Council's agent wants none to come alive from the mountains. I wonder if it is true, and why," pondered the first man.

"I wonder what Ariel suspects . . . or fears," said the third soldierguard.

After a long pause, the highlander shook himself like an ox. "I wonder only how long before my head rests on a real bed, an' my tongue tastes a sweet fement. . . ." he sighed plaintively.

"Never, if I catch you idling again when I have given an order!" came a new authoritative voice, so close my heart skipped a beat. Cautiously, I moved and saw that two more men had entered the clearing. From the markings on his collar, the tall, sallow-faced newcomer was the captain. The other stood hidden.

Then the captain moved and I caught sight of the person behind him, but it was no soldierguard. I stifled a gasp at the sight of Rushton!

Clad in shabby trews and a ragged jumper, he was grim faced and gaunt. The wild, dark gleam in his eyes told me why the soldierguards had judged him mad. He looked like a man possessed, and deep lines of suffering and despair made him appear far older than his years. There was a bitter twist to his lips that I had never noticed before, and I was filled with pity at the thought of what the destruction of Obernewtyn had meant to him. He must have loved it more than life for its demise to mark him so.

As if he sensed my scrutiny, his head turned and I shivered, for it seemed to me he stared straight into my eyes. I shuddered at the emptiness in his face and was glad when he turned aside to follow the captain and his men from the thicket.

I slumped back, aching all over from tension. I could not forget Rushton's face, for it warned me worse might have happened than I could even imagine.

I went afoot as we made our way back along the valley, but this time we went more warily and stayed close to the walls of Obernewtyn where trees grew thickly, offering shelter. I noticed fumes of faint blue smoke rising from the ruins and was struck by the feeling that I had seen them before. Gahltha stirred beside me.

"Elspeth?" came a voice from behind. I whirled in fright and found myself looking into the astounded face of Daffyd. Gahltha, who did not know him, moved aggressively between us, until I reassured him.

Daffyd came forward slowly, as if he thought I would disappear. "By Lud, it is you!" he cried. "I thought I was dreaming with my eyes open. But how? We thought you dead. Your feet..." He looked down.

"Are healed," I said firmly. "I coerced you to think them worse than they were because I knew I could not make it back to the mountains before the pass closed. But what has happened here? Was Obernewtyn like this when you arrived? Were any hurt in the firestorm? And when did the soldierguards come?"

Daffyd burst into laughter. "It must be a powerful illusion if it fools even the guildmistress of the Farseekers. But they do say little Dragon is as strong as you were... are," he added ruefully.

I felt my mouth drop open and a great joy welled up in me, "Then... this," I waved a trembling hand at the ruins. "This is all an *illusion?*"

"Of course," Daffyd said.

I sank to my knees, weak with relief. "No wonder Gahltha behaved so oddly. Dragon's illusions do not work on animals."

I sent an explanation to Gahltha, who still looked puzzled.

"Then everyone is inside?"

Daffyd shook his head. "Rushton thought that too much risk. We are using the Teknoguild cave network as a base. Only a few live in the camp for appearance's sake. Rushton, of course, Ceirwan, Dameon, and all others trained in empathy and farseeking."

"Not coercers?" I wondered.

"They are in another hidden camp very near the pass," Daffyd explained. "They are our insurance, in case this sleight of hand fails to deceive the soldierguards, and open battle is needed to stop them carrying tales to the Council." He frowned. "But how is it they did not see you come through the pass just now?"

I shrugged thinking fast. "I came very stealthily. And I have some coercive Talent..." I realized it would suit me well to have everyone think I had come from the highlands, rather than from the high mountains. "But we might have to fight despite this illusion." I told Daffyd what I had overheard.

"It is, true the soldierguards have stayed longer than we hoped," Daffyd said worriedly. "Tonight Rushton will come here, and you can tell him this news." He gave me a quick look. "He will be amazed to see you here. I think your death was a grievous thing to him."

I nodded absently. "I overhead one of the soldierguards say they have been here for three days. How is it Dragon can sustain an illusion so long?"

"She has practiced all wintertime," Daffyd said. "It is fortunate I was able to warn them, for as you feared the soldierguards came up here the moment the pass thawed. Dragon has proved our best defense. She is very powerful. Even so, it is a strain and she does not maintain it during the dark hours. Luck has made them come in the waning of the moon. The blue fumes are an added touch to give credence to Rushton's story that the ruins are contaminated. That stops the soldierguards wanting a closer look." He glanced at the ruin pensively. "I wonder what made them suspicious."

"From what I heard, it was something Ariel told them, before they came."

"Dragon is not far from here," Daffyd said. "It is easier for her to hold the illusion away from the distraction of people. Matthew stays with her to protect her. We three are camped not far from here. No one would dare come so close to Obernewtyn. They will be back after dark. In the meantime, what about some food?"

"I'm starving," I said fervently. "And so is Gahltha."

As we walked to the campsite, I explained to the black horse all that Daffyd had told me. It did not take Daffyd long to make a small fire and warm some fruit stew. Gahltha preferred grass to the bags of horse feed. I sat gratefully by the fire Daffyd made and accepted a cup of strong fement to warm me, once I had eaten.

"I meant to go back down to the Druid camp after delivering Dragon and your message, but that very night snow fell thick and closed the pass," Daffyd said, sitting beside me.

"You're worried about Gilaine and the others, I suppose..." I began, then faltered, seeing the grim look on the armsman's face.

"I don't know if they're still there. One of the soldierguards said the firestorm had all but burnt out the White Valley."

"Oh, Daffyd," I said, aghast.

Again he shook his head. "I don't believe they are dead. I would have known. Rushton has pledged Obernewtyn's help to find them when the soldierguards are gone." He sipped his drink as if it held a bitter draught.

We both froze at the sound of running feet. The brush parted and Roland burst into the open. "Where's Matthew?" he cried. "We need him to farseek the camp! Something has gone wrong. All contact has been severed, but we dare not go down there with the soldierguards..." He stopped dead, catching sight of me. "Elspeth?"

"Yes it's me," I said impatiently. "Are there no other farseekers but those in the camp?"

"None strong enough but Matthew," he said in a dazed fashion. His eyes lit up. "But you..."

I nodded impatiently and waved him to silence, closing my eyes to concentrate. I sent my mind flying toward the makeshift camp, seeking out any familiar pattern. It was as if all there slept, though it was not yet dark.

At last I located a weak sending. Focusing in, I discovered it was Ceirwan.

"Who... who is that?" he sent groggily. I was astounded at the weakness of his sending. His call was barely discernible.

"It is Elspeth," I sent clearly. "What has happened there?"

There was a pause. "Elspeth... impossible."

I felt his grief, but could waste no time on it. "I did not die. Now you must concentrate. I can hardly understand you. What has happened?"

I sensed his struggle to concentrate. "I... They drugged us. But I drank little of their draughts. The soldierguards have grown suspicious and think we hide evidence of Sedition in the ruins." His signal faded.

"Ceirwan," I sent strongly. "Are you hurt?"

"No one hurt. All... but me unconscious. Rushton bade me call in hope that someone would hear. You must stop the soldierguards from getting to Obernewtyn... Coercers..." He faded out again and this time it was impossible to recall him.

I opened my eyes. "The soldierguards have drugged them and are about to go and examine the ruins. We have to stop them."

"We'll have to fight. Can you call the coercers?" Daffyd asked.

I shook my head. "I've a better idea, Daffyd. You ride Gahltha and bring back one of the coercers. Gevan, if you can.

As well, I want you to get a group of those left to go down to the camp as soon as the soldierguards leave..." I outlined my plan quickly.

"It might just work," Roland said.

"And it would explain why Rushton was so anxious to keep them away from the ruins. But will the captain react as you expect?" Daffyd asked.

"It's my guess they'll prove a craven lot, more worried about their own skins than their duty. But if not, Gevan is a coercer, and so am I, at need."

"You?" Roland asked sharply. I ignored him, giving Daffyd a leg up onto Gahltha. The black horse allowed Daffyd to mount, then sped off, keeping close to the treeline.

"Come. We'll meet Gevan in front of Obernewtyn," I told the Healer guildmaster. "We'll have to make sure they don't come too close to the buildings. Now describe to me the symptoms of..."

∽

It was dusk when the soldierguards appeared, riding along the entrance road leading up to Obernewtyn. Catching sight of Gevan and me, the captain reined in his horse.

"Who are you, girl? I've not seen you before. What trickery is here?" he shouted harshly.

When I did not answer, he ordered one of his men to bind us. The man dismounted, but he paused when he was close enough to see my face clearly.

"Captain... I think there's something wrong with her..." he called uneasily.

I lurched toward him and he backed away hastily. "Help me!" I moaned. "Help me. I am ill."

The captain dismounted, staring at me suspiciously. "Ill? What do you mean? I won't stand for——" He stopped, having come close enough to see the black blisters on my lips. Gevan moaned loudly, making him jump. His face changed, contorting with horror and he spun away. "Lud's curse! This creature has the plague."

The soldierguards murmured in dismay.

"Shut up and let me think!" the captain snarled, mounting his horse. The other soldierguard did the same.

"What are we goin' to do, Captain? We won't be allowed to live if anyone finds out we've been in contact with the plague!" said one soldierguard in a frightened voice.

"We can't stay here. I don't want to die of plague!" wailed another man.

"We won't," said the captain tightly. "Now listen to me, all of you. It will take closed mouths and a tight story to save us from being burnt. We will tell the Council all was as Rushton had claimed—Obernewtyn a poor ruin, the valley tainted. We will tell them we found no one here. No one must ever know there was plague here. Even a whisper would be enough to see us dead."

The men nodded, ashen-faced.

"But are we not already infected?" asked one of the men.

"Thank Lud we made our own camp and did not sup or dally with these wretched people. 'Tis said plague spreads by close living. I think we will be safe if we leave at once."

"What about these two and the people in the camp? We can't leave them here alive," said another of the soldierguards.

The captain shook his head grimly. "There must be no witnesses. If anyone ever does come up here, it must be exactly as we have said. Do not bother with these half-dead wretches. The wolves will finish them. But while the others are drugged, we will burn the camp. Now let's ride. I want to be quit of this cursed valley before full night."

It was growing dark when the soldierguards torched the camp.

As I had hoped, they did not trouble to make sure their victims were inside, else they would have found the settlement deserted. The coercers had carried all the unconscious out and set them under the trees.

From the distance, we watched the huts blaze. Silhouetted in orange light, the soldierguards let out a hoarse cheer before mounting and riding out of the valley. None looked behind him.

"Are they all right?" Gevan asked, watching Roland lift Rushton's eyelid.

He nodded in satisfaction. "Only drugged, though I have not seen this kind of drug before." He moved to look at Ceirwan.

I leaned over Rushton and stared into his ravaged face. In repose, he looked so terribly sad.

Unexpectedly, his eyes fluttered open, flamed with longing, then he shook his head and groaned. "Ah, Elspeth, love," he sighed, then his eyes fell shut.

I stared down at him in wonder.

XXVII

"I am the Master of Obernewtyn. Who among you will choose a guild this night?" Rushton asked.

Those prepared crossed to stand in line facing him. "We choose our places," they spoke in unison.

Rushton handed each of the candidates a candle and then lit them all from his own, the flame guttering slightly. Usually the ceremony took place inside, but fortunately the wind was low. "May you choose well," he murmured.

"I am Merret, I choose the Coercer guild," said the first, a thin, dark-eyed girl.

There was a predictable buzz of surprise since Merrett's mother was a healer. Merrett crossed to the table and set her candle amidst the Coercer token.

Zarak, grinning with pride, held up his own candle. "With permission, I choose again the Farseeker guild." There was a burst of applause as he crossed to the Farseeker table and I smiled inwardly at the success of Ceirwan's negotiations.

There were no other surprises, and when all had chosen, the newly guilded led a toast to Obernewtyn.

Able to escape at last from his affectionate guild members, Dameon came to sit beside me. I was amused and flattered to hear some children begin to sing an idealized version of my own first journey to Obernewtyn.

"I had no idea how brave and wise I was." I laughed.

Dameon smiled. "I think they are already at work on the epic of the journey to the coast. But I doubt anyone will ever sing the complete story."

I looked at him. Dameon had always been able to see more than most people. Like Atthis, his judgment lay in some keener place than his eyes. I had not told anyone what had happened in the mountains, but for a moment I was tempted to tell the empath. Such a secret made me feel lonely, even in the midst of my friends. Then I remembered Atthis's final stern warning. "For your own sake, speak to no one of this quest, for it is yours alone."

Behind my seat, Gahltha stirred, as if he too heard an echo of the voice which had changed his life. The black horse had become my shadow whenever I moved outside Obernewtyn's halls, regarding himself as my special guardian. Fortunately this was not too noticeably odd, since he and Avra had become the first animals to attend guildmerge. Rushton had provided a direct entrance from the outside for them and they used it proudly.

Dameon patted my hand. "Some secrets are safer kept."

I smiled wanly. "I'm glad to be home, but I can't help worrying about what will happen next."

Dameon shrugged. "The battle is won but the war goes on. Do not dwell too much on yesterday's battles. Take things as they come. Today is a day for singing and laughing." Dameon laughed. "Do you suppose Kella and Domick will bond before they go back to the safe house in Sutrium?"

I stared at the empath. "They told you?"

Dameon smiled. "I am an empath master, but the greenest novice might guess, as easily. They might as well announce it and get it over."

I grinned. "They're working up courage. It will rock their

two guilds on their heels. Merrett's choosing will be nothing to that."

"It is well done. Such divisions are not good for Obernewtyn," Dameon said approvingly.

"I hear Dragon is doing well as an empath novice," I said, catching sight of the red-haired beauty.

Dameon shook his head. "She is a handful, that one. I do not envy Matthew her violent affections. Yet I would like to know more about her past. Her fear of water is extreme. Brydda has promised to find out what he can about her. We will see."

Lina ran up, grinning. "Dance with me, master?" she cried, taking his hands. I opened my mouth to rebuke her, but to my surprise, Dameon let himself be coaxed to his feet. As if sensing my surprise, he cast a smile over one shoulder. "Remember, today is for dancing, not worrying about the future."

I sat back in my seat astonished. So much had changed subtly at Obernewtyn, as if winning one battle, even if by trickery, had given everyone bolder hopes. I looked up, caught Roland's eyes, and looked hastily away not wanting to face more questions about my legs. What would he think if I told him a Guanette bird had healed me?

It was spring, and the choosing ceremony had been the high point of our own moon fair. It was the wrong season and the moon had waned, but the brief lovely spring and an increasing feeling of hope for the future insured its success. After the choosing, there were tests of skill between the coercers, a vision demonstration by Dragon, and various demonstrations by the other guilds. These were followed by a merry feast. Last of all, the musicians brought out their instruments.

Daffyd appeared beside me with a mug of fement. I motioned him to sit as the musicians began to tune and strains of discordant music filled the air.

Daffyd smiled, but his eyes were sad. "Gilaine would love to hear this," he said wistfully.

"Is there any news of them?"

He shrugged. "Nothing definite. You might remember Gilbert, the leader of the armsmen? He devised a plan some time back in case there was a need to evacuate the camp in a hurry. It was meant to be used in case of soldierguard attack, but it would have served well in the firestorm. If Gilbert survived to put it into operation, he would have kept the survivors together."

"Have you spoken to Maryon? She might be able to help pinpoint them."

"The Futuretell guildmistress thinks they're alive, but 'tis hard for her to get a definite reading because she dinna know them." Daffyd was sunk in thought for a minute. "I mean to leave when Domick and Kella go. I'll travel with them as far as Sutrium and then . . . well, I'll keep lookin'. Rushton has offered help, but until I find some clue as to where they are, I'm better working alone."

I felt a shadow touch my own heart at the thought that each had his own deeds to do, his own battles and quests. Mine lay in a dark chasm across endless Blackland plains.

I caught sight of Rushton deep in conversation with Brydda and Gevan, apparently oblivious to the music and laughter. As ever, he treated the festivities as yet another guildmerge, going from one group to the next in his effort to have everything organized before his departure. He was going down to the lowlands with Domick and Kella when they returned to Sutrium with Brydda. The big lowlander had been vastly impressed with all he had seen at Obernewtyn, and he and Rushton had taken an instant liking to one another. Brydda was eager to have Rushton meet his allies.

Addressing a guildmerge, Brydda had made it clear that though he had no prejudices about Misfits, he would not speak for his allies. But he was certain that in time the book I had found about mind powers would convince them that Misfits were not mutants or evil caused by the Great White, but a natural development of human abilities which had existed in the Beforetime.

Brydda had brought Katlyn and Grufyyd to Obernewtyn to stay. The group had arrived soon after we had sent word to Sutrium that the way was clear. Brydda told me his parents had hated the city, and had only been too glad to be invited to live at Obernewtyn. Katlyn had already begun to replant her collection of herbs, much to Roland's delight.

The news of Pavo's death had saddened me, though I had expected it, and the Teknoguild, still mourning his loss, had mounted an expedition to the city under Tor in his memory. It had made me think of Jik, and of Maryon's words.

"It is true, the prediction focused on the boy, but I think the dog would not have gone without the boy. Futuretelling is inexact even for a futureteller. Not long after you departed, I foresaw the boy's death, but not the dog's. But there is no sense in blaming yourself for Jik's death. Who knows what would have happened to him, if he had not left the cloister, or if he had not gone, and because of this Obernewtyn had failed. Only a fool plans his deeds by future plans. Who knows what will come to change matters. Dwell not on his death, but on his last happy days with us."

Brydda whirled Kella past me in a dance, rousing me from my memories. I smiled, already regretting that Brydda had to leave. He had a heartening manner and a cheery way of making everything seem possible.

As with all coming and going at Obernewtyn, they would travel across the now barren White Valley, and down the Olden way. Few dogs were as sensitive to poisonous taints as Darga, but with care it would be possible to find a safe path, retracing our own journey. It was no longer safe to come openly along the main way, and the mountain valley was supposed to be deserted and barren. Domick had gleefully reported that this was the report made by the soldierguards. It had been accepted by the Council and Ariel had lost some credibility over the matter. I wondered what he made of the disappearance of the Druid and his people.

I caught Rushton's eye, and he stared at me a moment before being accosted by the ever-diligent Miryum, who thought the fair a waste of valuable time.

Her words floated to me through the music and laughter: "Just this one detail that needs..."

I sighed. Miryum was a worthy person and strongly Talented, but she had few friends. No doubt she thought them frivolous.

From the corner of my eye, I watched Rushton. No emotion showed on his features. It struck me suddenly that he had spent a lifetime hiding his thoughts and feelings.

The memory of his words as he lay dazed after being drugged by the soldierguards came back to me with a queer thrill. No one had heard those words but me, and it was clear from Rushton's behavior afterwards that he did not remember having said them. Yet in the light of them, many things seemed clear: Kella's cryptic words about my inability to see the truth of things, and Rushton's reluctance to let me join the expedition to the lowlands.

I turned to find Rushton standing beside me and flushed at my thoughts, glad he had no ability to deep probe.

"You are always alone, even when there are people about you," he observed.

I shrugged. "Matthew tells me I'm too gloomy. But I find it hard to forget all the bad things. I feel sad for Jik. He was so young. All this is wonderful... but sometimes it seems like a pleasant dream that can't last. So many have died. It's a high price we pay for our place in the world."

"If we did not fight, there would still be deaths because Misfits will continue to be born. We want to stop the killing, and that means fighting."

"War to end war? It doesn't sound very sensible," I said.

We stared at the dancers for a moment in silence, then I felt his eyes on me.

"I could scarcely believe it when I heard you were alive," he said remotely. I did not know what to say. When I looked up, embarrassed by the long silence between us, his expression was stern and unsmiling.

"It will take much to convince me to let you go away again," he said gravely. "Yet, I sense you don't really belong to us or to Obernewtyn. There is something in you that holds you ever apart. You are like a piece of smoke in my hand."

"I am glad to be home," I said, not knowing what else to say.

A wintry smile lit his dark features. "Home? This is the first time I have heard you call Obernewtyn that."

I smiled. "You would be astonished at how often I thought of it that way, and longed to be here. What is that saying Louis has?"

"The greenest grass is home grass . . . something like that." He gave me a long look. "You are a strange one, Elspeth. Everything you do is mysterious and unexpected. Roland is sadly puzzled over the healing of your feet. He tells me even the scars have disappeared, something he assures me is impossible. The coercers talk of nothing but your ability to coerce as well as Gevan, and the healers praise your miraculous healing of Maruman. Not to mention the change in Gahltha. And what of your sudden appearance when we had thought you dead? How much more is there about you that you choose to keep hidden? I would swear you tell more to Gahltha and that cat than to any of us."

I suppressed an urge to smooth the frown from Rushton's forehead. I had never imagined loving anyone, and I had always believed Rushton incapable of doing so. Perhaps I was wrong in both cases. But something stayed my hand and tongue.

My life did not belong to me until I had fulfilled my vow to destroy the weapon machines. While that was undone, I could not truly belong anywhere, or to anyone; I had no right to think of Rushton as anything but the Master of Obernewtyn while my dark quest lay before me. That secret set a tiny chasm between us. Until that was gone, I did not belong even to myself.

"Tomorrow you go to the lowlands," I said, wanting to distract him.

He looked out beyond the walls of Obernewtyn. "Maryon said the time to take our stand is not far away. I want to meet Brydda's friends and see how they regard Misfits. There is no good our making allies of bigots and, despite his optimism, I think not all his friends will welcome us with open arms."

"What about Ariel?"

Rushton smiled grimly. "We have nothing to fear from him. But he has much to fear from me. Domick tells me he has fallen from favor with the Council since the soldierguards came to Obernewtyn and found all was as I had reported," he grinned.

"Hopefully, he no longer bothers to think of revenge then. Domick said he has taken vows to become a Herder," I mused.

Rushton shrugged. "We have nothing to fear from those dabblers in dresses. I'll deal with Ariel once I have dealt with the Council."

I stared at him, wondering if he was right about the Herder Faction, and about Ariel.

"We have come far, but the road is not yet ended," Rushton said.

I sighed. "Don't you think of anything but fighting battles and winning? There must be more to life than that."

"More? Perhaps," Rushton said. "But life is a fight just the same, whether you fight it with weapons, or with words. You have to fight for what you believe in, and for the things you want."

Abruptly he held out a hand. "Dance with me."

I stared at him, astonished. I had never seen Rushton dance, and I did not dance. I opened my mouth to say so, but the words died on my lips.

His arms went about me, lightly and impersonally as one might hold a piece of soap.

"I have always fought for what I want," Rushton said with calm determination.

Epilogue

It *was* raining.

"Soon the coldwhite will come again," Maruman sent.

I looked down at him, marveling at his recovery. His appearance was as disreputable as ever but his eyes shone with their old stringent light. We were in the Futuretell hall, waiting for Maryon.

"The time of cold is the time when Obernewtyn is safest, secure behind a barrier of snow and ice," I sent.

"There are some things no barrier can hold away," Maruman sent.

I stared at him, suddenly uneasy. "What do you mean?"

"When the others come, it will be time to make the dark journey," he sent.

I shivered, knowing at once what he meant, though we had barely spoken of it since the day I returned with Gahltha. "What others?" I sent.

"You will not go alone," Maruman responded. "The oldOne has promised." I received a vague mental picture from Maruman of what looked like many dogs. One, I knew.

"Darga?" I whispered, wondering if it were really possible Darga had survived and, if so, where he was. And what did he have to do with my quest?

"He will come, and when he returns, it will be time. Best to forget until then," Maruman sent.

I dared not ask him to explain. Maruman had only ever told what he wanted and no more. Besides, I thought morosely, I would know soon enough if what he said was true.

If Darga returned . . .

I wondered suddenly if this had anything to do with Maryon's request for me to call on her. I was aware she was more likely than anyone else to see what lay ahead in her futuretell dreaming. Already I had appeared in her dreams, but as yet she had not fathomed the meaning.

Abruptly, I felt cold with premonition. Unlike Maryon and those of the Futuretell guild, my ability to see the future was restricted and infrequent. Most often, my premonitions were no more than a strong feeling of danger, but I had become accustomed to trusting them.

Sensing my mood, Maruman looked at me, yellow eyes gleaming in the dull evening light. "Fear or no, you must do what must be done. You are the Seeker."

"That's what scares me most," I sent. "If I fail . . ."

Strangely, Rushton's face came into my thoughts, and his words on the day of our moon fair.

"Life is a battle. You have to fight for the things you care about and believe in. . . ."

"Even the funaga have their times of wisdom, rare though these come. . . ." Maruman said with oblique humor.

I laughed.